# Accomplishments & Accomplices

# Accomplishments & Accomplices

a New Glenbury Village novel

GRACE ELLEN QUEEN

ISBN (paperback): 979-8991061704
ISBN (ebook): 979-8991061711

Cover design by Hannah VanWoert
Edited by Erin Wilcox
Typesetting by Benita Thompson

For Kevin,
my happily-ever-after

# *Prologue*

Lady Elizabeth Dormer burst into the dining room, feeling as fresh and giddy as the day her husband died. On that day, some forty years ago, she might have been described as rosy and breathless. But now, at sixty-eight years old, she could only be called red-faced and out of breath.

Constance and her husband, the Reverend Samuel Astley, were just in the process of exchanging the London papers over their breakfast. Lady Elizabeth Dormer was not an uncommon visitor in the Astley parsonage. Indeed, she could be expected to arrive most days after luncheon. But this morning, she was very early. The looks of astonishment from her hosts begged the question why. Elizabeth was all too glad to answer, but not before helping herself to a jam tart. Upon its completion, she launched into expostulation.

"My dear Constance, I've just heard the most horrible news!" Elizabeth said, unable to conceal a grin. "The Langfords are in debt. Terrible debt."

The Astleys exchanged puzzled glances before Constance replied.

"That's hardly news. That's like saying farmers are expecting rain in the spring. It is a fact that the entire county has always taken for granted."

"Yes, well it seems this time their embarrassments are so great, they have been forced to vacate Langley Hall. Isn't it wonderful?"

Hearing this, the Reverend Samuel Astley considered it his duty as a clergyman to recall Elizabeth to the true human suffering she was overlooking in her reporting. He did this by coughing dryly three times. Elizabeth ignored him. Constance took up the part of her husband with less subtlety.

"Elizabeth, while this is certainly *new* news, I fail to see how—"

Before she could finish, Elizabeth gave a sharp yelp of sudden remembrance.

"I haven't told you the best part! Oh, Constance, wait until you hear this."

"I am waiting, Elizabeth."

Rather than end her friend's anticipation, Elizabeth helped herself to another jam tart. Constance and her husband cast knowing glances between themselves, each in silent acknowledgement of the folly of their friend and neighbor.

Constance and Elizabeth had been friends for more than thirty years. Though they were near opposites in temperament and taste, together they presided as dual matriarchal monarchs over their small town of New Glenbury. In the course of this friendship, Elizabeth's distinction of character was a frequent topic of discussion among the Astleys. Were the Reverend Samuel not so assured of his wife's quiet disapproval of Lady Dormer's more outrageous attitudes and behaviors, he was not sure he would have permitted the friendship. Many years ago, he had even gone so far as to say this to his wife. Constance had only laughed. That response still puzzled him.

When Elizabeth finished the tart, she clapped her hands together to call the room's attention to her singular presence.

"They have let Langley Hall to a young man from London. An *unmarried* young man from London. What do you think of that?"

Samuel looked at his wife to see how she would reply to this most benign of revelations and was surprised to find her gaping in awe.

It must be understood that both Mrs. Constance Astley and Lady Elizabeth Dormer delighted in nothing so much as matchmaking.

Owing to their contrasting dispositions, it was one of very few occupations they *both* deemed worthy of their talents. The pair of women fancied themselves responsible for ten marriages in the last twelve years. It had been ten marriages in the last ten years just two years prior, but after such a productive decade, single residents in their sleepy village had become scarce.

When Constance regained her composure, she peppered Elizabeth with questions.

"When will he arrive? Do you know his surname? Have you looked him up in the peerage? Will he be bringing any company? Do we know anything of his prospects or personality?"

She asked all of this as Elizabeth munched on the last of the jam tarts and waved her hand in an indecipherable gesture. At last, she answered.

"I haven't the faintest idea of any of that. I have told you all that I know, which I heard from Heloise who heard from Elsie Downs at the butcher yesterday. Though she only told me this morning, stupid girl, and I came here to tell you straightaway."

The Reverend Samuel Astley excused himself without anyone much minding. A lull in the conversation spoke what the two friends knew the other to be thinking: even with the exciting addition of an unmarried young man to the New Glenbury social scene, there remained no unattached girls of any merit with which to entice him.

Soured by this silent concession, they adjourned to the drawing room. There, Lady Elizabeth played solitaire while Constance knitted mittens, even though it was well past the last frost of the season.

"Put the eight of hearts on the nine," Constance said, glancing up at Elizabeth's cards.

"Constance, this is a game of solitaire. It is meant to be played solitarily."

Despite this rebuttal, Elizabeth moved the eight to the nine.

"You know, Elizabeth, the Fosters are due another child. Your help would be appreciated in making up a nightie or cap for the little one."

"Constance, in the thirty-odd years of our friendship, have you really learned so little of my character? I have no interest in making and mending, and certainly not for any children."

Rather than argue the point, Constance only commented, "Don't cover your queen yet. You're about to draw a jack."

"And just how exactly can you be sure of that?"

Elizabeth turned over the next card in the deck and it was, indeed, a jack. Constance smiled in spite of herself. Then, ever industrious, she picked up the thread of conversation and proceeded to make something of it.

"As I consider myself responsible for the happy marriage of the Fosters, I cannot help but feel some equal responsibility for the little children it produces."

"Constance Astley, you forget yourself. What's more, you forget me! Who was it that arranged that the Fosters should ride side by side on the wagon to market?"

"Yes, Elizabeth, that's very well. But considering that it was I who introduced them—"

"Never mind that! What's an introduction worth?"

Constance lowered her work and leaned forward in her chair to defend her position.

"As it was *I* who negotiated the terms with the girl's father, and it was *my husband* who performed the marriage on such short notice, I feel it is only right that I should be of some assistance in the clothing of their offspring. Elizabeth, if you can claim an equal responsibility for their marriage, then I wonder you do not adopt some responsibility for their continued matrimonial felicity."

Elizabeth, in her usual calm way, waved her hand in replying, "By that logic, we should be clothing every child in this neighborhood. You know neither of us has the appetite for such tedious needlework. As it is, you sew as much as an old maid!"

"I most certainly do not."

"You do, indeed!"

"How can you say such nonsense to me in my own drawing room?"

"I should be happy to say it to you in your dining room if you ever intend to serve luncheon."

With this reminder, the women examined the mantel clock. Luncheon was now a full half hour late. In Elizabeth's house this would have been excusable. Her French staff did not often adhere to the English habit of punctuality. But in the orderly and precise home of Constance Astley, this delay would have been enough to make the papers, if the town of New Glenbury had the use of a printing press.

Constance gently folded her yarn and needles back into her sewing basket. She rose and politely excused herself from the room. A few moments later she returned, looking grave.

"There has been a tragic accident."

"Good heavens, Constance. It's only luncheon. I'd hardly call it a tragedy."

"No, no. Something has happened at the mill. No one in the kitchen could tell me much about it. But . . . well, it seems there was a small fire."

"And some of the girls ran out to go see it?"

"Yes, that seems to be the case."

"Well, how perfectly ridiculous. As if they haven't their own small fire to look after in the kitchen. Is there washing and mending to be done at the mill as well? If so, you shall never see them again."

At that moment, there came a flurry of knocks on the rectory's door. Constance opened it to find a young lad, soot-stained and panting with his hat in hand.

"The reverend, mum? Is the reverend here?"

"Have you come from the mill?"

"Yes'm. I've been sent for the reverend. There's been an accident. Old Mr. Howard . . . I've been sent for the reverend."

Constance could hear her husband stirring in his study.

"Shouldn't you fetch the surgeon if there's been some accident? If Mr. Howard is injured, he should be seen by a surgeon."

The boy paused in uncertainty, twisting his hat brim in his hands before he answered.

"We've already had the surgeon. I've been sent for the reverend."

At this grave pronouncement, the Reverend Samuel Astley swept out of his study. Bible in hand, he made significant eye contact with his wife, wordlessly confirming that he heard all that the young man had reported and that he plainly understood its significance. He took his broad black hat from the hook by the door and said simply, "Lead the way, Donald. Run and tell them I'm coming."

The boy took off at a sprint and the reverend billowed after him in the direction of the Howard Linen Mill.

Constance turned back towards her friend in the drawing room, who had heard the exchange as well and looked deep in thought.

"What on earth was he doing there?" Elizabeth ventured.

"Who?"

"Robert Howard. What was he doing at the mill?"

"I'm sure we will know more once Samuel returns," Constance said. "I suppose in this time we can only be thankful that Mrs. Howard predeceased her husband. She would not have been strong enough to withstand the shock of this tragedy."

"Hence her predeceasing."

"Oh Elizabeth, don't be so sharp."

"You're the one who said you were glad she was dead."

Constance gave a great huff. "I most certainly said no such thing!"

"Well, not in those exact words. But anyway, if we're not going to have any luncheon, then I think I shall send for my carriage and partake of my own hospitality for the rest of the day. You are, of course, welcome to join me."

"I'll stay here and await Samuel's return. Thank you."

As the two friends waited for Elizabeth's carriage to pull around to the front of the rectory, Elizabeth turned to Constance.

"You know, I'm sure you'll think very poorly of me for bringing up such a thing at a time like this, in the wake of tragedy and all. But, you know, Mr. Howard leaves behind a son."

"That's right, Benjamin Howard."

"And he is what now, twenty-five? Twenty-six?"

"He was born in the August of 1794, making him twenty-eight."

"So, we shall have *two* unmarried men in the neighborhood this summer."

"Oh Elizabeth, I hardly think—"

"Yes, well, I shall think enough on this subject for the both of us."

# One

BENJAMIN HOWARD HAD the audacity to already be married. This fact was discovered upon his arrival in New Glenbury to attend his father's funeral. How old Mr. Howard had failed to report such monumental news about his only heir was inconceivable to Constance and Elizabeth. But as the man was quite dead, little could be done to make him feel the ire of his deeply offended neighbors.

The Reverend Samuel Astley gave the funeral service all the pomp and flair its subject would have demanded, for Robert Howard had been a man of much ostentation. And his glittering obelisk tombstone, which towered over the modest marker of his long-departed wife, felt very fitting to all who had been in New Glenbury long enough to remember the gentle simplicity of the late Mrs. Howard.

The *new* Mrs. Howard, Benjamin's wife, was the subject of much village speculation that day. Shrouded in mourning, she was also shrouded in mystery. It could not be discerned if, under her veil, she was shedding any tears for her father-in-law, nor could it be determined if she were pretty or plain.

Some of the housemaids at Wuster Park, the palatial estate of the lately departed, volunteered to skip the burial and get an early start on unpacking the trunks of the new master and mistress. But the ever-dedicated housekeeper, Mrs. Rollins, would not hear of it. She had been the manager of the entire Wuster Park household under the late Mr. Howard, and she had an unyielding idea of duty. She insisted, therefore, that all staff pay their respects for the entirety of the service. Then, she required the household staff to process behind the coach carrying their new master and mistress on their inaugural ride to the front door of their new home—even though it was raining.

Thus, Benjamin Howard and his new wife found themselves waiting patiently in one of the many drawing rooms of the great Wuster Park house. Upstairs, their trunks were deposited and their contents hurriedly unpacked. At last, Mrs. Rollins ushered the couple to their new chambers in the master suite of rooms on the second floor. Benjamin paused upon the threshold. This room had always belonged to his father. Looking in at the familiar chamber, he plunged his hands into his coat pockets and began a nervous tapping of his heels.

His wife, Maggie, knew this display of anxiety well. She turned to Mrs. Rollins and spoke directly to the woman for the first time since her arrival.

"We shall not take this room tonight, I think. Tomorrow, perhaps. Do you have another room which can be made ready?"

Mrs. Rollins inwardly chastised herself for not anticipating this discomfort. However, she was pleased to report that she kept all rooms at Wuster Park in a state of readiness and they might have their choice. Benjamin turned without speaking and led the way. This was his childhood home, and though he had not spent more than a few consecutive weeks here since the death of his mother, he knew perfectly well where each of the bedchambers was located. He opened a door farther down the hallway leading to the room he had occupied in childhood. The walls were a soft green, the carpets a rich golden yellow. Maggie entered the room and removed her shawl.

"Send someone up to deliver our nightclothes and make a fire," Benjamin instructed quietly.

Mrs. Rollins nodded and departed.

When the mundanities of the evening had been attended to and the candles extinguished, the couple settled into bed. There, Maggie found Benjamin's body in the darkness and encircled him in her arms. Softly, she said, "It's going to be all right, my love. Losing a father is a terrible thing . . ."

"He wasn't a father like your father," Benjamin said.

"No. But he was your father, and that's enough."

Benjamin said nothing, but his short, strained breathing betrayed an intensity of feeling which endeared him to his wife all the more. She rubbed his back in slow gentle circles, occasionally smoothing his hair. After some time, his breath calmed, and the newlyweds went to sleep in a wordless understanding that any challenges that tomorrow might bring would be faced by them together.

They were that most rare and obnoxious thing: a couple truly and completely in love.

# Two

"It is a shame about his wife," Elizabeth said.

Constance and Elizabeth were, as usual, passing the day together in Constance's drawing room. Elizabeth had consented to "assist" Constance with some of her projects. Thus, she was winding a skein of yarn in such a sloppy manner, she knew Constance would rewind it as soon as she departed.

"Is she ill? She certainly looked a little frail at the service. Just a wisp of a girl, really."

"I don't think she's ill."

"Then what is the shame about the new Mrs. Howard?"

"That there is a Mrs. Howard at all. I think it's quite ridiculous that we were not informed."

"Well, it is a very newly made marriage, and the banns were read in his London parish."

"They might have at least come here to the village."

"I assume they wanted to wait and see it in better weather. You must agree, Elizabeth, that New Glenbury is not at its most appealing until at least June."

"Oh, don't argue with me. You know exactly why I am feeling disappointed. All our plans for the summer are ruined. I simply cannot be expected to sit idly by for another year."

"Well, we shall still have our new neighbor in Langley Hall."

"If he ever arrives!"

"And you know, Elizabeth, there are many alternatives to idleness . . ."

"Kindly refrain from foisting your charity commitments onto me, Constance. I have neither aptitude nor interest."

~

It was just before luncheon when the two friends decided on taking a turn in the rectory's tidy kitchen garden. Constance was eager to show Elizabeth some newly planted fruit trees, and Elizabeth was eager to assert that she didn't give a fig for such considerations.

Then they spotted her. Though a stranger, the new Mrs. Howard was unmistakable in her drab mourning attire, even at a distance. Constance gave a small salutation.

"Now look what you've done," said Elizabeth. "She's coming towards us and will want to join us for luncheon."

"Yes, I hope so. Aren't you curious about her? I only spoke a few words to her at the funeral."

"Not in the least. Nor is she at all curious about us, I can tell you that. She will think we are old grandmothers with nothing but dotty notions and damp handkerchiefs."

"Elizabeth, that's very unfair of you."

All this was said through the gritted teeth of welcoming smiles as the women watched the slow progress of their new neighbor making her way towards the garden. Mrs. Howard looked bright and healthy, despite her dour mourning clothes. She was a small woman, shorter than Elizabeth, but she was not as wispy as she had appeared at a distance. Her light-brown hair was complemented by soft blue eyes. She moved with ease and her smile displayed a row of clean healthy teeth.

"Good afternoon, Lady Dormer, Mrs. Astley."

"Good afternoon, Mrs. Howard. I see you are enjoying this fine spring weather we are having," Constance replied.

"Indeed, I am. The rain we have had these past few days has kept me indoors. And it has been so dull. All the distant relatives finally left Wuster after Monday's reading of the will. Though I've been looking forward to their departure since they arrived, now that they are actually gone, I am terribly bored. Had we not fine enough weather for a long walk today, I am certain I would have gone mad with only sewing and books for company. Mr. Howard has been very much occupied with the mill. He takes himself there every day after breakfast. And so, you can just imagine my days are now quite solitary."

She said all of this without the slightest hesitation. The words simply flowed out of her as if she was a friend of many years. She was utterly unconscious of how odd it was to unburden oneself so entirely upon introduction. Constance was put off by the girl's loquaciousness. Elizabeth was intrigued by her easy and dramatic admissions. In hope of soliciting further confidences, Elizabeth took Mrs. Howard's arm in a way she hoped communicated the closeness of friendship (rather than the feebleness of age) and invited her indoors. Constance followed behind them, suspicious of her friend's sudden reversal of sentiment for the guest.

When luncheon had been laid before them, Elizabeth commenced her questioning.

"Mrs. Howard, you say you are quite alone. Have you no lady's maid? Did you not secure one before your honeymoon? In my day, and I admit that day was some time ago . . . Perhaps I am not as familiar with the goings-on of fashionable people as I used to be. But in my time, if a married woman were to travel without a lady's maid, well! It simply was not done."

"Oh, Lady Dormer, you are indeed correct. But you must call me Maggie."

"Could we call you Margaret?" the ever-fastidious Constance interjected.

"You could, but I might forget to answer. I have always been Maggie at home and to friends. Ever since I was a little girl—"

Elizabeth did not wish to risk losing the thread of her conversation with trifling details about names.

"Yes, Maggie it will be. And Maggie, why have you not secured a lady's maid?"

"I was going to while Benjamin—I mean, Mr. Howard—and I were on our honeymoon on the Continent. I rather liked the idea of having an Italian maid. Someone who could help with the travel arrangements. My husband's French is very good already. So that was our plan. Then we got the news of old Mr. Howard's unfortunate accident. Just as we were on the shores of Dover ready to cross, if you would believe it! We rushed back here, naturally. Since then, there has not been much time to settle such matters."

"But who does your hair and lays out your dresses?"

"I attend to many things myself. Mrs. Rollins, she is our housekeeper, do you know her? Yes, of course. She helps me in the mornings with fastenings and such."

Constance interjected.

"Have you placed an advertisement for a lady's maid? If not, I can assist you in drafting it."

There was an unusual pause in the flippant rapidity of Maggie's conversation before she replied.

"I have not. I know that I should . . . but . . . I seem to be getting along—"

"You say you are lonely, though. A lady's maid would solve such a problem."

"Very true, Mrs. Astley. But my mother has just written—"

"Ah, she will have opinions about securing a maid, no doubt."

"No, Mrs. Astley, it's not that. My mother has written to me saying that my aunt wishes to send my cousin to Wuster Park to act as my attendant."

"That seems very mean indeed. As if you cannot afford a proper lady's maid!" Elizabeth replied, bristling like a porcupine as she spoke. Before her own advantageous marriage to the late Lord Dormer, Lady Elizabeth had lived as her aunt's lady's maid. She remembered the experience with much bitterness.

"Those were my thoughts exactly! My mother's too. Though, I'm told my Aunt Mary specifically wishes it for her. My cousin is now seventeen—"

"Ah yes, I understand," Constance replied. "She quarrels too often with her mother. All girls do at seventeen. But why don't they send her to school for a year? Or perhaps she ought to go with her father to the seaside."

If Maggie had been in possession of any defenses, she now dropped them.

"I must confess I do not know. She is quite a stranger to me. I have never met any of my cousins. I only ever saw my Aunt Mary the one time when I was very small. They live so very far up north, nearly in Scotland! And while I can hardly mind the inconvenience of company, in truth, I had hoped that my marriage would keep me well out of the company of unmarried young girls. They are so tedious, dramatic, and fickle. Waiting so long to be wed, I was all the time thrown in at tables and parties with girls *supposedly* my equal. But there is a great difference between an unmarried girl of seventeen and an unmarried girl of twenty-seven."

"You are twenty-seven?" Elizabeth could not contain her surprise in this blunt question.

"I am twenty-eight."

"You look not yet twenty-one."

"Had you seen me at twenty-one, you would not say so now." Maggie gave a small laugh before resuming. "You can appreciate my predicament. I wish to refuse, and my mother recognizes the absurdity of the request. But my Aunt Mary specifically wishes it for her. Outright refusal feels impossible. Wuster Park is so large . . . But you agree that it is an odd request, do you not? Her father is *Baron* Huxley. To send his eldest daughter to be a lady's maid—"

"Your cousin is a *baron's daughter*?"

Elizabeth looked at Constance as she asked this question, observing that her friend's eyebrows had disappeared upward into the lace of her cap.

"Yes. Her name is Lady Diana Huxley. That's one of the only things I know about her."

Constance and Elizabeth simultaneously considered the considerable considerations of having a titled bachelorette in the neighborhood of New Glenbury.

"Obedience to one's parents is a commandment," Constance said firmly. "As such, your cousin must obey her parents. She *must* come to Wuster."

"But not as your lady's maid!" Elizabeth interjected. "Keep her as a companion or guest. You need not trust your toilette or tea to her, certainly not."

Maggie surveyed the women. Though she did not understand the satisfied smiles exchanged between them, she understood that these declarations counted as their final ruling on the subject. She nodded solemnly in acquiescence. That evening she would write to her mother, giving her consent to welcome her mysterious young cousin, Diana, to Wuster Park. What Maggie did not know was that Diana was already on her way.

# Three

DIANA WAS THIRTEEN when she learned the future wasn't something to look forward to. Up to that point, she had been prone to imagining things might one day get better, despite all her observed evidence to the contrary. Now, at seventeen, she knew with the certainty afforded only to seventeen-year-olds that things would only and always find a way to get worse. The conciliatory look of the coachman as he opened the post-carriage door told her that this was exactly what was about to happen.

"Glad you're awake, miss. We've had . . . well, we've got . . . there's these men here . . . I'm sorry. I'm afraid I have to ask you to give up your seat and ride topside."

The coachman did seem very sorry to deliver this news, but Diana was acquiescent. She had always known this was a possibility, having only paid as much fare as would secure her an outside seat. She smiled shyly.

"I thank you for letting me ride inside for as long as you were able."

She had been riding post for three days and nights. During that time, she'd met six drivers and seven other passengers. She had eaten two meals, and slept for a total of about twelve hours. With her instinct for disappointment, Diana had suspected, when the last passenger had disembarked a few hours before in the predawn light, that her luck would soon run out. Uninterrupted sleep was too much of a luxury to last.

"I'd let you keep riding inside, too. Only we've got these three men, and then also these crates, you see. I think you'll be more comfortable on top. Well, you might have been, but it's looking like rain. Do you have a coat?"

Diana shook her head, no. The coachman eyed her hard-worn dress, then looked around the dark cavern of his conveyance. Out from under a pile of mail bags he wrestled a tattered blanket.

"We use this for furniture. It will keep the rain off you for a while. You've not far to go today if I remember. Last driver said New Glenbury's your stop?"

Diana affirmed this as she made her way out of the cluttered compartment and climbed up the ladder to the roof. She drew her legs up under herself and wrapped the woolen blanket about her shoulders. The coachman assisted his new passengers into the carriage before checking that his fresh horses were secure and taking his seat. Then he turned back to Diana.

"Hold fast to that rope, especially in the turns."

Diana had only a moment to nod before he snapped the reins and the post carriage lurched onward.

Diana was not afraid of a little rain. She had made long walks in worse weather without the comfort of a borrowed blanket. Diana was not afraid of riding atop the hulking post carriage. She had been thrown from enough horses to know how to hang on. Diana was not even afraid of being away from home for the first time in her life. She had wanted nothing but escape from that place for as long as she could remember. Diana was only afraid of what she might find when she reached her destination. What would a place like Wuster Park be like? How could she ever convince anyone that she belonged there?

# *Four*

As IT HAPPENED, on that same rainy day, a mud-splattered coach pulled by four horses was making its brisk and bumpy way down the road towards New Glenbury. Inside sat three young men speaking in hushed but adamant tones and one woman of late middle age. The woman was asleep; her head bounced softly to the motion of the carriage, her needlepoint still in hand. Her name was Mrs. Sarah Bellwood.

Mrs. Sarah Bellwood was a tired woman. She found sleep easily and under all manner of circumstances. It was explained in the neighborhood where Mrs. Bellwood resided that the strain of raising her two twin boys had permanently depleted her energy and made her prone to dozing. This was, perhaps, true. Because her twins came of age in the nebulous and uncertain atmosphere of the new-moneyed London mercantile class, they had not received the benefit of a firm tutor or an away education. This was the sort of arrangement which all sensible parents of the more experienced city elites would have availed themselves of immediately. Mrs. Sarah Bellwood had decided instead to be a dedicated, dutiful mother to her darling boys. Thus her energy had been exhausted day after day as those boys grew from fierce, wild children into exuberant youths of opposing temperaments and perpetual needling annoyances.

She loved her dear boys, and they loved her. Perhaps the twins even loved her more owing to her appetite for naps. She was a great favorite of all the youths of their acquaintance in her role as chaperone. This preferential treatment gave Mrs. Bellwood great pride, though she never quite connected her popularity with her propensity to sleep during the events to which she was invited. On all occasions, her sons did their best to shield her from this self-awareness, worrying that it might spoil the arrangement.

Her boys, now grown men, sat across from her in the carriage. As children, they had been bright and wild, fond of pulling pranks on their servants and disappearing into market crowds. As young men of twenty, however, they had mellowed. Though they were each wealthy and handsome, with identical black hair and wide hazel eyes, they partook of no damaging vices. They did not gamble or drink to great excess. They stayed mostly within their allotted allowance each month. And they did not trifle with the affections of young women, though plenty of young women had made it clear that they longed to be trifled with.

The company they kept was mostly their own. Though they could also be found with their best friend and neighbor, Mr. Hudson Birch, who at that moment sat next to their mother in the same carriage.

While the Bellwood boys (as they were sometimes called) shared an almost identical appearance at first glance, Ellis and Noah were actually quite different. Noah, for his part, had taken an early and ardent interest in the illustrious Lord Byron. He had come of age devouring reports of that reckless poet in the society papers to which his mother subscribed. Now, as a result, he styled himself a brooding, mysterious character of secret romantic notions. He wore dark clothing and combed his wavy hair low across his brow. The prevailing impression Noah Bellwood gave to society was, regrettably, quite contrarian and dour. Still, for a certain type of girl who had also read too much of Lord Byron, he was alluring—the only confirmation he needed to continue his pretenses unabated.

Ellis, on the other hand, put a positive spin on all his thinking and doing. He favored cheerful colors in his dress and each morning used a scented beeswax pomade to style his dark hair high into a damp-looking confection. Possessed of an inborn optimism, he was never at a loss for a kind word or an agreeable affirmation. As a result, any conversation with him could be counted upon to take an exceedingly dull course. He was apt to agree with absolutely everyone on absolutely every subject, except his brother Noah. The two brothers together bickered about the merits of any and all situations that occurred in their lives. The tension between their ever-opposed viewpoints made for a constant stream of dialogue.

Their conversation, held in soft tones to avoid disturbing their mother, at this moment ran as follows:

"No, I'm simply saying that we cannot count on the weather getting better tomorrow, so there's no sense in making plans to go for a hunt at all."

"Yes, but Noah, what would you have us do instead? We've got the entire summer to enjoy, and I'd think we should start enjoying it as soon as possible."

"Ellis, surely there is nothing enjoyable about hunting in the rain. We should take at least a day to settle ourselves in the house. We don't even know what the servant situation is going to be. Or if they'll have the supplies on hand for a proper hunt."

"I'm certain they will! Whoever lived there before surely enjoyed hunts, and whatever supplies they had are certainly good enough for us."

"I wouldn't count on that at all."

"Well, I don't suppose you would. But I personally think this rain is going to clear right up, and you're going to be very sorry indeed that we didn't give instructions to the staff today to be ready for a hunt tomorrow. But anyway, let's ask Hudson what he thinks. It's his place, after all."

"Yes, Hudson. What do you say?"

Young Hudson was used to playing mediator and tiebreaker for his friends. Indeed, as the only son of a wealthy fishing fleet owner, he had the affable deportment of one accustomed to having his own way, always. His parents had raised him to think as highly of himself as they did of themselves. Given every allowance for ostentation, he dressed most fashionably and believed it wholeheartedly when his mother said he was the most handsome boy in all of London.

He was quite handsome. Though his stature was smaller than average, his physique was well formed and athletic. He had a wide smile and a strong jaw. His blue eyes were deeply expressive and, having never faced any real disappointments, he did not possess the self-awareness to hide the feelings they so openly displayed.

"I say, we shall inquire with the staff tonight what they think of the odds for rain tomorrow, and what the preparations for a hunt might entail."

"An excellent plan," Ellis said. "They'll know the weather patterns here, far better than we would."

"With our luck, though," Noah countered weakly, "it won't stop raining until the solstice, and we'll be stuck inside playing cards and reading books all day."

Ever the optimist, Ellis replied, "That wouldn't be so bad, really. And besides, I'm sure there are lots of neighbors who will be quite curious about us. You know how these country towns are when someone new comes to stay."

"You say that as if you've ever spent any time outside of London."

"Well, no it's true that I haven't. But one hears about such things, you know. It's only natural that the local people will want to meet us. Perhaps there will even be a special lady who has always longed for a Lord Byron of her own, eh Noah? What do you say about a double wedding? I and Melissa, and you and your country lady bride?"

"Please leave me out of your matrimonial plans. You know my opinion of your folly with Miss Greenby."

"Only because you yourself have not yet been in love like I am."

"Please, Ellis. Spare me."

"I'm only saying that the right girl would make you as happy as I am."

"To be as happy as you, one only needs a swift horse hoof to the head."

Sensing in her sleep her sons' hostile tones, Mrs. Bellwood was roused into half-waking long enough to say, "Stop that bickering, boys," rather sharply, before her eyes once again fluttered shut and her mouth resumed its slackened posture.

The carriage was silent for a while as all three boys let Mrs. Bellwood rest peacefully. Then, with an instructive confidence the Duke of Wellington might have envied, Hudson made a declaration.

"My friends, we must not forget: This summer is about preparing for our futures. If we are going to really be out in society—not just the society of our parents' set, but the true nobility of our nation—then we must prepare ourselves in the ways our education heretofore has not. So, I say then, let us not think of neighbors or country dances, but instead focus on perfecting the arts and activities of *true country gentlemen.*"

His loyal companions nodded in solemn agreement, as if they had any idea what the arts and activities of true country gentlemen entailed. It was then that their coach rounded a corner, and the three boys saw Langley Hall, their home for the summer, swing into view.

# *Five*

It felt good to walk again. Diana's stiff legs and ankles rejoiced at their return to animation. Having been deposited at the gates of Wuster Park by the post-carriage, she observed with pleasure the early spring blooms of hawthorns and hyacinths planted beside the road. It was only when Diana crested the hill and saw the wide facade of the Wuster Park house that she remembered the chill of her soaked apparel and her apprehension of this adventure into the unknown.

None of the general staff of Wuster Park had been given any advance expectation of Diana's arrival. Maggie had only recently mentioned to the housekeeper, Mrs. Rollins, that her cousin might join them sometime in the summer. It was lucky therefore that Mrs. Rollins happened to be near the door when the girl arrived. The footman reacted with such considerable confusion at the appearance of the applicant, she might not have otherwise been admitted to the house. Overhearing some commotion, Mrs. Rollins swept past the footman and took stock of the situation in only a few words. She whisked the visitor upstairs before she could be seen by anyone else. Then, bustling with an unusual urgency, Mrs. Rollins found Maggie in the south gallery.

"Mrs. Howard, your cousin Lady Huxley has arrived."

Maggie stared at her housekeeper in plain astonishment.

"Here? She is here, now? It has not been four days since I wrote to my mother."

Blinking her eyes in rapid succession and rising from her chair, Maggie continued, "Well, do send her in, I suppose."

"I do not think that wise, ma'am."

Though it had been a short time since her own arrival at Wuster Park, Maggie had developed a great faith in Mrs. Rollins' unimpeachable judgment. She approached the trusted housekeeper and closely observed her grave countenance.

"Something is wrong? Is she unwell?"

"I do not think so, ma'am. But . . . I would not have her shown in here without some attentions to her person."

Maggie thought she understood. "Oh, yes. Of course. She must be very tired from traveling, I'm sure. Please take every care getting her settled . . . in the blue bedroom, I think. Unless you think the yellow one better. I leave it to you."

"Yes, ma'am. Only, perhaps you would like to come and see the girl first?"

"No, no. I'm sure I can wait until she is made more comfortable. Thank you for letting me know she arrived. I'll send a note to Benjamin to tell him the good news."

"Very good, ma'am," Mrs. Rollins said, unconvincingly, as she removed herself from the room.

~

Diana stood rooted to the exact spot in the blue bedroom where Mrs. Rollins had planted her. This, Mrs. Rollins observed, boded well that the girl should not be a thief. Little else of her appearance boded so well. Diana was uncommonly tall, and she might have been pretty, though any good qualities were obfuscated by the filth and poverty which clung to her frame with the same determination as her tattered dress.

At last, Mrs. Rollins took a hard swallow of words unspoken and set forth with resolute determination to make right what was so obviously wrong.

"You say you are *Lady* Diana Huxley? Cousin to Mrs. Margaret Howard?"

The incongruous appearance of this skinny wretch was certainly enough to cast doubt on the relation. But the blue eyes that met Mrs. Rollins in answer to her question were such a perfect match for Maggie's own that the answer was unnecessary.

"Yes, ma'am. Is this Mrs. Howard's room? Is she to see me here?"

"She is not to see you at all looking like this."

"Pardon?"

"You are not fit to be seen by the lady of this house, nor anyone else in it. Undress while I call for water."

Mrs. Rollins turned from Diana and poked her head into the hallway. There, two under maids were attempting to look busy to disguise their efforts at eavesdropping.

"Clara, Sarah, go and fetch water for a bath. And bring fresh bath linens—four of them. Quickly now."

Returning to the room, Mrs. Rollins was irked to find that Diana had not disrobed. Before she could begin a chastisement, the girl meekly protested, "I'm sorry. I have no other dress to put on."

"No, you don't look as though you would. Tell me, did your family send you like this?"

"They sent me by post carriage. I was told this was the house where I was to go. Is this not Wuster Park?"

Despite her appearance, Diana's voice was soft and her accent genteel, touched lightly with a hint of her northern origins.

"You rode with the post? Alone?"

"Yes, ma'am. Is this Wuster Park?"

"Yes, yes. You've arrived. But what about your luggage? Have you no trunks?"

Diana looked down at her shoes. She shifted uneasily, watching muddy globules drip onto the fine carpet underfoot. She did not need to answer for her answer to be known. Inwardly, Mrs. Rollins burned with questions. But she did not let her curiosity give over to a full inquisition. She reminded herself that this girl, this pale reedlike creature with frightened eyes and trembling hands, was the daughter of a baron.

In the silence of unasked questions, Mrs. Rollins could hear water sloshed from buckets into the large tub in the adjoining bathing chamber. It would only be a few more minutes until it was ready for use. But then what?

"Wait here again. I shall be right back. And don't touch anything."

Mrs. Rollins betook herself up the servants' staircase. Her mind was cast back to the outline of a girl half-remembered. Joanne had been an under maid early in Mrs. Rollins' career as housekeeper at Wuster Park. Like Diana, she had been tall. This was most of what Mrs. Rollins remembered about her appearance now, because not three months after Joanne's arrival at Wuster Park, she took suddenly ill and died. She had left behind one solitary servant's box. Mrs. Rollins now silently prayed it had not been beset upon by mice. In the attic, she found it. Not wishing to waste time while her guest remained unattended, she conveyed the whole of the box back down the stairs and into the blue bedroom. There Diana stood, still as a statue.

Mrs. Rollins opened the small trunk, and a wave of relief expelled a small smile from her otherwise placid visage. She took out two dresses and several old-fashioned cotton shifts. She held one dress up by the shoulders across Diana's frame. The girl wordlessly submitted to this inspection.

"Come with me."

Mrs. Rollins led Diana through the connecting door to the blue bedroom's bathing chamber. The air was heavy and hot with steam from the great tub so recently filled. Despite this already impressive heat, Mrs. Rollins began to kindle a fire in the small hearth. When it was well ablaze, she turned to Diana.

"Take off your wet clothes and get in the tub."

Diana obeyed, and Mrs. Rollins saw with a pang that the girl was close to tears. But Mrs. Rollins was too consumed with her own thoughts and plans to offer words of comfort. After a small yelp at the shock of the heat, Diana settled into the water and drew her knees up to her chest, wrapping her arms tightly about them. Mrs. Rollins snatched her discarded clothes from the floor and tossed them into the fire without ceremony. Diana gasped, but said nothing of protestation. Only her tears, now flowing in earnest, betrayed her emotions. She surrendered wordlessly to being washed, scrubbed, doused, and scrubbed again.

Given over to the machinations of her task, Mrs. Rollins moved efficiently through the bathing ritual. It was only when she took Diana's hands in her own that she paused. These could not be the hands of a baron's daughter. Calloused palms and small scars spoke of hard labor and cold winters. The girl's nails were short, chipped, and unclean. A fresh cut, dry but not healed, ran from the base of her thumb to the center of her palm. Not even Mrs. Rollins' scullery girls had hands this rough. Diana saw the close inspection of her hands and attempted to draw them back to herself. Mrs. Rollins grasped them tighter.

"I'm sorry," Diana whispered.

"I see nothing to be sorry for," Mrs. Rollins answered firmly.

When Diana's skin was pink and clean, Mrs. Rollins remembered that her guest was unlikely to have eaten. Indeed, the girl looked as if she had not had a full meal in many months. Her ribs made a washboard of her back, and the sinewy muscles of her lithe figure showed plain under her skin.

Mrs. Rollins opened the door of the bathing chamber and motioned to Clara, still milling about in the hall.

"Go fetch whatever cold meats and things that might be made into a meal and bring it straightaway."

Clara departed in haste, and Mrs. Rollins resumed her reconfiguration of Diana's person. Helping her from the tub and wrapping her in the bath linens, she first combed and covertly inspected the girl's hair for signs of vermin. Finding none, she twisted the glossy dark mass and pinned it high on Diana's head. Then she dressed the girl as though she were an overgrown doll. Mrs. Rollins was pleased that the departed Joanne's dresses fit the newcomer. However, she resolved to set Tally and Clara to the manufacture of a more modern dress for Diana that very night.

The plate of meats and cheeses arrived. The curious Clara took its delivery as an opportunity to survey the mysterious guest sparking so much speculation downstairs. Mrs. Rollins cast a disapproving look in her direction and shooed her from the room. Then she conveyed Diana and her dishes back to the blue bedroom, where she could sit and eat.

Much to her relief, Mrs. Rollins observed that Diana's table manners were not so lacking as her earlier appearance might have suggested. Perhaps, she considered, poverty was a new condition for the baron's daughter. But no, recent impoverishment could not have made the callouses Mrs. Rollins had observed as she cleaned under Diana's fingernails. This girl had known at least a few years of hard labor. So why then had she been sent so suddenly to Wuster Park?

Mrs. Rollins tried not to devote much mental energy to such considerations, but they occurred to her, nonetheless.

*Six*

AFTER HER BATHING and dressing at the hands of Mrs. Rollins, Diana was shown downstairs. A brilliance of colors and textures asserted themselves at every corner and corridor in this palace of a place. Diana felt dizzy. Exhaustion was overtaking her, and the cold meats and cheese of her meal rumbled uncomfortably inside her. In a room that could only be described as violently yellow, she met her cousin Maggie for the very first time.

Overwhelmed by the strangeness of her surroundings, Diana was late to realize that after their introduction, Maggie was still speaking to her. It was with considerable effort that Diana drew her concentration to the words coming out of her cousin's mouth. Sadly, she found them to be as disorienting as everything else she had encountered in Wuster Park so far.

" . . . and you and I shall be the best of company, my dear, I'm sure. We must make sure to see about an extra crop for you, and you must inform Mrs. Rollins where we are to send for—Oh! And here he is! Benjamin! Benjamin, come and meet my dear cousin!"

Maggie said this as a tall, tolerably handsome man poked his head around the door frame. Spying his wife, his face broke into an enthusiastic smile. He bounded to her side, his long legs making quick work of the distance between them.

For an uncomfortably long time, the Howards stared rapturously at one another, grinning and blushing as they exchanged the most banal of greetings. Diana was a reluctant observer of this display. To avoid it, she first eyed the carpet and then the cushions of the settee. Her eyes had journeyed to the mantel by the time Maggie's mind was recalled to her guest.

"Oh, Benjamin, dearest. Meet my cousin, Lady Diana Huxley. Lady Huxley, this is my darling husband, Mr. Benjamin Howard."

Like two shy dogs, cousin and husband greeted each other politely. Then Benjamin turned his attention back to his wife, his face reigniting with obvious joy.

Over dinner, Maggie spoke in a near constant narration. She explained to Benjamin the very brief history of her correspondence which led to Diana's arrival, the surprise she had felt about said arrival, where Diana was now staying in the house, and all the gay plans she would make now that she had a female companion. Benjamin nodded along, matching her enthusiasm. Neither of them noticed the obvious wonderment Diana displayed as each new dish was placed before her.

When Maggie's lengthy telling of the short narrative had concluded, Benjamin turned to his new cousin by marriage and asked, "So, Diana, where are you from?"

Diana looked up at him. "Yansworth."

He waited for her to elaborate, but she did not. Maggie cut in.

"But I believe you live in a place outside of Yansworth, yes? A place . . . Coldflat? No, no. Caldflett Castle?"

"Yes."

There was an awkward pause before Maggie continued.

"Well how charming that must be. A castle. Your father's family's, is it not? An ancestral homeland. Very charming, I'm sure. And so grand. A castle!"

Diana did not know how to reply to this declaration, and so she ventured her first question of the night.

"How long have you been married?"

"Oh, my dear! We have been married, what is it now, Benjamin? Four months? Four months!"

"Four and a *half* months," Benjamin corrected.

"Yes, you're right. Four and a half months. What bliss it has been. You know, I'm not shy to say it, for it's very true. I was not always so sure about marriage. I waited a very long time. I am twenty-eight, you see."

Maggie paused to let Diana express surprise about this fact. When she did not, Maggie continued.

"Yes, I waited a very long time. But I'm so glad I did. For when we met . . . there was nothing like it in the world. It was meant to be. And every moment since that moment has been pure bliss. I am truly so lucky."

"No, it is I who am so fortunate to have you blessing my heart and home with your radiant, magnetic, poetic existence. I am forever indebted, in awe, inspired by your beauty, wit, and charm."

"Oh Benjamin," Maggie sighed, before continuing in her chipper tone. "Yes, we have been married four months. Which is almost as long as we knew each other before we were wed. Would you believe it? After waiting twenty-eight years to find a husband, I could not even endure a yearlong engagement!"

Benjamin began to protest that it was *he* who could not wait, but Maggie talked right over him.

"We met, oh it's such a droll story, my dear. So funny. Would you care to guess where we met? You shall never guess it. Would you like to try? Go ahead. You shall never guess. A dance! We met at a dance!"

Diana failed to grasp the humor of this revelation.

"It was a *public* dance," Maggie clarified, leaning forward and smiling at her cousin, hoping to coax some laughter from her at the obvious hilarity of the story.

The best Diana could manage in that moment was "Oh."

Maggie continued as if gratified by a standing ovation.

"We met at a public dance in Bath. Benjamin was looking so

handsome, but so uncomfortable."

"I was pinned in—"

"He was pinned in, you see. His friend Hempstead was making such a fool of himself. And I walked by, and saw him bouncing on his feet—"

"I was trying to spot my other friend, Cartwright."

"And I said, 'Well you look like you are just bursting to dance!' And what could he do? He had to ask me to dance. Though, I assure you, that was never my intention."

"Oh, I don't know about that."

"Don't tease me so, Benjamin! You know I was just making conversation."

"Well, I'm certainly glad you did. For it has been the catalyst of my greatest happiness. And indeed, any conversation you make is a gift to all who should chance to receive it."

The newlyweds stared deeply into each other's eyes and were lost to all else, especially the uncomfortable seventeen-year-old girl at their dining table. It was only when the footman began serving the third course that Maggie resumed her prattling discourse and dinner felt like it was trending towards a conclusion.

~

After dinner, Diana was led back into the magnificent blue bedroom where she had first arrived. The mud patch from her boots had already been cleared away. She was told this room would be hers for the duration of her stay at Wuster Park. Then she was left alone.

The silence of that room was an unsettling presence. The thick drapery and full carpet muffled sounds both interior and exterior. Diana could only hear her own breathing and the gentle crackle of the waning fire alight behind a screen in the hearth. With her candle in hand, she inspected the room minutely. Everything was so delicate. The hinges of the wardrobe were silent. The drawers of the writing desk slid effortlessly in and out of their places. Each small bottle on the vanity was made of glass thinner and clearer than any Diana had ever seen before.

But, by far, the most interesting object in the room was the tall cheval glass. Other mirrors Diana had seen were dull or distorted. The only mirror of this quality that she had known was her mother's small hand-mirror. When Diana was young, this hand-mirror sat on a rectangle of velvet upon her mother's bedside table, the last extravagance from a lifestyle long inaccessible. Once, at thirteen, Diana's mother caught her examining her face in the glass.

"Careful, Diana. You don't want to get too pretty. Your father might notice. A pretty girl, and a baron's daughter . . . You could be worth a lot of money. That means he'll lose you at cards, same as everything else."

Diana remembered the dark look in her mother's eyes as she had spoken those words. She had not fully understood what her mother meant by that warning. But that was the day she stopped imagining that things were going to get better.

Now, here at Wuster Park, alone in the room she was told was her own, after examining everything else, Diana examined herself in the cheval glass.

In the mirror she saw pieces of her sisters' faces. She saw her mother's eyes. She saw her father's dark hair. She saw the shape of herself, and she pressed the fabric of her dress flat against her body to see it better. She didn't look as old as she felt. She didn't feel as pretty as she looked. She remembered her mother's dark look once more, and she blew out the candle.

# Seven

DIANA WAS ROUSED from sleep the next morning by the arrival of a housemaid with a pitcher of water for her morning toilette. Next, Mrs. Rollins came in. To Diana, the stately housekeeper resembled a boxwood hedge. She was rigid, sharp, and directive. The woman combed and plaited Diana's dark hair, pinning it again before lacing her into the old-fashioned dress she had been given the day before. Finally, Mrs. Rollins presented Diana with a pair of gloves, lightly worn, which she insisted Diana put on right away and not remove unless necessary. Then Diana was left to wait in her room, unsure what she was waiting for.

It was with some irritation that the housekeeper knocked on the door later to inquire why she had not joined the family for breakfast. Diana sheepishly trotted down to the main level of the house. There, she commenced a search for her relations. She might have searched all morning if not for a footman pointing discreetly to the door on the far side of the long dining hall. Through that door, she located the breakfast room. In that room, she found her hosts eating breakfast. She joined them quietly, ate everything that was offered to her, and then sat in apprehensive silence until Benjamin announced he was headed out for the mill.

Upon his departure, Maggie turned her full attention to Diana.

"Well, how do you find Wuster Park so far? Is it much like your home? Caldflett Castle? Tell me, am I saying that right? Those northern places have such funny spellings, one can never be sure."

"Yes, ma'am."

"Oh, you must call me Maggie, dear. You must. Even being called Margaret makes me feel so strange. Maggie it must be. May I call you Diana? I hope so, for I already have."

Here, Maggie laughed at herself. Diana only nodded. Maggie's laugh tapered abruptly. An air of awkwardness settled in the room.

"What should you like to do today? It is your first full day at Wuster Park, and I suppose you'll want to see the place. Yes, we'll go for a drive on the grounds. I suppose we could take a turn in the formal gardens first. Or perhaps you'd like to see the house? Did Mrs. Rollins show you the house? No, I suppose not. You were very tired from your trip, I'm sure. How was your journey? Did your coachman have any trouble finding us? I am told that our gate can be easily missed in the low light if you're coming from the north, on account of the trees. But you must have found it, because you're here now."

It was with this cheerful, chattering narration that Diana was shown over the main floor of the house. She took in the splendors of the library, music room, three drawing rooms, and all other ornate chambers whose uses and necessity were foreign to her as she half-listened to Maggie describing more details of her abbreviated courtship and marriage. As the cousins took a turn in the small formal garden, Maggie explained the history of her husband's family. Benjamin's grandfather had invented some sort of extra efficient something in the manufacture of linen, and the wars on the Continent had created such a great demand that the profits financed the construction of Wuster Park. Over luncheon, Maggie told Diana of Benjamin's mother's tragic untimely death, and her father-in-law's more recent accidental departure from the land of the living. Finally, as the women were whisked around the expansive park grounds in an open carriage, Maggie shared with Diana her hopes and aspirations for her own future there at Wuster Park.

At last, when they arrived back at the grand house, Maggie announced that it was now time to prepare for dinner. Only then did Diana venture a sentence unprompted.

"Would you like my help getting ready, Cousin Maggie?"

"Oh yes, how dear and sweet you are. I would love that. And I can arrange your hair. I suppose Mrs. Rollins did it for you this morning, in a rush before she came to me. It looks very tidy, but I suspect you usually wear it in curls at your temples the way all the girls are wearing it this year. I can help you with those. I'll have some curl papers sent to your room so you may set them at night.

"Dear Mrs. Rollins told me about your missing luggage. Such a shame. But no matter, we will have you a new set of dresses made up in no time. I would offer to lend you mine, but you are so much taller than I am, I think the effect would be comical. As it's just family for dinner, your current dresses will be well enough. It makes perfect sense that the fashions would not change so quickly in the northern counties. Besides, it is nearly impossible to feel stylish when one must trim everything in black. You know, for the mourning period. Not that I don't grieve my father-in-law, I assure you. Only I didn't know him very well. Still, rules are rules . . ."

And Maggie prattled on unchecked through her evening preparations, until the dinner bell rang. Then she prattled on at dinner, to the evident delight of her husband, before they all settled into the drawing room for the evening. There, Benjamin read aloud from a novel, which neither cousin bothered to explain to Diana.

Upon returning to her blue bedroom that night, Diana was surprised to discover that the once imposing silence was now a balm to her soul. Alone at last, she relaxed, took down her hair, stretched her arms overhead, shook her limbs and spine to ward off the stiffness of so much sitting that day, and then fell into bed.

What a bed it was. Mattress, blanket, and pillows all gorged with feathers and wrapped in the smoothest cloth that had ever touched her skin. It was heavenly. But it was also cold. At Caldflett Castle, after cleaning up from dinner and putting out the fire, she would join little Nina on the straw bedroll under their shared wool blanket. The warmth of her sleeping sister was a rare comfort in an otherwise cold life. As she considered all the contrasts between life at Wuster Park and life in Caldflett Castle, she could not help but think this element to be one where Caldflett had the advantage.

# Eight

After almost a week of residence in Wuster Park, Maggie decided to take Diana to pay a visit to the village center of New Glenbury. In the time since her cousin's arrival, Maggie had found Diana's behavior to be most unusual. She was reluctant to speak, even when spoken to. She expressed no interest in offered amusements, opting instead only to observe Maggie in their pursuits. Diana's behavior towards Benjamin was even more reserved, and her obvious discomfort over their dinners in the dining hall put everyone on edge. This trip to town was an attempt by Maggie to rouse her cousin into some real conversation.

Built before the times of large carriages, the main street of New Glenbury was a narrow one that required all visitors to travel its modest distance by foot. Horses and carriages were left secured at either end. While some of the more modern visitors saw this as incredibly provincial and antiquated, the citizens and shopkeepers who frequented the village of New Glenbury felt great pride in the benefits of this arrangement, especially in comparison to the nearby town of Shrewsbern.

Unlike a wide and busy street teeming with horses, carriages, and the dust and debris that horses and carriages kick up, the little lane lined with shops was uncommonly clean and orderly. Owing to the regular and decent wages paid by the Howard Linen Mill, New Glenbury citizens had enjoyed many years of relative prosperity. This made for a stable economy supporting an abundance of quaint shops and vendors.

Maggie had not anticipated the amount of surprise the modest village of New Glenbury would inspire in her guest. From the moment of their arrival, Diana could not disguise her wonderment. Rather than endearing her to her cousin, this stirred Maggie to some vague discomfort at the girl's obvious lack of exposure to broader society. So far in their acquaintance, Maggie had come to understand that her cousin grew up near a very small hamlet in the mountainous countryside of the northlands. But, from Diana's reactions to the village of New Glenbury, Maggie came to see just how incredibly limited her society had been.

Yet, despite Diana's somewhat overexcited reaction to a rather small collection of shops and sellers, it was delightful to watch her in this new environment. Already in her short stay at Wuster Park, Diana had grown brighter and healthier in appearance. Though she remained clothed in the old-fashioned long-sleeve dress of a servant, her striking good looks and tall stature bestowed an unconscious elegance to the attire.

As Diana marveled aloud at the second hat shop they encountered, simply for it being the second of its ilk, Maggie felt a warm tickle of pleasant anticipation, knowing that down the lane Diana would encounter the third such business of their town.

As they approached this third hat shop, Diana's elation became rapturous. She spoke the largest collection of syllables she had henceforth shared with her cousin.

"A third! A third hat shop! And all these fine ribbons! A wonder you do not come here every day, Cousin Maggie. If my sisters could see this, they wouldn't believe it, not for a second. If I should write and tell them, they would call me a liar."

Maggie looked at her cousin, rosy-cheeked with excitement, and asked if she might like to go inside this third hat shop. She had asked this question at the first two hat shops as well. Each time, Diana had shyly declined. Now, as Diana was shaking her head again in gentle refusal, Maggie decided that she would simply lead the way. Into the hat shop she went, taking Diana by the hand.

Once indoors, Maggie watched as Diana scanned the small space until her eyes alighted on what all girls' eyes seek in a hat shop: the ribbon wall. To the ribbon wall they went. There, Diana stood in mute admiration. Maggie pushed for a little more conversation.

"Should we send some ribbons to your sisters?"

"Oh no, Cousin Maggie. Thank you, no."

"Perhaps this nice green trim for your mother, then?"

"She would like it well, but no, I cannot."

"Cannot or do not wish to?"

Diana only blushed and turned away, looking down at her hands as they nervously pulled at her borrowed gloves. Maggie was used to this silent reply, so used to it that it now became somewhat frustrating.

Taking her cousin's hands to stop her fidgeting, she said as sweetly as she could, "Let's pick out some ribbons for your sisters."

"Oh no, Miss . . . Mrs. . . . Maggie. I'm not to be any trouble to you."

"Trouble? What trouble is picking out ribbons?"

By now, the shopkeeper had come over to be of assistance, and the presence of a stranger sent Diana back under her veil of silence.

"Can I help you with anything today, Mrs. Howard?" the kindly old shopkeeper asked.

"Yes, please. We would like ribbon enough for three girls to trim their summer bonnets. What do you suggest?"

"They are not in mourning like yourself, ma'am?"

Maggie assured her that they were not. The shopkeeper wisely recommended three blue ribbons, all the same color but of varying patterns and widths. She explained that when young girls are trimming their bonnets together, it is best for them to have no colors to fight over, and instead a collection of ribbons which might be shared between them. When Maggie acknowledged this as most sensible, the shopkeeper smiled, explaining that she had three daughters close in age and was thus very familiar with the particular needs of young sisters' bonnets.

As Maggie approached the counter to collect the wrapped ribbons and settle her account, the shopkeeper suggested she might want to add some silk flowers to the bundle. She showed Maggie three white silk roses which she promised were sure to delight any young lady. All was going smoothly until the shopkeeper noted the total cost of the order. Hearing such a sum, Diana couldn't help but cry out in alarm. Both women turned to look at her. In the instant after her outburst, Diana turned and fled from the shop. Maggie moved to chase after her, but the shopkeeper placed an old, crooked hand atop her own.

"Give her a moment, ma'am. I've seen that look. Girls at that age . . . She'll need a moment before you get any sense out of her."

The old woman spoke with such unflappable confidence that it eased Maggie's worry. She concluded the transaction, thanked the shopkeeper warmly, and then calmly walked back into the neat and narrow cobblestone street.

She had seen Diana turn left upon her exit, so Maggie walked in that direction. A few buildings down, she found her cousin wringing her hands under the eave of a small doorway. Maggie attempted to hand her the little parcel of ribbons and flowers, but Diana would not take hold of it. This, more than anything else Diana had done that day, was vexing to Maggie, who finally vented her frustration.

"Diana, you had better just come out and tell me what is going on. What is the trouble? We are both adults, and if there is something upsetting you, I expect you to make it known."

Diana looked at her, and in that instant, Maggie caught a glimpse of the woman behind the childish behavior, saw the flash of true feeling behind the juvenile caprices.

"Speak, Diana. Speak plainly."

"I cannot afford those ribbons. I cannot afford them or the flowers. Mother said, she was very, *very* clear, that I was not to make my-self a burden to you. I was not to indulge in extravagances or be costly to you in any way. It is a favor that you have taken me as your lady's maid, and I'm to work and serve you and cause no trouble and add no expense."

It took Maggie a few moments to comprehend the full scope of this declaration and all the understanding it shone on all of Diana's previous behavior. Her unvarying silence unless spoken to, her tremendous deference to all of Maggie's suggestions, her skepticism at all offers to enhance her comfort . . . All these made sense now as Maggie realized the girl was operating under a very different under-standing of her place in Wuster Park. Of course she was. Maggie re-alized in a wave of mortification that the timing of Diana's arrival meant that no letter explaining the terms of her invitation to Wuster Park could have possibly arrived before she did.

Maggie could not help her next action, so moved was she by her sudden comprehension of this tender girl's anxiety. She threw her arms about her cousin in an unreturned embrace. After a few mo-ments of what she hoped was at least some consolation, she linked arms with Diana and led her slowly back to their ponies and gig. Along the way, she tried to explain.

"Diana, you are my cousin."

"Yes, but mother says that I am not to be giving myself airs on account of it, and I should serve you just as well as a stranger. You are a grand lady in a grand house and I'm not to be making assump-tions on your kindness."

This last phrase was said in such a way that Maggie knew it could only be a direct quotation from the girl's mother.

"But Diana dear, I do not see you as my lady's maid. Indeed, you are *not* my lady's maid. I wrote to my mother to invite you as a guest. She in turn was meant to write to your mother. I'm sure she must have. Of course you arrived so quickly, I did not consider that the letter would have missed you. I invited you to Wuster as a guest, and a guest you must be. When I have advertised for a lady's maid—"

"Then you shall send me back home?"

"No! Then I shall have a lady's maid. And you shall remain my cousin and remain a guest in my house for as long as it is comfortable to you and convenient for your family."

To this, Diana said nothing. But it was clear that she was deep in thought with this new information. Maggie remembered the wise shopkeeper and with great restraint gave Diana a quiet carriage ride home to devote to her concentration.

They arrived back to Wuster Park a half hour after tea was typically served. Mrs. Rollins had anticipated their late arrival, and the tea table was just set for them in the south gallery, where the light from the tall windows warmed the room to a gentle prelude of summer. The ladies ate in silence, but when they rose from the table, Maggie led them to Diana's room and closed the door. She then commenced with a speech she had been composing for the whole of their repast.

"Diana, I apologize. I can see now that your situation was unclear to you upon arrival. You have acted in your best abilities to recommend yourself to the position you believed yourself to occupy. But you were not correctly informed, and I did not know you well enough to see that this was a mistake. Please forgive me, Diana. Do you forgive me?"

Diana only nodded, though somewhat skeptically, Maggie thought.

Maggie continued.

"You are here in my home as a guest, and, I hope, as a friend. I want only your happiness and require none of your help. Do you understand?"

Again, Diana nodded.

"Now Diana, I'm going to speak plainly. It seems to me that your parents have done little to expose you to much society outside your own home and country life. As such, it's understandable that the new and different things around you might be confusing or daunting. But you are, by rank and relation, entitled to all the comforts and amusements of my home and hospitality. I know they are different from your own. While you are here, you are under my care. And under my care, you do not need to do anything . . ."

Here, Maggie lost her way. She wanted to say something about how Diana's lack of funds did not exclude her from the life that Maggie wanted to give her, but even for Maggie, this seemed like too mean a topic to approach head-on.

Diana must have considered Maggie's faltering speech to be its conclusion. She began to speak of her own accord in a way that Maggie had not yet seen.

"If I am not to be your lady's maid, I do not know that my mother will let me stay. I was sent here so I might send regular wages back home. My sister Nan—Nannette—she is just now thirteen and there is much work to be done every day at Caldflett. If I cannot be useful here, I must seek another position. I cannot even afford to send these ribbons!"

"But Diana, it will not cost *you* anything to send the ribbons. Postage is paid by the receiver, as surely you know. Don't you? Do they have the post in Yansworth? Oh dear, please tell me they do."

Diana smiled. "Yes Maggie, Yansworth has the post. But my sisters will not have the money to receive the parcel unless I include it. As I have no money of my own—"

"I can supply a sufficient amount, surely."

"That is very generous of you. But I still must seek another position. My mother was right when she said I was unprepared to be a lady's maid, so perhaps you could write me a reference for an easier—"

"Stop, stop. No more of this talk, Diana. You must stay here, my dear. You must. And if it's your wages your family requires then we shall supply them. How much does a lady's maid make in a month?"

"I do not know."

"Well, it cannot be very much. I shall ask Mrs. Rollins tomorrow. Think no more about it, dear."

Then, with great solemnity, Maggie took Diana's hand in her own before concluding in a tone of great sympathy.

"I only hope, in time, you can find some happiness here."

For the first time since her arrival at Wuster Park, Diana laughed. Seeing Maggie's look of confusion, though, she quickly clapped her hand over her mouth.

"Please, Diana, don't cease laughing on my account. Only explain to me why it is so funny."

"You say you hope I can find some happiness here, but look around." Diana swept her arm towards the tall windows, richly draped. "How could anyone be unhappy here?"

Maggie now saw the room as Diana saw it: sumptuous, grand, and imposing. The canopy, carpet, and walls all collided in harmonious blue damask. Maggie realized that she had spent too much time in high society to recall that many who made claim to her social rank were unacquainted with her privileged reality.

"Is it very different from your own home, then?"

"Yes. You could say that. You could indeed say that."

"But I assumed with a name like Caldflett Castle . . ."

"It is a castle, I suppose. But it is nothing like this house. Not at all."

"Tell me how. Explain for me, Diana dear, please. I want to understand."

"Well, I never had my own room before. Never had my own bed. Even now, though I am oldest, I share with little Nina. Caldflett was not a very big castle when it was built. I do not know when that was, but it was a very long time ago. We have the four stone walls mostly whole, but the roof has been leaking as long as I can remember. No one can go up to the top floor anymore because the timber is rotted and we've had to move the bedrooms down."

Maggie nodded as her eyebrows pressed together. As Diana expounded upon the daily labors required of her to keep a fire lit and food on the table for herself and her sisters, Maggie interrupted.

"Where is your father? My dear, he is a baron. Barons do not live like this. There are certain privileges that a man of his station—"

"I believe the only privilege of the peerage which applies to my father is his inability to be jailed for his debts."

"This is unimaginable."

"For you, perhaps."

"I can see that Wuster Park is indeed a great difference from what you are used to at home, Diana."

Diana replied with a nod, then added with a sudden anxiety, "What about Mr. Howard? Does he know you do not want me as your lady's maid? Will he let you keep me if I'm not to be of any use? I don't want to cause a fight between you. I see how much the expense of having me at your table must be. I promise I wouldn't mind eating my meals in the downstairs, or just here in my own room."

Maggie shook her head. "My dear, you leave Mr. Howard to me. He has such a kind and generous heart. He will have no hesitation, I'm sure."

"What about the wages?"

"The wages? Oh yes, the money to send your sisters. I'm sure we can manage it. It cannot be much. Think nothing of it, dear."

In the next hour before the dinner bell rang, Maggie soothed her own spirits by explaining in detail her own personal adjustments to life at Wuster Park. Diana was grateful that her cousin spoke so fluently and freely. Such discourse left only enough space for Diana to nod in agreement. Thus, her mind was free to grapple with this bewildering stroke of good fortune and what myriad of misfortunes must surely follow. To live at Wuster Park *not* as a servant was a scenario she had never imagined. What her mother would say of such circumstances she would not dare consider.

When the dinner bell rang, both women were surprised by it. For Maggie, the time had flown by. For Diana, an age had passed.

<h1 style="text-align:center">Nine</h1>

Diana's arrival at Wuster Park had not escaped the notice of Constance and Elizabeth. However, in the two weeks since her appearance, very little had been learned about the mysterious baron's daughter. Constance had spoken to her after church, of course. These exchanges could not be called conversations. They could barely be called exchanges. Diana's replies had been nearly inaudible, and the only conclusions Constance could make from the introduction were that Diana was very tall and very shy.

Elizabeth did not attend services at the New Glenbury church except on holidays. As such, she had not yet had the opportunity to meet Diana. The following Monday after Diana's second week in New Glenbury, Elizabeth arrived to the rectory after luncheon with many pressing questions for Constance on the subject.

"Have you heard what they are saying about her in town?"

"No, Elizabeth. What are they saying?"

"How should I know? That's why I'm asking you."

"Well, I've told you everything I know about her. She's as tall as an elm and as meek as a mouse. This week she wore a new dress to church, more modern than her previous frock. That is the extent of my observations. We have other parishioners, you know."

"What about the Langley party?"

Constance was just about to answer when a polite knocking was heard at the rectory's front door. Elizabeth rose from her seat and began to gather her belongings. She did not like to be present when Constance had other callers. They were invariably dull and often solicitous of help, a condition Elizabeth found most tedious. It was not that Elizabeth was ungenerous exactly, it was just that she hated being party to other people's complaints.

When Maggie and Diana entered the rectory's drawing room, however, Elizabeth quickly resumed her seat. If there was going to be an intrusion into her time spent gossiping with Constance, it was ideal that the subject of such gossip would be the one to intrude.

Both of the younger women were outfitted in riding habits. Maggie's ensemble was a complete set made of dark-grey velvet trimmed in black braid. Diana's jacket was obviously borrowed from her cousin. The sleeves were comically short and the color was in disharmony with her plain old-fashioned dress underneath.

After introductions were made, the formal requisites of conversation that stand as a ceremonial prelude to any real discourse between neighbors began.

Elizabeth loathed these tedious preambles. At long last, when the necessary comments on the weather, the weekly sermon, the health of everyone in their mutual acquaintance, and the fineness of the offered shortbread biscuits were dispensed with, Elizabeth led the conversation back to where she and Constance had left it.

"Have, by chance, either of you encountered the new tenants of Langley Hall?"

They had not. And, to Elizabeth's extreme pity, they had not even known that there were new tenants to be encountered.

"They have not come to the service on Sunday, which I think bodes extremely unwell," Constance remarked.

This was agreed to by all, mostly out of politeness, for none of them had so strong a feeling on this matter as their hostess.

Maggie then ventured a question that Elizabeth was all too happy to answer. More and more, she was beginning to appreciate the unreserved nature of her new neighbor.

"What are people saying about them?"

"Well, we know from reports in town that there are three young men, probably brothers. Though one is fair and the other two are dark. There is one woman, almost certainly their mother. We know that they are interested in hunting and fishing, for they have placed an order for all those necessary supplies in town." Elizabeth lowered her voice as she continued, "Which, to me, seems quite indicative of the utter ruination the Langfords must have been on the brink of. For, if they have let their house without any of the supplies for a hunting party, it can only mean that they sold all those things long ago. But, I digress. We know that they are four in total, with no young ladies. And until their supplies arrive, I imagine they are all probably stuck indoors playing cards."

This comprehensive report precluded any follow-up questions, and the conversation faltered before it veered directly towards Diana.

Both Constance and Elizabeth were very gentle in their inquiries. They asked where she had come from, what she thought of New Glenbury, and they even tried a few questions about her interests and accomplishments. Diana's answers fell decidedly short. Not one could count as a complete sentence. Elizabeth noted the sheen of nervous sweat that misted Diana's forehead as she mumbled these short utterances quietly to her fidgeting hands.

In an act of mercy, Constance shifted the conversation to her recent projects in the parish. Entirely inattentive to the new subject of discussion, Diana was soon looking longingly out the windows at the rectory's orderly garden. Elizabeth noticed this and nodded at Constance. The reverend's wife suggested that Diana might like to take a turn in the garden while the others finished their visit. After all, it was acknowledged, their neighborly discussion of people and places she did not yet know could not really hold much interest for her.

Without hesitation or reply, Diana pushed herself back from her chair and galloped out of doors. Upon her exit, Maggie became so obviously animated with a desire to speak, it took only the faintest prompting from her companions before she laid the whole story out upon them. Diana's sudden arrival, her mistaken role as lady's maid, the difficult communications, the ribbon scene in town, and her slow adaptation to life in Wuster Park.

All of this was related quickly and completely, with an earnest, straightforward manner that gratified Elizabeth's every curiosity before it could be spoken. At the end of her telling, Maggie looked to the two wise women before her. She clearly expected that they would bestow great praise at this feat of social maneuvering. Instead, there came a long pause.

Finally, Constance said, "I think no good can come of this."

Maggie glanced at Elizabeth, probably hoping for a rebuttal. But Elizabeth only nodded, as serious as her friend. It was up to Maggie to inquire what could possibly be the problem. On this point, Constance was evasive. But upon direct appeal, Elizabeth laid plain the issues that the women were both in apparent agreement upon.

"It's simply this, Maggie. You are raising this girl above her station. And when she leaves your house, she will never know peace again."

Maggie did not see how this was such a certainty. So, it was Constance's turn to gently explain.

"Your home at Wuster Park, being so graciously opened to her, will make her accustomed to a certain style of living. Had you taken her as your lady's maid, she would have understood her place there to be one earned, not entitled. But now, she will come to fancy herself as belonging in such a home. And we know she cannot ever settle in one so fine."

"But you both said I ought *not* to have her as a lady's maid, only as a companion, a guest."

"Yes, we did."

There was a pause—a rather uncomfortable one. It was obvious that Constance was not done speaking but was only gathering her words very carefully.

"But this was before I understood that her . . . upbringing was so different than your own. I assumed that because she was your cousin, and a baron's daughter, she would have had the same advantages of charm and—"

"She is indeed very charming. Very pretty!" Maggie could not help but interject.

Elizabeth cut to the quick of the matter, saving Constance further embarrassment: "Maggie, she gulps her tea like a child. She has no conversation. And while, yes, she is very pretty, she has had none of the refinements of an education befitting a lady."

"Oh, but she is very smart. Only today as we were riding over, she could name every tree, every plant, every bird quick as can be . . ."

Elizabeth waved her hand in replying, "So, she will make a fine farmer's wife. Or, I should say, she would have. For surely, now, she will not think herself so low as to have one. And you, my dear, have just adopted a very pretty young spinster."

This blunt admonishment caused Maggie to flush bright pink. She stammered, "H-how dare you speak of her like that? You do not know her at all. Fifteen minutes we've been here and you think—"

Here Constance interjected.

"Maggie, dear, we say this as your friends. And in friendship to your cousin, Diana. We say this because we have seen it happen before."

"Indeed, it is a circumstance most common."

"Please try to listen as we say, with only her best wishes at heart, that you must help Diana to understand that your way of life is never to be her way of life. The sooner she can reconcile this truth to her understanding, the sooner she will be able to be happy in the life pre-ordained for her."

"Who is to say what her future might hold? She is a baron's daughter, a titled lady. She could marry a duke. She could be a finer lady than any of us. Why couldn't she? She is beautiful. She is a very fine rider. She is . . ."

Here, Maggie's enumeration of her cousin's merits ceased, and she, too, recognized the futility of hope on such a grand scale for Diana's future. Constance and Elizabeth watched this understanding soften Maggie's resolve and weigh, undeniably, on her heart.

But Elizabeth would not let the subject perish on such a conclusion. Who knew what might have been said about her when she was Diana's age . . .

"Well, she could not be a duchess, certainly not. But she is what, seventeen? Not out at all in society, you say. Therefore, she has several more years to work at improving herself. With diligence and the right training, she might make an adequate match. For she is indeed very pretty. Even if her father and mother can do nothing for a dowry, surely you and Benjamin can provide some modest sum to keep her competitive to her set."

"If you don't mind me saying so," Constance contributed, "I think that the skills of an accomplished woman are a great benefit to the satisfaction of a long life, no matter the matrimonial outcome."

"And," Elizabeth added, with more practicality than tact, "if you do end up saddled with her for life, at least with an education, she may be a more agreeable companion . . . or even a governess when your own children are quite young."

Maggie's pinched eyebrows betrayed her doubt.

With redoubled optimism, Elizabeth continued, "And who is to say what a little polish might do for the girl? You could get her some nice dresses, take her to London, and foist her off on some equally ignorant second son of some old family looking to add a little height to their heirs. Who's to say? That she requires polish is certain."

"I'm not sure I know where to start," Maggie said.

Constance and Elizabeth exchanged a wordless look that called upon all their long years of friendship in ascertaining their mutual agreement before Constance spoke for them both.

"You shall not do it alone, dear. Elizabeth and I will help you. We have undertaken similar projects in the past. We will guide you in the most sensible way."

"We shall call on you tomorrow morning," Elizabeth said. "For now, we shall say goodbye. You should take Diana home and make a thorough catalogue of her wants and her wardrobe."

The three women then moved to join Diana outside in the garden. Elizabeth was just thinking about how new gloves and dresses would probably be the biggest benefit to Diana's marital prospects. After all, many men preferred a shy girl for a wife, especially if she was pretty. There was a moment of pause as everyone looked around for the subject of their conspiracy. Then they spotted her.

Diana was crawling on her hands and knees along the south border of the garden where some apple trees had been lately planted. She spotted her hosts as they came towards. Wiping the dirt from her hands across the skirt of her dress, she stood to greet them. No one knew what to say in this strange situation, but Diana spared them the trouble of asking what on earth she was doing.

"They are taking quite well to their root stock, Mrs. Astley. The canvas is ready to come off the graft."

In that moment, Elizabeth was able to see Diana at her best. She was calm, confident, and carrying herself with an upright vigor the old woman envied deep in her bones. It was a great pity that she was a baron's daughter, Elizabeth thought, for she would have made a very fine farmer's wife.

# Ten

ON THE RIDE back from the rectory, Diana struggled to engage her cousin. On the ride over, only an hour or so earlier, Maggie had seemed delighted by Diana's identification of meadow birds and wildflowers. Now, even when Diana pointed out a very fine and colorful male thrush, Maggie only hmmm'd inattentively. She must have done something wrong. That was the only explanation. She replayed the day, trying to pinpoint the moment when Maggie's mood shifted to disapproval. It was a difficult task. Upon reflection, there were a great many things Diana suspected she had been wrong in doing.

First, there was the matter of the horses. When Maggie had announced that they would pay a call to the rectory, Diana had asked if they might ride over on horseback. In the days since their misunderstanding had been cleared up, Maggie often reminded Diana that she was free to make requests. But Maggie had not specifically said that such requests could extend to the stables. Maggie had not seemed displeased by the riding request, though, only confused. When Maggie had seen how easily Diana took to her saddle, she had looked greatly relieved.

Their ride over together had been pleasant. Diana was almost sure of that. She had even made Maggie laugh, though she was not entirely sure why. Diana was only doing what she assumed everyone did on countryside rides—pointing out all the plants and animals encountered along the way. It was true that Maggie had not joined in the naming, but she had nodded and smiled with every identification Diana had made.

The arrival at the rectory had been daunting for Diana, but she thought she had handled it well. She tried her best to say as little as possible, which in her experience was the most advisable strategy to take in the company of adults. She left as soon as she felt she was being a nuisance, and she could not figure how she might have displeased her cousin Maggie while she was out of the room.

In the warmth and stillness of Mrs. Astley's fine garden, Diana was sure she had done no wrong. She had pulled a few weed seedlings from the beds, and had not eaten any of the early berries growing ripe in the spring sunshine.

Then it came to her. She looked down at her dress. What an ungrateful fool she was. To wipe her dirty hands on a dress just given to her, Maggie must be beyond furious. Diana knew she would have to apologize as soon as possible, and probably have to apologize to the maid who took it away to wash. No doubt she would not be given any other dresses to disgrace with her carelessness.

Diana had just reached this conclusion when the cousins were reining their horses towards the mounting blocks before the Wuster Park stables. It was only after the women were out of earshot of the stable boys that Diana launched into her apology.

"Cousin Maggie, I am so sorry. I know it was very wrong to wipe the mud on my new dress. I will never do it again, I promise and—"

Maggie turned to Diana and cocked her head to the side in consideration.

"Oh, my dear, think nothing of it. I mean, hand it over to the maids to be cleaned of course, but . . . tell me, Diana, how did you become such a fine rider? I do not mean to insinuate, but of course you have told me about the conditions of Caldflett Castle and it seems reasonable to suppose therefore that your family did not keep horses. Perhaps your father is a sportsman and oversaw your lessons?"

Diana had been ready to prostrate herself in apology for her bumbling blunder, but she was not prepared for a question that cut so deeply into her heart and history. She was unable to speak. How had she learned to ride? On the surface it was a simple question that should have had a simple answer. Why couldn't she make herself speak? Why couldn't she think of something simple to say?

The longer her silence persisted, the closer Maggie's eyebrows crept and the farther her head tilted. Diana forced herself to speak, not sure what she would hear herself say.

"I had . . . when I was thirteen . . . no. When I was fourteen . . . there was a farmer. There is a farmer. There is a farmer and he also has horses. He has a son. I met his son. Then he came to Caldflett, the farmer and his son. He gave me lessons. Not at Caldflett, at his farm. I learned to ride from a farmer with horses."

Diana shut her mouth and began walking at a brisk pace up the gentle hill to the Wuster Park house. Maggie followed behind her, her short legs needing twice as many steps to keep up with Diana's stride. Both women were breathless by the time they reached the door. Maggie caught hold of Diana's sleeve.

"Wait. Please. Tell me more. A farmer does not ride sidesaddle. Do not tell me you learned to ride astride—"

"No, I learned sidesaddle. It's a long story. It doesn't matter now, does it?"

Diana wanted desperately to pull herself free from the tether of Maggie's light hold. Even though her cousin was smiling plaintively at her with innocent curiosity, her questions came too close to subjects Diana was unwilling to think about, let alone discuss. How could she tell Maggie about Charlie? About how they met and what he meant to her. She wouldn't understand.

"We should change, shouldn't we, Cousin Maggie?"

It looked for a moment as if Maggie was determined to push the issue and demand a full explanation. Then she only smiled.

"Yes, let's go and get freshened up. I'll call for baths."

# Eleven

Hudson, Ellis, and Noah were out of doors. Their expected hunting gear had not yet arrived, but the prospect of another day spent in indoor pursuits was deemed unbearable, even by the ever-affable Ellis. So, they took an exploratory walk about the grounds of the Langfords' estate.

The grounds of Langley Hall, in comparison to those of its neighbors, were shabby, small, and rather poorly planned. But for the three young men accustomed only to the trimmed and trampled tread of London's parks and the technologically enhanced pleasure grounds of Vauxhall and Ranelagh, these overgrown surroundings seemed a perfect wilderness of natural delights.

Each young man had conceived this countryside summer to serve his own purpose. While Noah claimed it was the romantic seclusion of nature he craved, in truth he hoped that the trip would distract his brother, Ellis, from his early and ardent attachment to one Melissa Greenby. Ellis fancied himself quite in love with this young lady and professed himself ready to give up all the best years of his youth to settle and be her husband. Noah abhorred this plan. He felt it would rob him of his chief companion years before he had any intention of securing a wife of his own—*if* he ever came to want a wife of his own.

Ellis had come to the country in hopes of perfecting the country arts away from the judgmental eyes of his prospective father-in-law, Mr. Greenby. Mr. Greenby had the distinction among his peers of owning a country estate. Though he was just a wine merchant, he was ever so keen to put on tremendous airs about his distaste for city life. Unfortunately, city life was the only life Ellis (and Noah and Hudson) had ever known. So, Ellis had ventured to the remote New Glenbury estate to ride and shoot and fish and farm, or whatever it was that country gentlemen were supposed to do without the entertainments of the city to occupy them.

Hudson's reasons for this country summer were more nebulous. It was the twins who first suggested the adventure to him. At the time, Hudson had simply agreed that he, too, fancied a change of scenery. In truth, he was seeking something closer to escape. As the rules and responsibilities of manhood coalesced about him, he longed to throw off these impositions and discover true freedom. In his urban imaginings, it was only in the countryside where a man might be free—free from the watchful eyes of social responsibility, free from the obligation of endless leaving and receiving of cards, free from the halfhearted amusements of theater and spectacle designed only to make a man seen by as many of his neighbors as possible. So, when a man by the name of Langford posted notice of an available estate, to the country he gladly went.

These young men, with their scant knowledge of the nature around them, could not contain their enthusiasm for the pleasures that they now indulged in. For more than a week, they had been mostly indoors. In the lightly furnished Langley Hall, they spoke in hushed tones as they played cards or chess. In the evenings, they read books. All this was to keep Mrs. Bellwood comfortable in her near-constant doze, but the monotony of such an existence was stifling. Now, out of doors and out of earshot, they whistled and yelled as they had done together as boys. In those days, the sounds of their play echoed up the long grey alleyway that ran behind the row of townhouses where they had grown up.

It wasn't long before each young man had a long stick in hand, "fencing" up and down the overgrown lanes of the Langley grounds. The sound of their merriment dissipated in the spring foliage and was swept away in the rustle of the wind overhead. Together, the trio was getting more enjoyment out of the Langford estate than any owner of the property had felt in at least three generations.

Panting and sweating in the warm spring air, Hudson took a seat and watched his friends continue their ceaseless sword-stick battle. There he contemplated the fallacy of time. Time told him that he was twenty, and time told him that because he was twenty, he was a grown man. But time had not, he felt, supplied him with the knowledge of what a grown man should know. He felt closer to eight than eighteen. He knew he was not alone in these feelings.

Once, he had confessed his surprise at Ellis's eagerness to marry when he himself felt so unequal to the responsibility. Then, Ellis had confided that he, too, still felt himself a boy dressed up in his father's long trousers. Nonetheless, Ellis believed that a marriage (and especially a marriage to the incredibly sensible Melissa Greenby) would make him equal to the task of adulthood. Perhaps this was true, Hudson thought. But he could not bring himself to rationalize such an action considering the risk that it would rob him of his precious little freedom, without the reward of the wisdom he sought.

Hudson knew that since Waterloo and the Congress of Vienna, other young men of his age and station were once again making grand tours of the Continent. Hudson saw much to envy in this. His family situation was one which could easily afford him such an excursion. However, he felt keenly that his education was unequal to the task of traveling even as far as France. He knew any trip he took would only put himself in the company of other English citizens. He did not like the idea of being dependent on servants for communications. And he suspected that he would be excluded by way of rank rather than fortune from the most elegant and interesting of diversions, just like he was in London. He had not sworn off the grand tour entirely, but he doubted himself equal to it just now. So, to

avoid another summer in London with its exhausting parade of parties, promenades, and plays, he absconded to the country. He hoped
that this summer might make him more of the man he felt he was
failing in finding.

All this he turned over in his mind as he watched the sparring of
his two friends. There among the weeds and wilds was a world that
felt to Hudson entirely free from responsibility. This freedom was
simply because he did not yet know the demands of a polite country
life.

# Twelve

THE NEXT MORNING, in anticipation of her new collaboration with Constance, Elizabeth awoke early. She had instructed her staff to make her breakfast ready at seven, and yet no breakfast was waiting for her. Elizabeth kept a staff of entirely French citizens. This practice was adopted shortly after her husband's death, to ensure the discretion of her help. Though she was now well past the age and inclination when a discreet staff was needed, she had grown quite fond of the extra instruction, maintenance, and management that a foreign team afforded her. Put plainly, Elizabeth liked to be needed. Under the care of such a capable housekeeper as Wuster Park's Mrs. Rollins, she would have been bored to tears. Furthermore, her "fluency" in the French language (which she considered her greatest accomplishment) would have deteriorated to passé phrases.

It was not uncommon for Elizabeth to request that her breakfast and toilette be ready early. But since none of her household was permitted to wake her, and she often slept past her own stated intentions, the staff had come to regard these requests as being purely ceremonial. So, it was with great alarm that her lady's maid, Heloise, replied to the ringing of an early-morning bell summons.

"Bonjour, Madame. Avez-vous un problème?"

"C'est sept heur, Heloise! Ou est ma breakfast? Ou est ma café?"

"Oh Madame! Excuse moi!"

The maid fled from the great room of her mistress to rouse the rest of the house into action. When she returned, Heloise tried her best to distract Lady Elizabeth from the delay by taking great pains with her personal appearance. She brushed and restyled her hair twice more than was necessary, continuing until she heard the gentle tap on the door which signaled that one of the under maids had arrived with breakfast. Elizabeth ate quickly, rushed the rest of her routine, and called for a carriage as she bundled up a folio of papers she had been working on the night before.

Many of Elizabeth's household watched from the abbey windows as her carriage sped off that morning. Then they collected around their own breakfast table to engage in speculation about the meaning of this uncommon occurrence. Had they not been so certain of their mistress's confirmed and continued idleness, they might have imagined that the old woman had somewhere to be and something of great importance to do that day.

In the carriage, on the way to the rectory, Elizabeth braved the possibility of motion sickness to read over her notes from the night before. She had felt very proud of her efforts upon settling into bed. Because she had written most of the document with the added inspiration of a few glasses of claret, she thought it best to check over it just once more by the light of day before showing it to Constance.

It was a list of the skills and attributes Elizabeth thought it both prudent and possible to impart on a girl, already seventeen, for the purpose of making her a more eligible match. It read as follows:


*Dancing—a must!*
*French conversational basics*
*New dresses—not to skimp on the gloves!*
*The flute*
*Bonnet trimming*


In her memory, the list had seemed longer, but it was no matter.

She did not doubt that Constance would have her own ideas about what to teach the girl.

Indeed, Constance did. She, too, had committed her ideas to paper. The ladies exchanged their lists in a tone of mutual mirth at their parallel thoughts on the way to Wuster Park. Constance's list ran as follows:

*Reading—major classics and contemporary poetry*
*History of England, France, and modern political systems*
*French*
*Arithmetic and the neat management of a small household*
*Needlework: fancy and plain*
*Lace making and ribbon work*
*Penmanship and polite correspondence*
*Darning and knitting*
*Pianoforte*
*Drawing—landscapes*
*Painting—still life*
*Polite conversation*
*Moral and ethical enlightenment*
*Dancing*

Elizabeth and Constance shared a small chuckle as they read the other's list, and then cast sidelong glances at one another, each wondering what was so funny about her own list. Constance broached the topic first.

"Why do you suggest she learn the flute?"

"I think it quite clever, actually. With the flute, she would only need to learn a few songs, maybe three. Then, since no one keeps a spare flute lying about, she will never be called on to play outside the days and times of her choosing. She can exhibit, but she can never be asked to accompany."

"Oh, that is rather clever," Constance admitted without a hint of disapprobation before she continued.

"Last night, I was considering the difficulty of teaching such an unpolished girl all the essential skills in a mere three years. To cut piano out of the equation will save a great deal of time. And it will probably save the girl a good bit of embarrassment. Because, no matter how much she might practice, she could never achieve proficiency with the pianoforte in comparison to a girl who had lessons since childhood."

Elizabeth nodded in agreement. "I am glad we both agree on French."

"It seems most sensible. Though, I do have a plan if she finds it too difficult. For, I must admit, Elizabeth, she did not impose an impression of keen intelligence. I worry we may have our work cut out for us in this tutelage."

"Oh yes, she seems blessed only in face, rather than head. But as you were saying . . ."

"Yes, well, if French becomes too difficult for her, I was thinking the reverend could impart some of the rudiments of German to her—little phrases, a few key sentences, nothing substantial. No grammar. And, since she would never be in the path of any who could speak German, it will never be known how ill she might sound."

"Yes, for all German words sound ill, and who can say if they are right or wrong?"

This was pronounced just as the two women alighted from the carriage at the front court of Wuster Park. As they were expected, they were shown right away into the breakfast room, where Maggie and Diana waited.

The formalities of greeting commenced. As they had just seen each other yesterday, the polite conversational topics of neighborhood gossip and recent weather were all soon exhausted alongside the delicious breakfast prepared for them. As the footmen were clearing away the dishes, Constance took the liberty of suggesting they all move to the library.

Settled comfortably away from the watchful eyes of the house staff, Constance and Elizabeth were eager to begin the discussion of their plans with Maggie. Whether or not Diana should be included in this conversation was discussed, but not with words.

Elizabeth looked at Constance, then Diana, then Constance again.

Constance looked at Elizabeth and nodded, but then looked at Maggie, and then Diana.

Maggie observed all of this and looked around confusedly.

Diana observed nothing but her own gloved hands.

Finally, it was settled between Constance and Elizabeth that Diana should not be present. Both women looked at Maggie, then Diana, and then back at Maggie most pointedly, until finally Maggie said, "Diana, do you think you should perhaps go for a walk this morning?"

"Am I allowed to go for a walk by myself?"

"Yes, of course you are. What a silly question."

"Or perhaps you might like to do some reading?" Constance suggested.

Diana was already halfway across the room.

When the door slammed behind her, Elizabeth said, "Add entrances and exits to your list, Constance."

That was the entire introduction this absorbing subject needed to get all three women collaboratively charting the course of the next three years in Diana's life.

By lunch, it was settled that French lessons with Elizabeth would commence as soon as possible. A reading list was started, and Constance agreed to come twice a week to Wuster Park to give Diana practice in polite, rational conversation about books. The flute was universally approved as an excellent musical option, and Maggie was tasked with finding a master to come with those instructions when the time was right. Maggie was also in charge of determining the girl's skill with sewing and decorating. A few possible plans of instruction sprang from the speculation of what she might discover.

The morning hours passed so quickly and agreeably that the group was quite startled by the arrival of Benjamin and the call to luncheon. Though there was plenty of food to welcome them to table, Constance and Elizabeth begged the excuse of prior obligation. They departed in Elizabeth's carriage just as Diana was coming back to the great house.

In their few remaining moments together, Elizabeth, Maggie, and Constance conferred on one final detail: what should Diana be told about their plans? Each woman had her own reasoning why the only answer to this question could be *nothing*.

Elizabeth felt that the girl would surely rebel, as all girls of seventeen feel impelled to do when informed of plans made on their behalf.

Constance posited that the information of their purpose might raise the girl's hopes of a marriage beyond her abilities to secure one.

Maggie insisted that Diana would feel the added instructions on her behalf to be an abuse of kindness for which her mother would admonish her greatly.

So, it was decided by all to say nothing and, rather, try and pass off all their instruction as simple, well-meaning, neighborly interest.

As the carriage carried Elizabeth and Constance back to the rectory, where they could share their own meal and the comfortable conversation of two longtime friends, Elizabeth could not contain her happiness. She reached out and squeezed Constance's hand across the carriage seat.

"I know just what you mean," her friend warmly replied. "It is certainly nice to have some real meaningful occupation again after these two years."

# Thirteen

IN THE TIME when her female acquaintances were plotting her future, Diana took to the garden. At first, she stayed nearby, not sure if she would be summoned soon. Round and round, she made slow circles in the little formal flower garden in front of the grand vista that was Wuster Park. But the rolling green hills and soft breeze tempted her greatly, and she longed to place herself out of summoning distance. So, after one last look at the wide windows of the great house, she set off. First, she headed north towards the main road to New Glenbury. Before reaching the gate of Wuster Park, she turned west into a great stand of trees.

There she followed one of the lesser-used walking trails of the park. On most days with fine weather, she would accompany Maggie on a walk in the Wuster grounds. Maggie favored the routes that took her east on the bare hills so she might look over and see the mill at a distance and enjoy the sunshine of an unobstructed day. The path that Diana took now was deeply shaded. Because she was walking without her cousin's constant chatter, she was able to hear the birds calling to each other from the treetops and the low grumbling of an occasional frog near the clear brook that served as companion for the wooded path. Sweet violets bloomed in patches too sporadic to be intentional. Diana picked a few of their small purple flowers and turned them idly in her hands.

As the wooded trail wound further to the south and the brook grew wide and still, she saw the beginnings of marshy irises shooting their sword-like fronds straight up from the reedy banks. It was a beautiful place. Diana sat on a rock, careful to place her handkerchief down first to keep from soiling her new pale-yellow dress. Turning her face to the sky, she caught a glimmer of sunshine filtered through the leaves of the great trees overhead. The warmth of it permeated her closed eyelids.

She breathed slow and deep, and without thinking, she found there were tears wetting the corners of her eyes. She dashed them away on the sleeve of her short jacket and shook herself like a foal beset by a fly. What could she be crying about? She reprimanded her own folly. She knew she could not be homesick. That much was certain.

How could she be homesick for a place that had none of this charm? None of this gentle beauty? She had heard the north counties called "enchanted," of course. But the people who said such things were the ones who saw it only from carriage windows and from comfortable travelers' inns. None who really knew it could call it en- chanting. Wild, yes. Harsh, often. Rugged, certainly. However, when she thought of her own home, as she tried so hard not to do, she could only call it bitter—bitter and cold.

Caldflett Castle was a crumbling stone ruin, worse even than the way she had described it to her cousin. Sitting high on a crag, it was far from everything, and the only visitor was the howling wind. In winter, the rains leaked in from every window and door. The yard turned to mud and then froze. She shivered now to think of it.

It was a harsh place, and the only things that grew on the grounds were heather, heath, and sharp grasses that even the sheep pastured there seemed to resent. While she could see why the wide mountainous vistas might appeal to flat-landed visitors seeking an afternoon walk, living there was an exercise in unrewarded persever- ance. It was nothing like Wuster Park.

Wuster Park was all calmness, all gentility. Rain misted politely on the soft meadows. Sunshine blanketed the earth, every inch of which seemed aching to bloom; everything planted seemed to thrive. Diana wondered if she too might thrive here. So why, then, were her eyes wet with tears?

She continued her walk, trying to put a physical and emotional distance between herself and those intrusive memories that seemed always just a few steps from catching up with her. She listened to the birds and the frogs and tried to keep her mind on more present matters. She thought of her new life and the strange intricacies that were forever revealing themselves to her. She thought of her new acquaintances.

Right away, she had felt that Mrs. Rollins was a boxwood hedge personified. In recent days, she had come to think of the maids as a tangle of creeping loosestrife. They blanketed Wuster in their presence but were not easily seen unless looked for. Benjamin was the upright and ever-bouncing ox-eye daisy. His slender body bent and bobbed as he peeped wide-eyed around a doorframe before springing to his wife's side, forever nodding along at her cheerful chatter.

And what could her cousin Maggie be except a rose? A sweet-smelling, full-blooming, sunshine-seeking rose of the lushest description.

Diana had tried to grow a rose once. Farmer McFaden had given her a small rose bush after returning from a journey to market. The thorny shrub had been dutifully planted in the only place where it had any chance of survival: at the base of Caldflett Castle's west-facing wall. All spring and summer, Diana had watered and watched the little rose bush, making note of each new leaf and every bit of fresh green growth. The first flower bud had rendered her breathless in amazement. Then, wonder of wonders, the little bush bloomed. With each new blossom came a scattering of white petals over the rocky landscape, but bloom it did. Then, the winter came, and the bush went dormant.

Diana had still visited it every day, waiting for new growth to signal that imperceptible first herald of spring. But, for the little rose bush, spring never came. It remained there still, a dry brown husk of thorny sticks demonstrating what Diana already felt, that nothing beautiful could grow at Caldflett Castle. No amount of love or care could compete with the brutal reality of life there.

Maggie had never known a brutal life. Only sweetness and gentleness surrounded her. She made the most innocent assumptions of all situations. When Diana had confided that she was unfamiliar with the use of curl papers, Maggie was quick to say that the trend had probably not reached the north counties yet. When Diana expressed wonderment at the heap of bright-white sugar cubes made available with tea, Maggie assumed it was the painting on the sugar bowl she was admiring.

At first, Maggie's naivete made her seem to Diana much like a living doll, incapable of any real feeling or comprehension. But by degrees, she saw that Maggie was not the vacant, sparkling marble of perfection that she appeared to be. No, she was only innocent, coddled, and indulged. An acquaintance with Maggie would have been infuriating, were she not so gentle and so kind. She had an adorable, pathetic softness to her. Having never known scarcity, she was always eager to share. To Diana, she was a rare creature. Instinctively, Diana felt that the uncomplicated innocence of Maggie's existence was a thing to be protected. A rose could not grow except in such tender conditions, and Diana did not want to live in a world without roses.

She walked on, letting the rhythm of her steps lull her thoughts. It felt good to walk at her natural speed. When she walked with Maggie, she was always mindful about keeping her steps short to match her cousin's. Now, she swung her arms and let her bonnet rest upon her back as she made her way down a soft hill and into the rich timberland of Wuster Park.

She let her thoughts wander too, and soon she was lost in memory.

~

It had been an uncommonly warm day in early spring. Birds were feeding on the catkins of the aspen trees which lined the lower road on the last mile of her walk into Yansworth. She had come, as always, to collect her family's allowance and purchase the necessary ingredients of their modest existence. She was just fourteen then, a year older than Nan was now.

Outside of Yansworth's lone tavern and inn, some post boys were milling about. Though they were only a few years older than herself, their gainful employment and nomadic existence emboldened them. Some ale might have also been involved. The cluster of youths called after her, first in friendly solicitude of a smile, then in indignant condemnation of her inattention. Diana paid them no mind. This was not the first time such unwanted attentions had been lavished upon her. She trusted that in the absence of reply, they would tire of their exertions and find other outlets for amusement.

She visited the butcher first, tucking the parcel of tough mutton into the small basket on her arm. Upon her exiting that establishment, the post boys resumed their taunting. Diana continued to ignore them. She visited the miller and collected flour and oats enough for another week of tasteless mush and dense doughy rolls. This was her last stop, and she tied her shawl close over her shoulders before exiting to begin her long journey homeward. This was when the trouble began.

Upon exiting the miller, she once again heard the clamor of the post boys, their dialogue now veering into the vulgar. Diana was not familiar with most of the phrases they employed, but she understood their tone perfectly. Content to make a hasty retreat to the hills, she kept her head down. She did not see from where the new voice came. She heard only its clear and loud pronouncement.

"That is a lady you are speaking to!"

There was a pause and then a chorus of cackles. Diana knew she should walk on even faster, but curiosity halted her step and commanded her gaze. There, in front of the inn, stood a young man unfamiliar to her. He was tall, with brown hair and freckles across his tall cheekbones and strong nose. He wore the long workshirt of a farmer. He could not have been more than sixteen, easily the age of the post boys he was admonishing. But unlike their sinewy, slouching selves, he stood tall and well built. He wasn't looking at her.

The post boys made him the object of their insults as Diana watched in mute discomfort. He countered all their base remarks with firm rebuttals. There were five post boys, and yet not one of them seemed willing to get within an arm's reach of the young stranger, though the pitch of their abuses steadily increased. Diana felt certain that if they should attack the young man, it would be unquestionably her fault. She didn't know what to do. She wanted to call out, yell *stop*, scatter the group like a flock of fowl. But she couldn't. She couldn't move or speak or even look away.

Finally, the moment of violence arrived. One of the post boys lunged at the farmer, striking him with a meaty thud as fist collided with abdomen before quickly retreating out of reach. The farmer did not fall or even falter. He took but a half step back.

"If you're not afraid of a fight," he said calmly, "don't fight like you're afraid."

Something in his tone spooked the foul youths. They conversed quickly amongst themselves and then beat a hasty retreat around back to the stable yard. At their departure, the spell was broken and Diana regained her animation. She rushed to the stranger's side, fearing a return with redoubled violence.

"Quickly, before they come back!"

She pulled him along the dirt footpath that served as a shortcut through country that a carriage couldn't navigate. When the pair was safely out of sight, tucked into the folds of the hills that surrounded the valley, Diana came to a stop and caught her breath. She turned around to face her defender.

"What is wrong with you?!"

He wasn't expecting this question and had no reply.

"They could have killed you!"

"Beggin' your pardon, but it's not likely I'd be killed by them."

"If they had a knife!"

"What if they did? Someone should teach them not to talk to ladies in such a way."

"You think just because I am a titled lady that I need you defending my honor to a bunch of noisy carriage hoppers?"

"Beggin' your pardon, but I didn't know you were a *titled* lady. Only that you were a lady. And ladies ought to be able to go about their business—"

"Never mind me going about my business. I was going about my business just fine until you got involved!"

"Beggin' your pardon, miss—"

"Stop begging my pardon and leave me alone!"

Diana could not account for the animation of her spirit at that time. Later, she would conclude that it was a delayed expression of all she had felt while watching powerless as the young man defended her honor to the unruly ruffians.

"I will go on my way, miss. But I have to say it was *you* that dragged *me* out here."

Diana glowered at him in lieu of any sensible rebuttal. She turned and departed in a huff, mumbling to herself a million mean things she wished she had said. That night in bed, she earnestly hoped to never see that young man again. Yet each week when she ventured into Yansworth, she looked anxiously over her shoulder and searched for his face on every stranger.

That was how she first met Charlie McFaden. It would be another year before they met again.

Now, deep in the woods of the Wuster Park estate, Diana found her tears freely flowing and no self-chastisement to cease them. She missed Charlie McFaden. She knew she would miss him for the rest of her life. For him, she would mourn. For him, she would be homesick.

# Fourteen

As PART OF Constance and Elizabeth's plans for their new neighbor, Maggie had been tasked to determine Diana's proficiency in the skills deemed important for her education. So, for several weeks, each day brought a novel task for her cousin to attempt.

Diana proved herself to be an efficient seamstress, working quickly to make and mend. However, she was entirely lacking in the knowledge of decorative stitches, even the French knot. For this deficit, Constance supplied several projects to provide practice. Diana seemed happy to be helpful, and Maggie sensed that her young cousin even felt some pride as progress with this work was examined.

Maggie was also pleased to discover that Diana was a neat draftswoman. Her pencil drawings, though long in their production, were well ordered and proportional to their subjects. The girl seemed to have a natural sense for art. However, when Maggie gave Diana the opportunity to enhance her drawings with watercolors, she was shocked to learn she had never used paints. Maggie provided some basic instruction in the mechanics of brush and water. Then she watched in wonderment as Diana spent two solid hours mixing colors on her little porcelain palette without putting a single drop of pigment upon her paper.

Elizabeth expressed a strong conviction that the decoration of bonnets was a vital ingredient in the development of an individual aesthetic. Maggie had warned Elizabeth about Diana's extreme discomfort regarding the purchasing of bonnet ribbons. Elizabeth was not deterred. She visited all three hat shops in New Glenbury, where she purchased an alarming assemblage of bonnet bases, ribbons, feathers, fabrics, and fancies. These she heaped in a tangle on a table in one of the many drawing rooms in Eastbey Abbey.

The next time Maggie and Diana paid her a call, Elizabeth made a prodigious fuss about the inconvenience of such a hoard. She then begged that both women would assist her in its disposal. Maggie could not help but be amused at how well the ruse worked. Diana, it seemed, wanted nothing more than to be useful.

At each subsequent visit, as Diana pleated ribbons and stitched fasteners, Elizabeth would speak slowly and gently to her in French. Holding up ribbons of various colors, she would name them in French, asking Diana to repeat them back to her. By these means, and many others, the women in her acquaintance attempted to impart upon Diana all the knowledge she might need to be an eligible match for marriage.

Benjamin had been informed of the conspiracy surrounding his young guest, but he did not give much consideration to its progress. He was happy simply to know that his wife was happy.

Prior to his recent return with his new bride, Benjamin had not spent much more than a few consecutive weeks in New Glenbury since the death of his mother. He had been nine when she succumbed to her illness, and as soon as the headstone was carved he had been shipped off to school. Of course, he would come back to Wuster Park occasionally on breaks and holidays. Those experiences did little to endear the place to him. Most of his memories were colored by his father's continuous complaints. Nothing could please the man. Every fault required discussion.

From his father's grumbling grievances, Benjamin's idea of New Glenbury was one of bad weather, dull neighbors, and infuriatingly inconsistent post service. Because of this (and because his father had been in excellent health and of reasonable age), Benjamin never imagined he would have to live at Wuster Park so soon after his marriage. It was forever a distant thing, though only a long day's carriage ride from London. He had spoken of the place to Maggie in the vaguest terms before they arrived for the funeral. He remembered the cold clench of guilt in his sternum as their carriage first stopped before the wide portico. In that moment, he felt it was unfortunate that his father had died so suddenly, but it was a *tragedy* that someone so vibrant, lovely, and wonderful as his darling, dearest Maggie would have to reside in such a dull, dreary little village as New Glenbury.

Then, of course, Maggie did what she always did: she surprised him. She was charmed by the house. She got along well with the staff. She appreciated the modest mercantile offerings of the village. And now, just a few months after their arrival, she had found both friendship and occupation for herself. To Benjamin, she was a marvel of yet undiscovered magnificence. He spent each evening in awe as she would recount the delights of her day. At night, he lay by her side and listened to her breathing, awash in gratitude that fate had chosen to unite them.

Maggie's occupation with Diana had practical advantages, too. The scope of the project made Benjamin feel less guilty about how much of his time was required by the Howard Linen Mill. Old Mr. Howard had been the sole bookkeeper and accounts manager for the business, trusting no one else with such sensitive information. As such, his sudden death left everything in a state of profound confusion. Without such diversions for Maggie, Benjamin imagined she might have resented that her new husband was so obligated by his interest in trade. But because both their days were filled with activities each deemed essential and important, their time together was made all the more precious and leisurely.

# Fifteen

Diana did her best to keep up with the schedule of life in the Wuster Park house.

She woke in the morning with the sun and patiently awaited the arrival of a maid to secure her dress and hair before descending to the breakfast room. After Benjamin's departure from the table, Maggie would announce any plans for their day. Usually, these plans were edifying pursuits with Constance or Lady Elizabeth. But, at least once a week, their day included a visit to one of the tenant cottages on Wuster Park.

At first, Diana understood these visits to be social calls akin to those they paid to the rectory or Lady Elizabeth's home, Eastbey Abbey. She was surprised to discover that they were intended as visits of charity. To Diana, the tidy cottages of the farmers and their families seemed more comfortable than her own room in Wuster Park. To learn then that Maggie felt sympathy for such an existence which could only be assuaged by the deposits of heaping baskets of bread, game, butter, and cheese, made Diana blush.

With time, however, she learned to conduct herself like Maggie on these calls. She did not lift any children. She did not assist in any ongoing housework. She did not ask prying questions about the specific health concerns of pigs or goats. She nodded and smiled quietly.

She let the children tug on her skirts. She watched silently as the stew boiled over into the fire. And she said nothing when one farmer's wife reported she was planting a crop of leeks in the small plot south of her cottage, even though it was clear to Diana that the soil was much too wet for them to grow.

Yes, thanks to her ongoing observations, Diana did her best to accustom herself to the new reality of her life by Maggie's side at Wuster Park. But there were some adjustments she just couldn't find a comfort with, no matter how she tried. Daily baths were one such adjustment.

Most days, Maggie and Diana's errands or adventures would return them home in the mid-afternoon, two or three hours before dinner. Handing her walking accessories over to a maid upon entering the Wuster Park house, Maggie would politely request that two baths be drawn. Then Maggie would disappear into her bedroom and leave Diana waiting uncomfortably in her own room as the scurry of servant girls stopped their other projects to complete the request.

Maggie's bathing chamber was spacious, with a long window covered in white linen so fine that sunlight filtered through with an outline of the landscape outside. Diana's bathing chamber was tiny, with hardly enough room for the copper tub it housed. Within these constricted confines, there managed to also exist a small fireplace. There, a large copper kettle was filled and refilled with water from the supply of the tub. This provided an infusion of heat to the tub which counteracted the natural cooling of the water on its journey from belowstairs.

Diana hated every single thing about the bathing process. She disliked the inconvenience it gave the servants. She disliked the copious amounts of water it consumed. She hated that a whole half-shovel of coal was used for the small fire in her bathing chamber. And she hated that after all that trouble and expense, she was expected to undress and luxuriate in the blissful comfort of such opulence while one of the women responsible for assembling it stood by and watched her.

After weeks of tolerating this daily mortification, Diana made herself bold enough to beg the maids to kindly omit her bathing chamber from their services and attend solely to Maggie's bath. This request was met with confusion, which further frustrated Diana in her efforts to be unobtrusive.

Word of Diana's request soon reached Maggie. Her kind cousin was quick to come to her rescue. But not in the way Diana so desperately wished.

Maggie swept into Diana's bedroom with her usual tone of blithe, cheerful chatter. She assured Diana that bathing every day was quite modern. All the ladies and gentlemen in London did it. Many doctors agreed it was very good for the constitution. Maggie herself had quite come to depend on it. Diana tried to persuade her cousin that a basin and cloth were all she required for her daily toilette. She pleaded that the added expenditure of an additional bath was an unnecessary extravagance. Maggie had taken this to mean that her cousin was shy about being fussed over by the servants.

"If you like, Diana, I could come and brush out your hair for you. It would be no trouble at all. I know how awkward it can be to have a servant do it for you when you're still so new to a place."

Diana answered honestly that no servant had ever brushed her hair. Then, much to Diana's surprise, Maggie clasped her hands to her heart.

"Oh, my mother always brushed my hair in the bath, too," she intoned. "It was some of the sweetest time we ever spent. It's no surprise your mother did the same for you. I'm sure it must have been something Grandmama did for them when they were little girls."

Diana was too stunned by the sudden realization that her mother had once been a tiny child in a bathtub to correct her cousin's most earnest and innocent assumption. This silence Maggie interpreted as acquiescence, and she smiled warmly at her cousin before departing back to her own chamber.

Diana took her daily baths with no further protestation.

# Sixteen

As Diana was adjusting to her new life at Wuster Park, over at Langley Hall, Hudson, Noah, and Ellis received their shooting supplies at last. They were then instructed in the use of such supplies only until they were no longer in danger of killing themselves or each other. Tom Downs, the Langley Hall grounds manager and absentminded head butler, gave this minimal instruction. Afterwards, the boys spent nearly every day out of doors chasing the Langfords' old spaniel, Hercules, shooting at birds and things resembling birds.

Had they been better shots, they would have depopulated the entire grounds in a week. But the local fauna were more fortunate than that. Still, the number of partridges, ducks, and pheasants the boys managed to kill was enough to ensure that everyone at Langley Hall, from guestrooms to garrets, dined heartily on fowl every night of the week.

The summer the youths had imagined for themselves was going exactly according to plan. It might have continued to go according to plan were it not for a chance meeting between Hudson Birch and Lady Diana Huxley.

The boys were riding to New Glenbury for no reason at all except that the weather was fine and they had little better to do. After all, a man might go deaf shooting birds day in and day out. It had also been one of their country-summer ambitions to find firmer comfort in the saddle and familiarity with riding in the open atmosphere of lanes and downs.

Hudson would say later that he knew it to be love at first sight when he laid eyes upon Diana. This might have been true. Though Hudson nearly missed seeing Diana altogether, as he was having a rather frustrated argument with his horse at the moment of her appearance. When the well-timed "ahem" of Ellis alerted him to her presence, though, his reaction was utter astonishment. Her response appeared very much the same. It was not clear if this astonishment was owing to any particular regard or just the surprise of encountering strangers of the opposite sex. That the strangers should also be handsome, well, that was certainly a factor in some of the next proceedings.

Ellis was the first to speak, leading his horse alongside Maggie's. "Good afternoon!"

Greetings were all exchanged. This accomplished, Ellis had very little left to contribute. None of the young men were sure what rules existed regarding country civility while astride a horse. But, as they were all riding in the same direction, conversation did not seem as much an inconvenience as an inevitability. Maggie, untroubled by the awkwardness of faltering youths, helped the young men by introducing herself and her cousin. This prompted their own introductions in return.

When the introducing was concluded, Diana ventured a question. "Are you the three brothers who are over at the rented house?"

"We are but two brothers."

"Oh, which two?"

Luckily for Diana, the sincerity of this question was instantly dismissed and put down for a joke. No one seeing Noah or Ellis could be in any way confused about their relationship. She blushed as they chuckled, and then Hudson pulled his horse alongside her own.

"And where are you from?"

"I am the daughter of Baron Alester Huxley of Caldflett Castle near Yansworth. But I am lately staying with my dear cousin, Mrs.

Margaret Howard, at Wuster Park in New Glenbury."

She uttered this well-practiced introduction (rehearsed many times under the supervision of her esteemed lady friends) as gently and prettily as anyone could have hoped, and Maggie swelled with pride. Maggie's delight was short-lived. Almost as soon as Diana had recited her biography, she went off-book.

"Why do we never see you in church on Sunday? Everyone says it speaks very ill of your characters."

This too, mercifully, was taken in jest by Mr. Birch and his companions. Maggie, knowing the sincerity of her remark, whispered "Diana!" rather sharply.

Hudson had not known it was expected of them to attend church while away from their own parish. Now, realizing that it was foolish of him to have assumed otherwise, he blushed in a way that betrayed just what a boy he still was.

"I say, we would have gone. We shall go! Only . . . we didn't know where it was."

He said this, and Diana broke into a wide grin, for just ahead of them the spire of the church was quite plain.

"Well, it is a good thing we ran into you, then." She gestured gently. Hudson instantly lamented his ridiculous mistake. "Now you have your directions well worked out, I think."

"I say, indeed. Indeed."

This was all the young man was capable of saying, and he repeated it several times. Maggie watched this hopeless, ham-fisted flirting with the sudden understanding of why courtship was treated as a spectator sport by parents, aunts, and uncles. It was both hilarious and hilariously ill-fated without the intervention of a disinterested party. So, she took up the charge as she thought all married women responsible for an eligible girl must.

"Now that we've made your acquaintance," she said, "you three shall join us for dinner at Wuster Park, I hope."

"Yes, we should be delighted!" Ellis replied, happy to have something he could agree to.

"Our mother, is she also invited?" Noah asked.

"Of course. And any other in your party."

"When, um . . ." Ellis faltered, not sure if this were a real invitation or the sort of situation one sometimes encounters in the high-bred circles of London's fashionable folk, wherein calling cards are dropped back and forth but the parties never actually meet.

"We are still in mourning," Maggie said, gesturing to her dark ribbons and shawl, "so we have very few engagements. You may name the day of dinner most convenient to your party, and I'm sure we have no prior obligations."

The boys exchanged confused looks, for none of them had any obligations either. As such, all days were equal. Finally, not wanting to appear too eager for company, Mr. Birch ventured, "Tuesday?"

Tuesday, it was settled.

When it was time for the groups to part, Diana and Maggie turned off from the main road and headed farther north to the rectory, while the boys continued east in search of their own diversion.

"We shall see you Tuesday!" Mr. Birch called out in a manner he hoped conveyed his comfort both on horseback and in the role of real country gentleman.

"On Sunday first!" Diana glibly replied.

It did not take long, once parted from the ladies, for the boys to pronounce this final remark a most certain flirtation.

"What other reason could there be for her wanting us to go to church?" Noah stated, as if all of religion were organized for the enjoyment of young people.

"Perhaps she is very devout?" Hudson countered.

"Not likely at all. She's too pretty. Only ugly girls are continually in need of prayer. For how else can they expect to get husbands!?"

The tone of the boys' conversation continued in similarly playful spirits all the rest of the day.

# Seventeen

In the sunny sitting room of the rectory, Maggie related the meeting of the Langley Hall party to Constance. Originally, she spared the details of Diana's interjection regarding the church's whereabouts. Diana, proud of herself, remedied this omission. Constance appeared bemused by this tactless blunder being so well received. She could not suppress a small smile before lightly chastising Diana for her impertinence.

Diana had heard the words "impertinent" and "impertinence" a lot in the last few weeks. She did not know exactly what it meant. But she knew it was wrong and that she seemed to be very often guilty of it. In some of her quiet moments, this troubled her. In many more of her quiet moments, it did not. It was hard to be troubled for very long when kept in such constant comfort and occupation.

When Diana was settled in Constance's best sewing chair and tasked with adding about one hundred French knots to a piece of work Constance was making for a family in town, Maggie asked Constance if she might be favored with her company for a turn through the garden. It was there that Maggie expanded on the situation. The dinner party plans with the Langley Hall tenants had been made so easily, but now she confessed herself to be a bit out of her depth. Maggie had never played the role of chaperone to a party of single people, having so recently been a single person herself. It was only today, she explained, that she had become sensible to the vital role of reasonable adults in the socializations of the unattached.

Constance was gratified immensely by this appeal to her wisdom. For indeed, she felt herself to be a true blessing to Maggie and Diana, so gifted was she in the arranging of these things.

"Leave it all to me, my dear. You will see. Tuesday, you say? Set two extra plates for the reverend and me. No, better make it three. Elizabeth would quit our company forever if she were not included."

So, it was settled. Dinner on Tuesday would be just a small party of ten. Constance then asked very minute details about the three young men, knowing she might draw more from the encounter than even Maggie had perceived. Luckily for Constance, Maggie had a good memory and a sharp eye, unlike the Reverend Samuel Astley.

From Maggie's description of the boys' shiny boots, unsteady horsemanship, quaffed hair, tight coats, and unfreckled complexions, Constance determined them to be untitled, somewhat wealthy, idle sons of fathers in trade, and very new to the countryside and its customs. She would be, surprisingly (to everyone except herself), proved quite correct in many of these assumptions at dinner on Tuesday.

Before the ladies rejoined Diana in the rectory, Constance pronounced one final conclusion in favor of the upcoming dinner.

"It will be very good for Diana, I think, to practice being in company. These boys can be of no serious consequence. If she should be awkward or make some blunder, it will only give us a better idea of how we might improve her for better company in the future. For she is the daughter of a baron, and her studies are progressing admirably. Indeed, I think our new neighbors shall serve this purpose perfectly."

But before Tuesday's dinner came church on Sunday.

# Eighteen

Maggie observed that Diana was dressed with special care that Sunday morning before the church service. She had opted for the first time to wear one of the several bonnets Elizabeth had insisted she make for herself, instead of the plain one she normally favored.

Maggie warmly remarked on the new bonnet and instantly regretted it. Uncomfortable with such close observation, Diana desired at once to remedy the variation from her usual wardrobe, though it was already several minutes past when they could arrive on time by foot. It was too late to call for the carriage, as the coachmen and crew were already begun in their own walk to the village church.

So, the Howard party arrived late, after everyone had already been seated. It might have been suspected of a more conniving girl that this tardiness was arranged by design, so she might be more fully observed by all those in attendance. Diana, however, was too obviously artless in these vain ways to be suspected of such schemes. Still, the effect of her lateness was a profound one on Mr. Hudson Birch.

As she entered the chapel and made her way behind her cousins to the Howard box, Hudson, seated in the low walled visitors' section, had ample opportunity to see her tall, lithe limbs, the graceful sway of her hips, and the full gentle curve of her (ahem) smile. Prim and pressed in her new bonnet and her best Sunday dress, she was, without a doubt, the prettiest girl Hudson had ever spoken to in his short life. He was very much looking forward to speaking to her again.

While Mr. Birch was watching Diana, the Bellwood boys were watching their friend. They saw his mouth drop open, his eyes quickly blinking. They saw him fumble his hymnbook and miss the cue for the congregation to be seated. His rapture swelled from obvious to annoying. Each twin noted this, and a few glances between them confirmed that they were seeing the same thing.

Finally, to remove any doubt of his interest, Hudson stumbled bodily into the Reverend Samuel Astley on his way down the church steps at the precise moment when Diana turned and smiled at him. After recovering his balance, and some of his dignity, he made his way directly to Diana. With a studied jovial irony, he greeted her.

"I say, is that you, Lady Diana Huxley? What a coincidence. I never imagined I'd meet you here."

"You didn't meet me here, Mr. Birch. You met me while astride a horse four days ago."

Maggie, standing at Diana's elbow, had to feign a fit of coughing to disguise her shock at this swift jest from her shy cousin. Hudson's eyes sparkled with laughter behind his long eyelashes. He had not expected her to be so quick and clever in reply. He had no retort of his own prepared. But Diana's open countenance set him at ease.

"May I have the pleasure of joining your journey home?" he asked with a smile.

Hudson extended his elbow for her grasp. Diana was not sure what to make of this gesture. After a quick glance at her cousin to be assured of her acquiescence, Diana rested her hand lightly on the extended forearm. Hudson sauntered forth, feeling as lucky as a rabbit with a rutabaga. Noah, Ellis, and Mrs. Bellwood made hasty polite greetings to Mr. and Mrs. Howard as they joined the throng of Wuster Park residents walking east to the main gate of that property.

The air smelled like sweet early-season hay. It had not rained in a few days, and the sunlight shimmered over the hills. It was the perfect temperature. Warmth from the sun was tempered by a cool breeze. Diana's cheeks were bright pink, and life lit up her blue eyes. She felt giddy. No one had ever offered her their arm in such a manner or addressed her with such formality, but something about Hudson Birch still felt warm and familiar. She walked beside him. Their steps fell into unconscious rhythm. They spoke. She laughed. What had he said that made her laugh so much? She could never remember. But she remembered how that laughter made her feel, how the echoes of it would reverberate inside her like a bell for days and days.

As they approached the gate of Wuster Park, Hudson slowed their pace. Servants cast glances at the pair as they overtook them on the road. Benjamin and Maggie, walking arm and arm even slower, were only a few steps away when Hudson released Diana's arm and turned to face her. Was she blushing, or was it just the wind? She felt her heart fluttering high in her breast. He bid her cousins goodbye, most politely. Then, in full view of everyone on the road, Hudson doffed his hat and bowed at Diana with such an earnest, ridiculous flourish, Diana burst out laughing. Hudson's beaming, blushing face was all the confirmation anyone needed to see that he considered her laughter a most sincere compliment.

# Nineteen

After Sunday's stirring effects, Tuesday arrived in a blink. Though Mrs. Rollins had nodded with absolute equanimity at the request for a dinner of ten, Maggie remained unconvinced by her confidence. Because this was her first time hosting a dinner party as a married woman, she felt sure that something was guaranteed to go wrong. She felt equally certain that only women of age and experience could guide her. This sentiment was heartily supported by Constance and Elizabeth. After all, they had been the ones who first suggested such perils of party planning to the young hostess. To ease Maggie's anxieties, they graciously agreed to come Tuesday morning and help with the preparations.

Being informed that the dinner was to be for only ten persons, Mrs. Rollins had assumed that the best place to serve this meal would be in the breakfast room. It was called the breakfast room because it was where the family took their breakfasts. It was, in actuality, a second dining room containing a table that seated exactly ten persons. Admittedly, the room was much smaller than the great dining hall, but the soft carpeting and tastefully executed decoration made the space both pleasant and comfortable.

By contrast, the great dining hall was long and narrow with soaring ceilings. Benjamin, Maggie, and Diana took their dinners together there each night at the impressive thirty-six-seat table. At those intimate family meals, all were seated at one end of the table, with Benjamin at the head. However, for a party of ten, the large table was simply too large.

To Maggie's inexperienced abilities, she assumed that Mrs. Rollins had been correct in her placement of the dinner in the breakfast room. Constance and Elizabeth would not hear of it. They implored her to consider what offense the Langley party would take at being seen in such a small room after passing through such a large one. What would they think of country hospitality? This argument was especially persuasive because Maggie did not wish to be accused of either miserliness or snobbery. Constance and Elizabeth calmly explained that the only option was to host the party in the great hall and count on the youths to make lively conversations flow across the wide expanse of the great table.

In an uncommon occurrence, Diana took a stance in this debate. Even more shocking was the fact that she took a position of disagreement. She insisted over and over that the breakfast room was more pleasing and more comfortable. She maintained that their guests would feel more at home and more welcomed by its choice. She derided the great hall as being cold, loud, and spooky. Finally, all three women decided that she should be sent out from underfoot until things were better settled. So, Diana was instructed to go forth and collect all the ready flowers from garden and field to make up the centerpieces of the great hall table. (The centerpiece made by Mrs. Rollins for the breakfast room now appeared comically small.) Feeling the futility of her protestations, Diana departed with very little reluctance.

Next came the matter of the seating arrangement. Round and round the great table the three women went, adding and subtracting the name cards from each place in a constant bid at perfection. Maggie and Benjamin would occupy either end of the table; this was certain. That Hudson and Diana should be seated next to each other was equally certain, for all had observed his attentions to her on Sunday, and all were eager to see how Diana would respond to such obvious admiration. But both Elizabeth and Constance wanted the honor of being seated on the other side of Mr. Birch. Each hoped she might observe the conversation between the pair and make some polite inquiries regarding Mr. Birch's family and situation—very delicately, of course. Each woman pointedly reminded Maggie that she was the very soul of tact and discretion.

Around the table they went, again and again. By the time the seating was settled, Maggie needed a rest. Elizabeth and Constance also longed for a reprieve. After a quick, quiet luncheon, they both departed for their own homes in Elizabeth's carriage to rest and ready themselves for the evening's festivities.

<h1 style="text-align:center">Twenty</h1>

Relieved by her dismissal from the scene of debate taking place in the great dining hall, Diana borrowed a large flower basket from its hanging place in the larder. Armed with a small pruning knife, she went in search of foliage for the evening's centerpieces. It was still early summer, and the small formal flower gardens that began at the foot of the wide stairs to the south of the Wuster Park house were not yet in abundance. Diana still managed to gather a few large bearded irises and some broom branches before heading to the meadows to gather the wildflowers that were more plentiful.

As she walked forth, Diana mused about her new friends—not the young gentlemen staying at Langley Hall, but her more frequent female companions. Staring at the stout stalks of the irises in her basket, she was reminded of Lady Elizabeth Dormer. Yes, that woman was a great yellow iris personified, all frills and whiskers, too. While the woman had a cross look about her nearly always, Diana had noticed that hers was the keenest humor of all the neighbors'. In one of their afternoons together, as Elizabeth had been attempting to teach Diana a few key phrases in French, she had asked Diana if there were any phrases she should particularly like to know. Diana had considered for a few moments and then answered, "Take your hands off of me."

Lady Elizabeth had looked at her for a few moments before inquiring why she would wish to know such a hostile expression. Diana answered, "I've heard that French men can be very . . . impertinent?"

Elizabeth had laughed and laughed and called her a wise little chicken. Yes, Lady Elizabeth was every bit an iris. Utterly superfluous and ostentatious, with a thick and unbending stalk of character holding her up.

If Lady Elizabeth was an iris, then what was Mrs. Constance? Distracted by such considerations, Diana was now walking at a cheerful, brisk pace. She could see a few scattered groups of sheep on the hills. She stopped frequently to gather handfuls of bittercress, buttercups, and yellow weasel's snout for her basket.

Constance was very certainly a forget-me-not, Diana concluded. Because she was forever saying, "Now don't forget, Diana . . ." and then following that phrase with something that Diana had never known, much less had the time to forget.

"Now don't forget, Diana, it is always the order of rank that determines the order of entrance into a drawing room."

"Now don't forget, Diana, it is not polite to speak to the footman while you are at table."

"Now don't forget, Diana, more than one lump of sugar is considered very childish."

"Now don't forget, Diana, it is necessary to wait and be helped from the carriage no matter what a hurry you're in."

On and on. Just like forget-me-not flowers, Constance spread herself into everything. Diana saw evidence of her needlework in the cottages of the tenant farmers where she and Maggie would bring charity baskets. She saw signs of her industrious instruction in the orderly plantings of the churchyard and the perpetual repainting of the shutters of every business on the New Glenbury market street. Yes, Constance was a forget-me-not.

Diana made note of this in her mental catalogue and felt a sudden pang. It was a funny thing, this plant-person parallel. Yet she had no one to share the jest with. Maggie would not be interested in more talk of flowers and trees. Diana could sense her cousin was easily bored with such topics. And she could not write such nonsense in one of her infrequent letters home. Home. Was it home still? Was a place home if you never wanted to go back? Did the place of one's birth always lay claim to that title?

Diana turned around to begin her return journey and was struck suddenly by the magnificent view of the Wuster Park house, shining in the daylight. A little more than a month ago, it had appeared a hulking fortress looming in the rain. Now she had a favorite chair that her cousins always reserved for her in the evenings. Could Wuster Park be her home? Diana asked this question, earnestly hoping in her heart for an affirmative. But her heart could not admit it to be so. Her heart was still longing for some greater comfort, some other place where she might share her musings with someone who would want to hear them, where she might sit comfortably without occupation or obligation, and just be herself.

She had known such a place, once . . .

~

Nearly a year after Diana's chance meeting with Charlie McFaden, the elder Mr. McFaden had come into the possession of a short gelding perfect for a lady's daily rider. He was complaining to his son, once again, that there was no one to help him train the creature for proper sidesaddle riding. Charlie saw his chance.

"I've heard the Huxley household to the north has a daughter who might could help. Being a lady, she would know how to ride. They might even buy the horse for her."

Tempted more by the possibility of a local sale than a sidesaddle assistant, Farmer McFaden rode with his son in the direction of Caldflett Castle the next day.

Neither man had ever been to Caldflett Castle, and no one that Charlie had inquired with had made the trip either. It was said to be very strategically situated for defense, which was just a nice way of saying it was damn hard to get to. Astride their own horses, with the short gelding in tow, they made relatively quick work of the walk that normally took Diana a full two hours in fine weather. In the year since their first meeting, Charlie had spent a lot of time imagining the residence of the mysterious young lady. But not even his discrete questions in town about the Huxley family or their habits prepared him for what they beheld when they made their final turn in the winding road up the steep mountain.

It was a castle in the purest sense of the word—a castle that was built as a stronghold and perhaps, at one point, a lookout. There was a tower or two. Rather, there were several piles of stones that greatly resembled the lower half of a tower. The rest of the building was thick, moss covered, and crumbling from the top down. A small child clothed in a worn dress ran towards them calling, "Daddy! Daddy!" until she was close enough to see that neither man was familiar to her. Then she ran away screaming. She was barefoot even though it was early spring and the ground was cold and wet.

The McFadens exchanged silent glances, each in confirmation that this was not what either had expected. Charlie was tempted to think that there was some mistake. Perhaps this was only an outcropping on the Huxley estate, and Caldflett Castle was farther still. Diana's appearance at the door dispelled the notion.

Diana was somewhere between terrified and furious. Terrified because with no man in the household, they were more vulnerable than she cared to consider. Furious because she recognized the young farmer on the horse right away and hated that he should see her in this place. Affecting great confidence, she strode up to the men on horseback.

"What do you want?"

The elder Mr. McFaden answered in a warm tone.

"Good afternoon, miss. We've come with a humble request. Might we speak to the lady of the house?"

"What is this about?"

"Well, we've this horse here—"

"We've no use for a horse."

"No. I see that."

What Mr. McFaden saw was that there was no stable for a horse and not even enough good pastureland near at hand to keep one fed.

"I see that. I take in horses to train and sell."

"We have no horses to sell."

"I see that. I see that. But I am in need of assistance. This horse here is a very good horse and would make a very good lady's horse. For he is small, and gentle. I need the help of a lady to acquaint him with the sidesaddle. I was hoping you, or one of your sisters might be able to assist me."

For the first time, Diana looked directly at Charlie, wordless in her wonder. Charlie only nodded in a manner he hoped was reassuring.

"But I . . . I don't know how to ride."

"There's no bother in that. It's easy as can be. I'd teach you. We just need someone of the right size, and then of course with skirts too. Horses are funny creatures and they don't like surprises."

"They sound like very sensible creatures."

"That's how I know you haven't known many a horse."

Then Mr. McFaden gave a chuckle, and Diana gave a tight-lipped smile. Charlie noticed that three little faces were watching them from the doorway of the castle. He was just about to wave them over when a small angular woman shoved past them and marched up to Diana's side, barking.

"Get gone, the both of you! I don't know who told you what, but he's not here and if he knows what's good for him—"

"Mama, stop! They're neighbors."

Mr. McFaden dismounted and bowed in greeting, removing his knit cap to reveal a tuft of white hair underneath. Charlie followed his father's actions, then gathered the leads of all the horses in his large hands.

"What do you want then?"

Mr. McFaden explained again the situation with the horse and was interrupted at least twice as often as he had been the first time. His patience and skill as a horse trainer were on full display as he led Lady Huxley through the logic of his request. Diana stared at her feet, unwilling to observe the young farmer's appraisal of the situation. When Mr. McFaden had concluded his request, Diana's mother spoke.

"As you can very well see, we may not have much. But we do have our pride, and I would not have any child of mine, a *titled lady* mind you, be put to work as a farm laborer."

"No, m'lady. No, indeed. I invite your daughter *because* she is a lady. I know good breeding, you see. I could have got a farm girl for the job. Only, I know that a lady carries herself in such a way. Just as you do, very upright and elegant. A farm girl could only train a horse for farm riding. It will take a lady to make a ladies' horse."

The pride of Lady Huxley was appeased. Charlie could see that she had once been a great beauty, though her skin now looked slack and papery, with hard lines around her mouth—not from smiling. Mr. McFaden continued.

"I could not call her a laborer either, for a laborer would be paid. I, alas, cannot offer such, having so very little myself. But, my wife does keep a very fine garden and if your daughter would be so kind as to help me in this project, we would return her to you after each visit with anything we could spare. Though I only have the one child myself, I know how much they do eat as they're growing up."

Now Diana looked at her mother in plain desperation. Fresh vegetables would be more valuable to them than gold. Lord Huxley's meager contributions rarely covered more than their flour and meat for the week. Diana could see that her mother was sensible to this. Not to appear too eager though, she measured her words slowly.

"I suppose that might be agreeable. But we cannot spare her more than one day a week. Already she goes to town on Tuesdays."

"Might we see her on Thursdays, then?"

"Yes."

Diana was nearly overcome by shock. But Lady Huxley was not done speaking.

"And when your ladies' horse here sells, we want our share. And a share of any she helps you with after that."

Mr. McFaden bowed low in an unmistakable gesture of acquiescence.

"We shall meet the young Lady Huxley at Yansworth, next Thursday morning. I thank you for your generous help, m'lady."

Lady Huxley only turned on her heel and retreated to the castle. Diana was agape, burning with a million questions. But the McFadens both remounted their horses and made a hasty departure before she could find words to voice them.

Diana met the McFadens the next Thursday, as promised. She met them again the Thursday after that. Then she met them nearly every Thursday for the next three years. She brought back to Caldflett Castle the bounty of Mrs. McFaden's garden and an occasional sum of money more substantial than any received from Lord Huxley. But what Diana really took with her from those visits was the knowledge that a house could be warm and inviting, a family could be affectionate and close, a man could be gentle and kind, and a girl could be herself when she felt safe.

Had Diana not come to know all of this, she might have been able to imagine happiness for herself being entirely dependent on material circumstances. She might have been able to see Wuster Park as the answer to all her hopes and dreams. But because she had seen the loving, tender ways of the McFaden family, she could never be truly happy with anything less.

~

When Diana returned to Wuster Park, laden with meadow flowers to be stuffed in silver vases, she found the drama of the table seating to be entirely resolved. She joined her female companions for lunch and then spent the afternoon quietly perfecting her rolled hem stitch in the privacy of her bedroom. It was only when Clara the under maid brought up a basin of warm water for her toilette that she began to think of the night ahead.

# Twenty-One

THE ESTEEMED AND much considered guests of the impending dinner party spent their day in far less ardent negotiation than Constance, Elizabeth, and Maggie. In fact, the only debate they held was
on the subject of who *nearly* shot the most birds. Hudson actually
shot four. This was agreed to be very impressive. However, Ellis insisted that he *nearly* shot six, which merited some acknowledgement. Noah disagreed that this was worth discussing. They discussed the finer points of this competition until it was time to escort
Mrs. Bellwood to the carriage and take the ride to Wuster Park.

Privately, each of the boys (and even Mrs. Bellwood) felt some
hesitation about their visit to Wuster Park. The estate was known
to be very large and very grand. Considering that the mistress was
niece to a baron and that her husband was the wealthiest man in
the county, the Langley Hall party felt their own connections and
consequence lacking in comparison. To tell the truth, they were all
a little nervous for their visit. But none of them would tell the
truth, not to each other and certainly not to themselves. Instead,
everyone prepared for the evening as if dining at massive estates
staffed with dozens (maybe even hundreds!) of servants, all of
whom were surely watching them for any signs of irregularity, was
their idea of a regular Tuesday evening. They did such a good im-

pression of this confidence that each of them (even Mrs. Bellwood) was fooled into thinking that they were alone in their insecurities. In this way, they found a degree of confidence which none of them actually possessed.

Ere long, their carriage pulled up to the front of the Wuster Park mansion. Tall iron torches lit their path to the front door, and the glittering of an ungodly assemblage of candles shone through the windows. By this time, they were nearly jovial, and the happy party entered the magnificent home.

As this was to be an easy evening event, they were received in the library instead of a drawing room. The rich wood of the shelves coupled with the dark leather of the books made for a warm, inviting scene. Such a place might have been called cozy if it were not so massive. Under these comfortable circumstances, Noah and Ellis wordlessly agreed that Mrs. Bellwood must be prevented by the constant attention of her two sons from sitting on anything except the most unyielding straight-backed chair. They feared that in such comfort and warmth, she would succumb to sleep.

This left Mr. Hudson Birch to do most of the socializing with the other guests of the evening: the Reverend Samuel Astley, his rather harsh-looking wife, and the rich old widow who still curtseyed in the old-fashioned way. He did his best. His best was admirable. The adults all saw that he was trying and that he had the good sense to try. This boded well.

Dinner around the great table was far more awkward in realization than it had been in imagination. The places had not seemed so very far apart when the seating arrangement consisted of plates on a table. But when a humble human form occupied its assigned seat, the table dwarfed the party. All the guests found themselves sitting absurdly far apart. It was not too far apart to hear one another—unless one had been out of doors shooting birds all day.

Alas, an over-powdered shot had gone off, a bit too close and too loud, between Noah and Ellis that same afternoon. This accident had rendered one of each of their ears a trifle deaf for the time being.

They had not noticed this impairment until the echoing acoustics of the great hall enveloped them, and a persistent ringing drowned out the quiet attempts at conversation from their left-side partners. Hudson, it seemed, had been spared such a fate. Or perhaps his choice to ignore Constance, his right-side dining partner, was out of an equal affliction and not his eager attentions to Diana, who sat to his left.

If we imagine the table as a rectangular clock, we can orient our understanding of the seating as such: Benjamin sat at the head of the table, 12 on the clock face. Moving clockwise from Mr. Howard, the guests were Elizabeth, Noah, the Reverend Samuel Astley, and Mrs. Bellwood. Then Maggie occupied the other end of the table at the 6 hour. Continuing around the clock face from her up to Benjamin, the seating was Ellis, Constance, Hudson, and Diana.

The general happenings of dinner conversation can be summarized thus: On the side of the table to Benjamin's right, Diana and Mr. Birch were wholly absorbed in each other's company. Hudson was having a great deal of success in making Diana laugh by telling exaggerated stories of his own adventures and mishaps since arriving at Langley Hall. The subject of this discussion was never known to the larger group because Constance, seated to Mr. Birch's right, was fully absorbed in talking to Ellis. Though she had originally claimed the seat to Hudson's right so she might observe the young man, Constance found her conversation with Ellis Bellwood to be irresistible. This was because, half deaf, Ellis compensated for his deficient understandings with vigorous nodding and smiling at Constance's conversation. Indeed, Constance found this to be one of the most engaging and lively conversations she had been privilege to at a dinner party in a very long time.

Maggie, at the end of the table, talked mostly to Mrs. Bellwood, seated to her right. Ellis, seated to her left, was quite absent in his attentions to Maggie as his vigorous nods were needed to add to Constance's conversation. Maggie soon discovered that Mrs. Bellwood was one of those women who formed the habit in early motherhood of relying on her two children as a substitute for conventional conversational contributions. Now, with two fully grown children, she had the full stock of stories of their early antics. As Maggie had yet heard none of these, over the course of the evening, she received them all.

Meanwhile, the Reverend Samuel Astley and Noah were engaged in a debate, not exactly lively, but deeply stimulating. At least it was perceived to be so by the reverend, who found Noah's continual disapproval and disagreements (given vaguely because his temporary hearing loss made it a challenge to know the exact points to which he was disagreeing) to be most thoroughly thought-provoking. At first, Noah felt the old man of the cloth seated to his left to be an annoyance. But as the reverend continued to engage Noah's surly rebuffs of his old-man notions, Noah soon found that he enjoyed challenging the reverend. He would watch his dining partner think hard for some time, present a solution carefully for consideration, and have it dashed by a few short words from Noah, all with a beatific smile, and all without a pause in his consumption of the multitude of courses served throughout the night.

This left just Elizabeth and Benjamin. If they had ventured into conversation, it might have been the start of a beautiful friendship. Elizabeth was sharp in the ways of business and would have been an excellent counsel for some of Benjamin's mill-related quandaries. This was never discovered, because Elizabeth shushed all of his attempts at starting the opening movements of conversation in her futile hopes of hearing what Diana and Hudson were discussing across the table. So, Benjamin found himself alone, at the head of his table, looking down at the plates (not at the absurd spacing of guests, which he never really noticed).

He recognized these plates from a childhood so long unremembered that it felt like it belonged to someone else. These formal Sevres plates had been picked out by Benjamin's parents in the first year of their marriage. They were once considered so fashionable that his father often made a point of recalling their origins to dinner guests. Now, with their thick pink rims and the absurd abundance of gilded floral wreaths and fat cupids cavorting, they looked foppish and outdated.

The daily breakfast dishes at Wuster Park also recalled his childhood; the less formal plate they ate family dinners upon was something newer that his father must have purchased in Benjamin's adulthood. But these plates—these plates reminded him of times long ago—some happy, many sad. In that moment, it felt like they'd been staring up at him his whole life, just waiting to see what he would do with it. This feeling oppressed him, and, though the room was cold, he felt stifled. For him, dinner could not end fast enough.

As the second to last courses were being cleared away, a most unusual thing occurred. A bee, previously dozing in the petals of some field flower Diana had collected for the centerpiece, now roused itself to wakefulness. Perhaps it was prompted into action by the promise of dessert. Or perhaps the bee, feeling itself sufficiently observed of polite society, felt ready to take its place among the party.

Simply put, a bee found its way out of Diana's bountiful and somewhat sloppily conceived centerpieces. From there, it began to take a grand tour of the great hall. Buzzing as bees do, the tiny terror swirled about the room. In only a few moments, the entire party was in a panic. Mrs. Bellwood shrieked. Noah and Ellis both stood up in identical actions that sent their chairs crashing behind them. Benjamin was just about to direct everyone to flee towards the library until the hall could be reconquered. But then the bee, already tired of its grand adventure, began to swirl in loud, lazy circles about Hudson Birch's head. Finally, it settled on the lapel of his dinner jacket. Panic paralyzed the youth; terror reigned at the table.

Amidst the sudden movement of her surroundings, the screeching of her neighbors, and the clamoring of nearby servants, Diana calmly reached out both hands and cupped the bee from its resting place on Hudson's shoulder. Bee in hand, she walked placidly to the far doorway. Then, to the utter astonishment and confusion of all her company, she exited. She made her way through a few more doorways until finally, away from everyone else in person and consideration, she released the bee into the damp chill of the early-summer night air.

Alone, she stood a few moments. In the back of the great house where no lamps were burning, looking up, she could see the full bright dazzle of the stars through a clear sky overhead. And though the sky was clear, when Diana drew in a deep breath, she knew it would rain the next day. This was what she said when she reentered the great hall.

"It's going to rain tomorrow."

Her cousin ran to her. "My dear, are you all right? Were you stung?"

"No. I just carried it outside. It's going to rain."

"Is it raining right now? Should we call for carriages?"

"Oh no, it won't rain until tomorrow."

She said all of this, and said nothing else, before resuming her seat and enjoying the remaining dinner with the stunned Hudson's eyes transfixed upon her in speechless veneration.

It was only when the men rejoined the ladies in the drawing room for coffee and more conversation that Hudson found a coherent assemblage for the words he wanted to say.

"I say, Lady Huxley, how ever did you know how to catch that bee?"

"The bee? It was simple. How do you catch anything?"

"And, I say, how do you know it is going to rain tomorrow?"

"The smell outside. It's the smell of rain."

His astonishment was unabated.

"Well, I say . . . but how do you know all of this?"

As he put forth the question, Hudson took his seat beside her on the small yellow couch of the drawing room, awash in the warmth of candles and filled with the rich aroma of boiling coffee. Constance, Elizabeth, and Maggie all exchanged glances with each other, confirming their mutual observation of this situation. Each longed to be nearer to the scene to better comprehend Diana's reaction to it.

"Growing up, I suppose. Yansworth is a small village. We do things differently there."

"I say. How so?"

Hudson's question was the first sign of true interest about Diana's home from anyone since Maggie's grand declaration and ensuing lengthy lecture a few weeks ago. It prompted in her a look of such tender regret that Hudson began to long for Yansworth without having heard another word about it. Yet Diana had more words to impart.

"It's not so orderly there. One goes about with less rules and such. It's very free compared to here."

"Free?"

"Yes, compared to here."

"I say, I think I should like to go there very much."

"Oh no, you wouldn't. You have come from London, haven't you? Yansworth has nothing that London has."

"Well, to be sure it has some."

"No, I don't think so."

Hudson did not wish to argue, but he desperately wanted her to keep talking. And, miracle of miracles, she did.

"You come from London, but where are you from before that?"

"Oh yes, London. London all my life. I was born there, and I have lived nowhere else."

The admission seemed to shock Diana, and Hudson quickly worked to find another phrase that might pacify her look of astonishment.

"Though I have traveled, to be sure. I have been to Bath and to Manchester."

"Why did you go to Manchester?"

"My father had . . . business to attend to there." He colored at the admission that his father had *business*. Hudson knew that her father, a true gentleman, would not.

"What business does your father do?"

Her question, so sweetly asked, filled Hudson with dread. He could not answer as he would have liked. He wished, wholeheartedly, that his father had been something as fine as a wine merchant or even something so vulgar but important as a bond speculator.

"He deals in . . . fish."

"Fish! That is very interesting."

"But I do not have anything at all to do with the business. I say, I have no business at all."

"Why not? Don't you want to work with your father?"

"Certainly not."

"Don't you want to work at all? I think it would be exciting to have business. Going to make deals and sign papers. Adding sums and then talking about the sums with other men and their additions of sums."

"I say, yes, well . . . I think that if I were to pursue anything at all, I say, I might pursue something dignified. The law, perhaps. Though there is little of sums in that, I think."

"That's too bad. The sums seem to be the most fun of business."

"It is equally probable I should never work at all. There is no need for it, you understand."

This blunt admission was gauche, and Hudson knew it, but he could not resist trying to right himself in the opinion of this high-born lady of the northlands.

"Tell me," he said, returning to an earlier subject, "have you been much to town?"

"Oh yes, Cousin Maggie has taken me several times."

"And how do you find it?"

"I like it very well. There are *three* hat shops. I do like to go look in their windows. New Glenbury is much grander than Yansworth, to be sure."

"Oh no, I say. I meant London. Have you been much to London?"

"No, never."

"Never?"

"Not once."

She said this with a smile, as if her words were not an utter bewilderment to the young gentleman before her.

"It's not that I wouldn't like to go. I would, and I expect I will at some time. I have seen maps."

Diana felt suddenly on edge about how her inexperience with the innumerable joys of London would color her companion's opinion of her. She made sure to say the word "maps" with great confidence. Only, remembering the one map she had seen of London, she did not feel this great confidence. Her next question made this clear.

"I wonder, are you often lost in London? I would be very lost. There are so many streets and ways. How a person gets from one place to another is not clear to me."

"Well, that is simple enough. To get anywhere in London, one needs only money. Money for a hackney coach. You are quite right when you assume that those in London are often lost. For if you ask three people for directions to the same address, I say, they shall each of them tell you a different way to go. But the surest way to get to where you need to go is just to hire a cab. I say, there are no places in London you cannot get to with the help of a cab."

He said this suavely enough that, for a moment, he almost believed it. A moment later, however, his mind was recalled to all the places in London where a man with all the fortune of a genie could not gain admittance unless his grandfather had the right title. There were plenty of places where no cab ride or money paid could gain a man entrance. But to point out this fact, he thought, would only remind Diana of his place below her. So, he only smiled and hoped she did not doubt his confidence in himself.

In point of fact, Diana was thinking just how very lost she would be in London if the only way to go anywhere was with money. How nice for him, she thought, and tried to keep resentment from clouding her picture of this handsome young man before her.

# Twenty-Two

ON THE CARRIAGE ride home from Wuster Park, the Reverend and Mrs. Astley shared their impressions of the evening. They were both in excellent spirits owing to the wonderful discussions they enjoyed during dinner. Constance was quick to say how utterly agreeable she found Mr. Ellis Bellwood. He was such a fine young man of good taste and breeding, wise beyond his years to be certain, and destined for great things.

The Reverend Samuel Astley was happy to report that his conversational companion, the young Mr. Noah Bellwood, was equally blessed. Bursting with keen intelligence, and having displayed such an inquisitive mind, the boy had prompted considerations that the reverend knew would influence his own theology going forward. The young man was of few words, to be sure. His debating style, however simple, was nearly Socratic in its effect. The reverend felt sure this young man would find himself in positions of great power and influence before long.

Then, much to Constance's shock, the reverend added the following observation.

"And, my dear, did you observe the way the blond young man looked at our friend Diana? He is smitten, that is clear."

If this was clear to her husband, Constance thought, then there could be no doubt of it at all to anyone else in observation. Constance knew her husband's inattention could only be penetrated by the most certain and strong demonstrations. On this occasion, for her own amusement, she ventured to ask what her dear husband thought of the prospective attachment.

"Well, I think neither of them could want better. She is a titled daughter from an old family, and he is a nice young man from a . . . newer type of people. They would each provide what the other cannot. I confess, with such obvious interest on his part, I think there is little reason to wait. So suitable a connection can be of no objection to anyone, and such obvious attachment . . . Well, I'll say this, if they came to me tomorrow morning with a special license, I'd marry them right there in the doorway. And I would not be for an instant surprised."

This was the most detailed voluntary conjecture on any person's situation her husband had ever offered, and Constance was shocked to find herself in perfect agreement.

~

While Mrs. Bellwood got a head start on her sleep during the carriage ride home, the Bellwood boys exchanged a series of most alarmed glances. Hudson was looking out the glass window, obviously too far off in his own thoughts to consider the thoughts of his friends.

What his friends thought was most characteristic of their dispositions. Noah thought that Hudson was being foolish, displaying such an interest so obviously so early in an acquaintance and so early in life—twenty years of age being too young for any sensible man to marry. Noah held that the only men who married at that age were those who either had no say in their own fate or no hope of a second possible option.

Ellis, of course, was happy for his friend. Already, he was composing his description of Diana for his own dear Melissa, so she might begin to admire her and form a fast friendship upon their eventual meeting. Indeed, Hudson's prospective marriage was a great boon for Ellis. The young man had harbored some secret anxieties about leaving the realm of his single friends to join in his father's set as a married man. Now, with Hudson in the same boat . . . Well, to Ellis, the boat was starting to look a lot more like a pleasure cruise than an exploration into uncharted waters.

All of this the twins told to each other with their eyes. Then, with their eyes, they argued who held the correct opinion. Though no words were exchanged, the animated facial expressions and hand gestures soon progressed to such a degree that the argument was quite heated. They sulked off to their rooms that night, eager to resume their disagreement on the morrow.

Hudson remained insensible to all of this. What he knew was simple: Diana was the most remarkable of all women of all time. She knew secrets of the earth and stars. She was a nobleman's daughter. She was beautiful. She was so far beyond his own realm that to imagine a union with her was an impossibility. He could never be worthy of her. He could never hope to make her happy. He was twenty years old, and he knew that he would suffer the whole rest of his life in regret of ever meeting her. Though the sound logic of his heartbreak prevailed upon him in every instant, he could not help but also feel an eerie prickling—almost like joy—which kept him wide awake that night, though he longed for sleep.

~

After both the Bellwood-Birch party and the reverend and Constance had departed, Elizabeth called for her own carriage. She then invited Maggie to join her outside under the great stone archway as she waited.

The night remained clear, but Elizabeth silently agreed with Diana's prediction that there would be rain the next day. She felt it in her knuckles. As soon as they went outside, Maggie began an earnest speech thanking Elizabeth for her help. This was waved quickly away. The older woman cut to the point, knowing that her carriage would be conveyed soon and that Maggie would need the night to think on the quick action Elizabeth felt was next required.

"The boy, Mr. Birch, if he is not yet in love with Diana, he soon will be. I think we should make the most of this opportunity."

"I did see that they were quite engaged in conversation."

"I should like to see them engaged outside of conversation."

Maggie did not immediately understand.

"I should like to see them engaged, and then *married*," Elizabeth clarified.

"Oh, but they are quite young, don't you—"

"They are a good match, of sufficient sentiment, equal enough standing, and, if you don't mind me saying so, a man like Mr. Birch can only come to have higher standards the longer he is left in society to consider his worth. Young as he is, he does not yet have the experience to see Diana's deficiencies. To him, she is everything she should be. They should be wed."

The carriage pulled up, and Elizabeth imparted one final pronouncement before taking her leave of the stunned Maggie.

"Consider what I have said, my dear. And consider as well the odds that Diana should ever find herself in a position to tempt a match of Mr. Birch's equal. Consider it well."

Maggie did consider it. She lay awake in her bed and considered it all. Diana, exhausted from the day's festivities, fell asleep with no such considerations. Benjamin was considering a different matter altogether.

# Twenty-Three

THE NEXT DAY, a few hours after Benjamin departed for the mill, Constance and Elizabeth arrived at Wuster Park unexpectedly.

The two older women bustled in out of the rain with an obvious agenda. Diana was promptly placed in the music room with a lace-making box and some very vague directions, leading her to create a ruination of tangles. But the diversion was sufficient to buy the three women of her supervision some time to discuss her future.

With great animation and debate, the subject of her prospective match with Mr. Hudson Birch was argued until all three women realized that they were already in perfect agreement. Then, the discussion took a more tactical tone. It was decided that the rigorous plans for Diana's improvement should be placed on hold. The efforts of their group henceforth should focus on engineering a summer throwing Diana and Hudson together so agreeably and frequently that an autumn wedding would surely result. Picnics, parties, balls, and banquets all would have to be arranged. And the process would have to begin now, for the start of summer was already nearing its end. The rest of the season would fly by if they were not careful to entrap it in the amber sap of excessive merriment.

Right away, it was settled that Elizabeth should host a ball. Though the Wuster Park ballroom was bigger, Maggie and Benjamin remained in mourning and unable to host lively events of any real size. Elizabeth typically only opened her house to the wear and tear of a ball once a year in October, but another ball was to be arranged as soon as possible. The date was named as the last Friday of that month, just two and a half weeks away. To plan a party so quickly would be no small undertaking. Sending the invitations was the first order of business. As it had to be begun right away, Elizabeth and Constance departed directly back to Eastbey Abbey just after the luncheon bell sounded.

By this time, Diana had given up her lace making and had wandered to the library. It was there that Maggie found her. When Maggie concluded her announcement about the newly conceived ball, she began to prod the girl for details about her interactions with Mr. Birch the night before.

Diana answered her cousin's questions plainly and with no return curiosity. In truth, she was happy to finally know so many answers to her cousin's questions. Often, when Maggie asked her about things, she did not know how to answer so easily. Questions like "What do you and your siblings usually do in the evenings?" and "How is your mother?" were inexplicable to Diana.

From Maggie's perspective, Diana's easy volunteering of information about Mr. Birch betrayed a great admiration of him. For, outside the subjects of flowers and trees, Diana rarely found fluent conversation. This obvious attachment softened some of Maggie's hesitations on the rather disappointing news that Hudson's father was in the fish business.

# Twenty-Four

MAGGIE WAS EAGER to relate all of this new information to her husband. She felt it had been ages since they'd really spoken. The lead-up to their first dinner party had been quite diverting. After its conclusion, Benjamin had been tired, and Maggie preoccupied. She had not even had a chance to apologize to him for the rather peculiar details of the evening.

Despite her eagerness to enlighten her husband on the unfolding ambitions for Hudson and Diana, she could not discuss her plans with him at dinner. It had been reaffirmed by all three women that Diana should be kept ignorant of the purposes of their planning. It was supposed that it would make Diana feel terribly uncomfortable to know that any efforts were being extended on her behalf. But also, if there was to be some disappointment, it would be best if the relationship had never been acknowledged in any official capacity.

So, at dinner Maggie contented herself with asking Benjamin about his day at the mill without much listening to his answer. At last, when Diana went up to her room and Benjamin and Maggie were left on their own in the candlelight of the drawing room, Maggie was quick to settle near him on the sofa and say, "Benjamin, there is something I want desperately to discuss with you."

He looked at her in such amazement, she was sure he must have misheard her.

"Dearest," he replied, "there is something I must discuss with you!" Then, without waiting to confirm his assumption that they were of one mind, he plunged into the topic weighing on his heart.

"You're absolutely right. We must go to London. This house is in terrible need of better appointments and I can tolerate it no longer."

Maggie surveyed the immaculate finery that surrounded her on all sides.

"Benjamin, I . . ."

"Dearest, I know you're having such fun here with Diana, and I do admire how you've made yourself so agreeable to the society of our neighbors, but I simply cannot abide. I simply cannot abide. I cannot."

His face clouded in consternation as he could find no other words to make his meaning known. His heels began to thump in rapid succession against the carpet under his feet. He was agitated indeed. Though Maggie did not understand the cause, she felt it was only right to reassure his disconcerted soul. She took his hand with one of her own, and with the other, she drew his chin in her direction. Their eyes met. The percussion of his feet abated.

"My love . . ."

It was all she had to say, apparently, because he replied immediately, in a great sigh: "I knew you would understand."

"Yes of course, but—"

When Benjamin heard the word "but," his heels resumed their clamoring. Maggie could not think of a gentle enough way to ask him the meaning of his urgent need to go to London without giving the impression that she questioned the plan. Instead, she opted for a simpler question.

"Can we be back by the last Friday of this month, some two and a half weeks from now? Elizabeth has decided to throw a ball, and I know she is counting on us to help make up the dancers."

A wide smile broke out across Benjamin's face. Here, he thought, his wife only wanted for his happiness.

"Yes, my love, anything you like. But we shall have to leave here right away. Do you think that you and Diana can be ready the day after tomorrow?"

This urgency of action seemed highly unwarranted to Maggie, but she agreed, nonetheless. She reminded herself of another urgent, seemingly random insistence from Benjamin—his insistence that she was the woman he had been looking for all his life. It was a declaration he made after knowing her less than five days. The recollection reminded her that many of Benjamin's best decisions were made rather suddenly. To place confidence in him in these moments had not yet yielded any disappointment to her. So, to London they would go.

# Twenty-Five

THE FIRST THING to be done by Maggie in preparation for their sudden departure to town was the dispatch of notes to Constance and Elizabeth.

In reply, Constance wrote:

*Margaret,*
*Time apart can only increase admiration when those who leave depart on the best of terms. We shall welcome your soon return. Do write if you should need anything.*
*Your Faithful Neighbor,*
*Mrs. Reverend Astley*

Elizabeth's reply was as follows:

*Maggie,*
*What a dreadful thing to do, leaving us just as we've decided on a ball. No matter. Constance and I shall handle all. Your job now is to get Diana outfitted in all the finery she will carry. Paste will do just as well as real stones; the boy shall not tell the difference. But do not skimp on the gloves! I have enclosed a list of such shops where you will find most elegant and recent fashions. Bring back extra muslins! She shall want them as the summer goes on. Tell her they are for you if she protests.*

*Again, your timing is abominable. But I do understand that in marriage there are some things we women can never hope to control. A man's urgent need to go to town is one such thing. Count yourself very lucky indeed that you are invited.*

*Yours Etc.,*

*E—*

No note was sent by Maggie or Diana to Langley Hall, as such a gesture would be highly presumptuous on such a lately made acquaintance. However, as it happened, Elizabeth found she suddenly had too many eggs. These eggs needed to be hastily given away to her nearest neighbors, or given instead to her *nearly* nearest neighbors. (Her nearest neighbors were a large family on a small farm which had supplied the eggs originally.) So, the excess of eggs was dispatched to Langley Hall by Elizabeth's lady's maid, Heloise. Of all the Eastbey Abbey servants, Heloise spoke the best plain English and she was tasked with delivering both eggs *and* the news that the Wuster Park household was soon departing for London.

Once delivered, this information had the exact effect Elizabeth hoped it would. The three young men, led by Hudson of course, walked to Wuster Park for a short call of farewell.

With their hats in hand and the bustle of a hasty departure ringing through the large house, the boys made polite conversation when Maggie alone received them in the drawing room. Hudson tried his best to affect an aloof attitude, but his inner anxiety was betrayed by a constant glancing over his shoulder. Before long, his waiting was gratified. Diana entered the room. Upon seeing the familiar but unexpected party, she stopped short. She was unsure if she should join her cousin in receiving the guests until Maggie motioned for her to come and sit.

From there, Hudson became rapidly more animated. It was clear the object of his visit had arrived. From their recent conversation, Hudson knew that Diana had never been to London before. He was eager, therefore, to tell her all of the best sights, best amusements, most enjoyable productions, and finest teahouses that she should be sure not to miss. He also asked, as if in an afterthought, if she would be so kind as to deliver a note to his parents. Maggie noted with tender satisfaction the quaver in his voice as he made this significant request.

This rather obvious ploy was lost on Diana, however, and it was left to Maggie to assure Hudson that they would indeed make a point of calling on his family. The boy beamed so brightly that even his friends were embarrassed for him. Shortly after these assurances were given, the young men made their quick bows and departed.

"What do you think of that, Diana?" Maggie asked when they had gone.

"I don't think I can remember any of the places he was saying."

"Well, you shall remember to visit his parents, I think?"

Diana faced Maggie in a panic.

"But you are coming with me, aren't you?!"

Maggie was quick to console her. It was unfair, Maggie felt, to tease the girl about such things.

# Twenty-Six

DIANA WAS ASTOUNDED by the bounty of property she had acquired in her short residence at Wuster Park. Having arrived with only the dress on her back and the boots on her feet, she was shocked to discover that now an entire trunk was required to transport her wardrobe and belongings to London. She still had the dresses and underclothes which Mrs. Rollins had given her the day of her arrival, the initials of the original owner still embroidered at the necklines. She also had five day dresses that Mrs. Rollins had commissioned the maids to make her. Her cousin Maggie had undertaken the necessary alterations to two of her own dresses to supply Diana with proper Sunday attire. Then, of course, Lady Dormer was forever heaping accessories upon her when she came to call at Eastbey Abbey. Thanks to that lady's generosity, Diana now had four pairs of shoes and a plethora of gloves, bonnets, stockings, and wraps.

As she beheld this abundance, she wanted to weep. She did not deserve this. She had done nothing to warrant this kindness. She was unworthy, but unable to articulate to herself why. She had been sent away so she might not be a burden on her family. This is what she told Maggie. This is what she told herself. So why then did she feel so guilty for having found a life so much better than the one she left behind? All this she turned over in her mind as the carriage wheels crunched over the road from New Glenbury to London.

~

Late in his bachelorhood, when the annoyances of lodging at a gentleman's club outweighed the advantages, Benjamin had acquired a townhouse in London. It was neither modest nor grand, located neither fashionably nor unfavorably. In the time since his marriage, it had been closed up. Only his former valet, Simpson, and his wife, Mrs. Simpson, resided there as caretakers. As news of the Howards' impending arrival barely preceded their actual arrival, it was understandable that the place was still in a state of half-readiness when the carriage doors swung open before it.

This reasonable unreadiness embarrassed Benjamin greatly. He spent all of the tour of that townhome making apologies to his wife. In the moments between his regrets, Maggie filled the air with her sincerest compliments. Diana gave very little thought to either of them. Since they had reached the outskirts of the great metropolis, she had been too enamored with the fascinating bustle of city living happening all around to give heed to anything else. When her attention was not directly called upon, she would slip away and press her face up against any nearby window, surveying the street below. Only the smell of London was displeasing to her. Everything else seemed a marvel: rows of identical buildings, wide streets, and dozens upon dozens of people moving endlessly on errands she could not begin to imagine.

The kitchen was still in the process of stocking up for their visit, so the family dined out that night. The experience was so wholly enchanting to Diana that even Benjamin was delighted by something other than his wife. Indeed, the two married adults had each seen so many London seasons that they had grown a bit exhausted by the city's many demands. Now, seeing the *ton* for the first time through the wonderment of Diana, they found their enthusiasm for urban pleasures reinvigorated. To forestall the end of the night, they rode their carriage up and down all the major streets. Through the windows, they saw theatergoers and nighttime revelers aplenty. But it was the hundreds of lighted gas lamps that dazzled Diana more than any other spectacle.

The next morning, Maggie expected that Benjamin would take his leave of the ladies for the day. She was surprised, therefore, when her husband signaled that she should accompany him on his morning's errand.

"Are you not going to the bank?"

"No, I'm not going to the bank. What would make you think that?"

"Well, we have come to town, and I assumed it was so you might . . . go to the bank?"

"No, my dear, I told you why we have come. It is time for us to make the necessary alterations so we may be finally comfortable in our home."

Diana snorted her tea at this. Though Maggie sent her a reproaching look, she could not help but agree with the sentiments such a snort betrayed. But with her husband she would go. So, having made no other plans for her young charge, Maggie set Diana up by a window with the lace box. She knew very well that the only thing the girl would make was a mess. Still, Maggie shared a few words of encouragement with her cousin as she donned her bonnet and shawl. Arm in arm with her husband, she went to seek such comforts which she could not yet imagine.

When the couple returned to the townhouse that afternoon, Benjamin delighted in describing all his dear wife's décor choices to Diana. Diana demonstrated a polite enthusiasm for these selections as she waited to report the occurrences of her own day. In her turn, she described with excitement the passing of nearly *one hundred* carriages in front of their house. She regretted that she could not be sure the exact number of carriages. Diversions had sometimes carried her away from the window. That the number of carriages topped one hundred, she was certain, for that many she had counted herself.

Benjamin and Maggie nodded respectfully, each at a loss to discover an appropriate reply.

That evening, they took Diana to the theater. They did not bother to arrive early enough to find a place in the box seats, as surely some of their connections would have facilitated. Instead, because they were still technically in mourning, they came in with the lower crowds and watched the show, rather than the spectacle of all the fine attendees. Diana was, again, delighted.

The next day proceeded in much the same fashion, with Benjamin and Maggie taking another trip to the warehouses and storefronts. Then the whole party passed the evening attending a concert.

At the concert, it struck Maggie that Diana, ever delighted and blissfully unaware, was receiving a great number of curious glances from men *and* women around them. Maggie understood the men's looks. Diana was very pretty, and her delight rendered her radiant. However, the ladies' lingering glances were a mystery to Maggie until she had the opportunity to observe Diana at a distance. She was uncommonly tall, which Maggie had forgotten, spending so much time in her proximity. Maggie also realized, with no little mortification, that Diana was dressed in a very out-of-fashion way. It was a wonder to herself that she had not recognized it before. Maggie rationalized that because she had been in the countryside where fashion follows function, such matters had naturally slipped from her perception.

Maggie then recalled Elizabeth's letter, and she marveled at the woman's wisdom. That evening, she informed Benjamin that she would be taking Diana to have some clothes made at the earliest convenience. He agreed that the next day should be spent by the ladies in this pursuit.

The next *three* days were spent in such pursuit. Benjamin whiled away this time at his club, doing whatever silly things men do at their clubs, while Maggie and Diana perused and purchased.

Diana, at last, had surrendered herself to the care of her cousin. Much to Maggie's relief, she made no objections to being draped and dressed. She made no fuss about the expense and no mention of what her mother might think of such extravagance.

Inwardly, Diana knew that she would not take even half of the clothing with her at the end of her stay at Wuster Park. She could easily imagine the reaction her mother would have at even that fraction of Maggie's generosity, but she never intended her mother to discover it. Therefore, she saw no harm in letting her cousin buy her plenty of new dresses, shawls, hats, gloves, scarves, stockings, ribbons, lace, and so on; it would almost all end up back in Maggie's own wardrobe, in the end. On that assumption, she acquiesced to be dressed.

This was how Diana ended up with seven new dresses, four new hats, five pairs of gloves, countless ribbons and laces, two shawls, a pair of walking shoes, a pair of dancing shoes, and a second trunk to hold this great bounty. There was also a large quantity of muslins purchased, which were destined to be made into even more dresses, in their time.

Maggie always prided herself on her indifference to shopping as an occupation. She looked down on the young ladies of her set whose entire existence revolved around the acquisition of new and fashionable items to be cast off ere they were owned. As she was still reveling in the joys of her wedding wardrobe and bound by the conventions of the mourning period for her father-in-law, Maggie limited herself to purchasing only the items she really, truly, deeply admired.

This was how she ended up with six new dresses, four new hats, three pairs of gloves, countless ribbons and laces, two shawls, a new pair of walking shoes, a new pair of dancing shoes, a new trunk to hold all of these, and her own store of muslins, too.

Once, while being fitted at the modiste, Maggie attempted to gently tease Diana. She wanted to make it clear to her young cousin that she saw as well as any New Glenbury villager the warm regard between herself and Hudson Birch.

Diana reacted with considerable surprise. She was quick to deny that any attachment existed. She insisted that Hudson was just being polite and treating her as he would any young lady, only there were no other young ladies around to prove this point. The quickness of her rebuff suggested to Maggie that this was not the first time the girl had considered such matters. Maggie pressed on, urging Diana to judge his behavior as a serious display of interest.

"Why would he be interested in me?"

"Oh, why indeed! As if you do not know!" Maggie replied with a light laugh.

Stirred to some sharpness, Diana began to reply, "I do not! I am without the faintest—" Then, certainly for no reason at all, she caught a glimpse of Hudson in her mind's eye.

She saw him as he had been on their walk back to Wuster Park from the New Glenbury church. In a moment of conversational quiet, his perpetual grin had dissipated. His smiling eyes rounded into sincere, searching orbs. He looked at her as if she was the first of her kind. He looked at her like a man in a moment of great discovery. And when he had looked at her like that, Diana had felt how much he wanted to look at her, to be with her, to know her.

Since coming to Wuster Park, Diana had found it difficult to know what the people around her wanted. Things back in Yansworth were much simpler. In Yansworth, the people she knew wanted money, food, and a dry place to warm their boots. In New Glenbury, everyone had so much more than Diana could ever imagine wanting. So, what could they want? Only with Hudson, when he looked at her so ardently, did she understand that *she* was wanted. This knowledge of his sincere desire to spend time with her, to listen to her, to look at her . . . it felt overwhelming. It felt impossible.

"Why would he be interested in me?" she repeated, her voice a shadow of what it had been. She looked down at her hands shielding her face from the eyes of her cousin.

Maggie, seeing Diana's profound embarrassment, relented and regretted. It must be such a trial, she thought, to be so young and so in love.

Maggie did believe it was love, for Maggie believed most whole-heartedly in love at first sight. Benjamin had fallen in love with her at first sight, and just behold the fruits of such a seed. Maggie sincerely wished that everyone would be so lucky. But then, perhaps it was not so lucky to fall in love while still so young. Maggie had learned a lot about herself in those long years as a single girl. She had seen many flirtations fizzle and many warm regards kindle into the flames of passion. She had watched as each of her friends took their chances and made their choices. Yes, she learned a great deal in those years. And with that knowledge, she felt there were the makings of a rare and beautiful love blooming between Hudson and Diana. But was Diana wise enough to see it, too? That, Maggie could not know.

# Twenty-Seven

A FULL WEEK into their two-week stay in London, outfitted in her new finery, Maggie felt it was finally time for Diana to deliver Mr. Birch's letter to his parents. On the coach ride over to the address Hudson had supplied, Maggie carefully instructed Diana on exactly what to say to the footman who would answer the door. Though Maggie knew that the Birches were very new in their consequence, their townhome sat in a nice enough neighborhood. Upon arrival, Maggie noted that the front of the house displayed none of the ill-conceived ostentation of some of its neighbors.

Standing bravely next to her cousin, Diana knocked upon the door as she had been instructed. The door was quickly opened, and Diana delivered her practiced dialogue to the man before her.

"Good afternoon, my name is Diana Huxley. Mr. Hudson Birch has asked me to deliver a letter to Mr. James Birch—"

Before she could finish her speech in requesting to know if Mr. James Birch were at home, the man standing before her broke in and said, "I am Mr. James Birch. Thank you, girlie." He then took the letter, placed a small coin in her hand, and closed the door in her face.

For a moment, the two cousins stood on the front step in a stasis of general amazement. Even Diana, so new to the world of town manners, was sure that something about this exchange had not gone as it should.

Inside, Mr. James Birch had rejoined his wife in their parlor. There she admonished him, as he knew she would, for answering his own door.

"Well, I was not going to wait for old Henry to come from the back to get it. Besides, it was only a letter."

"Who is the letter from?"

Having not really listened to the messenger, Mr. Birch now examined the handwriting on the envelope to discover the answer. It was the loopy, oversized scrawl of his son.

"It's from Hudson."

"Well, read it then, do," Mrs. Birch intoned. They did not receive letters as often as she would have liked from their only son.

Mr. Birch read to himself the following scant lines:

*Dearest Father and Mother,*
*I send this letter in trust of a girl I am most eager for you to meet. Do write to me, please, and tell me what you think of her.*
*Your loving son,*
*Hudson Birch*

As the letter had been only a pretext for Diana to call on his parents, Hudson had not troubled himself with composing any reason for writing outside of this. Reading and comprehending these lines, Mr. Birch blanched at his own mistake and anticipated the wrath that was sure to flow swiftly from his wife.

"What does it say, Mr. Birch?"

"Ah well, nothing. Nothing of importance. Nothing."

Mrs. Birch knew the ways of her husband all too well. She read in his face that there was trouble afoot. She leaned over and snatched the letter from his hands. Reading it swiftly, even more swiftly she jumped up from her chair and raced to the front door. Throwing it open, she surveyed the whole of the street, hoping to see the object of her son's inquiry. She did not.

Diana and Maggie had, after their moment of confusion, retreated to their carriage and departed in the time it had taken for the truth of the situation to be discovered.

Seething mad at her husband's foolish mistake, Mrs. Birch could not help but also feel righteously justified. She had scolded Mr. Birch for many years about the terrible habit of opening his own door. Now, she thought, *now* he would see the error of his ways. With this high and mighty ire, Mrs. Birch rejoined her husband.

For a long moment, she said nothing, letting him marinate in the possibilities of her remonstrance. Then, thinking to lure him into false confidence, she inquired, as steadily as she could, "Well then, what did she look like?"

"What?"

"The girl with the letter. What did she look like?"

The first word that came to Mr. Birch's mind was "surprised," but he knew this would not do for an answer unlikely to upset his wife. He tried to recall the girl at the door.

"She was very tall, I think."

"Very tall, you think."

"Very tall. I'm sure."

"And did she give you her name, this tall girl?"

"She did! But I must own I have forgotten it."

He said this and cast a sideways glance at his wife, who was growing redder by the moment.

"Yes, of course you have. Well, do you remember anything at all about this tall girl?"

"There was a second lady."

"No doubt her mother. What a lovely first impression we have made on the family, I'm sure."

"No, she was too young to be her mother."

"Then how do you know it was not her that the letter describes?"

"She was not the one holding the letter."

"I see. And were they finely dressed, these two ladies?"

"I do believe they were. Though it was hard to say exactly because they had on wraps. But yes, I believe they were fine wraps."

"Well then, I suppose we should write to Hudson and give our blessing to his marriage."

This drew a response of astonished silence from her husband, to whom the question of matrimony had never occurred. Mrs. Birch was thus given the task of explaining just how grievous a mistake Mr. Birch's answering the door had been. It was true that she did not know with any *certainty* if this girl was to be her son's intended. (In fact, as she considered it at length, she realized it may have just been some casual kindness to send her to call on them.) But in that moment, she wished to impress upon her husband the serious consequences of his actions, in the hopes of breaking him of his door-answering habit for life.

It was not exactly successful. As soon as the tall stranger had been considered through the lens of matrimony, Mr. Birch suddenly recalled a very many more details that recommended the young girl to his favor. She was very pretty, he suspected—tall and pretty. She had hair that was nice, its color being somewhere between dark and light. Her name had started with a B or N or something between those letters, possibly. Her accent had been a clear one, maybe from the north, or the south.

All this he recounted with much softness to his wife. In her disagreeable temper, she could only oppose his suggestion that they should write to Hudson and admit the mistake. She scoffed at the idea that they should tell their son that they liked the girl terrifically despite not having spoken to her. And she balked at the notion that Hudson might give them instructions to make a second, more successful, introduction.

When pressed by her husband to account why this was not a most perfect solution, Mrs. Birch could only huff and explain, "Why, we know nothing about her! We do not know if she is indeed even worth knowing. She might be a governess or some other sort of type out in the country looking for a rich husband. The countryside is full, teeming full I tell you, of young penniless, title-less, family-less, unscrupulous girls looking to ensnare a sweet, innocent, wealthy boy like our Hudson."

"My dear, I seem to recall that you yourself once worked as a governess."

"That was for one summer, and utterly beside the point. We cannot be ignorant of our station, James. We cannot pretend that our son is not a prize many a young lady is trying to catch. We cannot go about opening our own doors as if we do not employ a person for that exact purpose!"

With this, the conversation was closed. The Birches each privately resolved to write their son their own letter. His mother was at that moment constructing an argument warning him of fortune-hunting lady's maids, dairy maids, chamber maids, and all their ilk. His father was planning to write and admit that he, too, had always been partial to a tall woman.

# Twenty-Eight

MAGGIE DID NOT know what to say to Diana about the unfortunate occurrence at the Birch house. She pitied the girl immensely. Maggie felt, on Diana's behalf, all the pain of this dismissal from a family she should be so desperate to impress. Now, without having met them, Diana would likely have even more difficulty securing a proposal from Mr. Birch for a fall wedding. For who could engage themselves to a woman without first introducing her to his family?

Maggie's pity was interrupted by the recollection that she herself had not met her own father-in-law until the day before her own wedding. In this recollection, the current situation did not seem so dire.

She therefore resolved not to mention the trouble to Diana. Instead, she hoped that the story might become one of those amusing in-law anecdotes which married people tell in the company of their married friends.

Diana interpreted her cousin's uncharacteristic silence as grave disappointment. She was not sure what about her own appearance or attitude had rendered her unpalatable to Mr. Birch. It seemed likely that she bore markers of inferiority that Maggie, being her cousin, affected to ignore out of politeness. Mr. Birch, being a serious businessman in a serious city, would have no time for her country coarseness.

The remaining week of their time in London was drawing to a

close, but Benjamin had in no way slowed his ambition for the redecoration of his home. He and Maggie had ordered paper for six rooms. Then, because Maggie had offhandedly suggested that a lighter color paper might make the breakfast room not feel so close, they had ordered paper for that, too. All the rooms that were getting new paper naturally needed new drapes and upholstery, which was also ordered. In addition, they had stopped at a silversmith to see the latest in candelabras and coffee pots. They had even ordered a new chandelier for the townhome because Maggie liked the look of one in a shop window, and it was too small for any use in Wuster Park.

Maggie still felt that all this extravagance was strangely timed and wholly unneeded; but she contented herself with the consolation that if Benjamin's father had not died so shortly after their marriage, she and her husband would have spent at least this much money on fitting their own home. Perhaps, she thought, the act of redecoration was one Benjamin had always associated as a benefit of matrimony. She had no reason to dislike the process, for Benjamin was always most encouraging of her own ideas and tastes.

The household got along well as a trio. Benjamin and Maggie had the pleasure of each other's company throughout the day, and then the joys of adventuring out with Diana in the evenings. There was something delicious about observing the whole of eligible London society performing its elaborate social rituals without having any stake in the outcome. As Diana was not out, they did not attend any dances or receptions. They did take her to Hyde Park to promenade, and it made them feel very wise and secure in their own happily settled state.

Indeed, for two people in the early days of wedded bliss, there can be no more enjoyable an activity than watching the absurd posturing and preening of the unattached in their hopes of securing a match. In the name of demystifying the spectacle for Diana, Maggie and Benjamin confessed to each other the tactics, trials, and insecurities that had transpired in their own unmarried years.

Diana's age and inexperience recalled to them their earliest seasons, many years ago, when blunders and gaffes felt insurmountable.

It was fascinating for Maggie to hear the inner workings of a man's life before matrimony. Maggie did not realize that men employed as much strategy as women in their appearance and in the displays of their accomplishments. Benjamin enlightened them both until Maggie's eyes streamed in tears of laughter. She could not imagine, as she insisted to him, that he had ever been desperate enough to buy another man's sketches for his own portfolio. He insisted that he had, and he promised to show them both upon their return to the house.

Had it not been for Elizabeth's upcoming ball, which a letter from Constance assured her was going to be a lively success, and which a letter from Elizabeth assured her would be an unforgettable disaster, they might have stayed in London many weeks more. Alas, as there were only two full days remaining before their scheduled departure, Benjamin insisted that now must be the time to select their china patterns.

Unlike on their trips to the paper warehouses and the drapers, Benjamin was in subdued spirits that morning. Unlike the playful, flirtatious outings of previous days, the process of china-showroom inspection and supervised catalogue perusals he treated with the utmost sincerity. They visited the studios in unceasing succession, not even stopping for an afternoon refreshment of tea and cake before returning home. There, over dinner, Benjamin pressed his wife. Which of the studios had she liked best? Did she think the French style of soup tureen would be suitable? What would the effect of a highly gilded pattern be in conjunction with their silver? He was continually making references to a pocket notebook, naming patterns and specifics that Maggie was at a loss to recall.

Frustrated by this lapse in her memory, he said firmly, "Maggie, it's very important to me that we order our new formal plate tomorrow. It is our last day in town, and I should not like to conduct the order via post."

In her airy voice, Maggie replied, "Maybe this visit, we do not pick out the plates. Indeed, with so many things soon to be changing in the house, perhaps the plates can wait."

"No, Maggie. The plates cannot wait." He said this sternly, and Diana began to glance rapidly back and forth between the couple. There was an unsettling ringing in her ears.

"I do not see why the plates are so important," Maggie continued.

"The plates are the whole reason we've come to London!" Benjamin barked, stomping his foot loudly under the table and rattling the dishes in his ire. Benjamin had never raised his voice to Maggie, and it was startling.

"Do not shout at me!" she shouted.

Diana fled the room.

Suddenly alone, both Benjamin and Maggie sat stunned and embarrassed by their outbursts.

At last, Benjamin mastered his voice. "I am so sorry. I shouldn't have shouted. Please understand, Maggie, if we don't order new plates tomorrow, then it will take ages to get the order settled before it can be placed. Even still, we are looking at those same formal plates for the rest of the summer, at least."

"Well, I like those old formal plates."

"That's not the point."

"Then what is the point? What is wrong with our plates, Benjamin?"

"They are not *our* plates. That's the problem. They're my father's plates. He and my mother picked them out, together, from the Sevres showroom."

"Yes, I know."

An edge of bitterness colored Benjamin's words, and he scowled at the floor as he spoke.

"Well, I do not like them. They make me sad. They remind me of them. Them, the two of them. The plates. I think those damned plates were the last thing they ever agreed upon."

Things were becoming clearer for Maggie, now.

"And you would like different plates which we may *always* agree upon?"

He looked at her and smiled a sad smile that answered her in the affirmative where words could not. In a few moments, Maggie remembered their guest.

"I should go to Diana. I think she was frightened?"

Benjamin only nodded, still mired by his own thoughts.

Maggie went to the door of Diana's bedroom. Knocking gently, Maggie entreated her to come join them in the drawing room. Diana emerged. Neither cousin directly acknowledged the situation or resulting discomfort. Instead, Maggie squeezed Diana's hand, smiled a conciliatory smile, and led them to the townhouse's drawing room. There, without saying much more than a few brief words, the group took up their usual after-dinner occupations. Diana was still working on the embroidery of a decorative table linen marked by Constance. Maggie settled by her on the sofa and began to work one corner as Benjamin read aloud from a novel.

Later that night, when Maggie and Benjamin had snuffed the candles and climbed into the bed, both lay for some time on their backs before he turned and spoke to the night.

"The plates make me feel like a little boy. I look at them and it's like I can hear them arguing in the next room. I feel trapped, trapped in that house sometimes. Trapped in the past. And I just don't want . . . I just don't want our life to look like their lives. Maggie, you are the first person who has ever made me feel like I have any bid at true happiness. I want my house, our house, all of Wuster Park to echo with your laughter. I want the whole place to remind me of you. I want everything I touch to be first touched with your light.

"Before I met you, my life was a series of little annoyances and petty grievances, like the whole world was filled with the sound of a whining carriage wheel or the grating of a rusty door hinge. I was always looking at my watch, wondering when the next thing was to happen. When I met you, all of that lifted off of me, and the world was made new. I want to make a new world with you and for you, Maggie. And that"—he closed this grand declaration with a shy laugh —"is why we need new plates."

"I had no idea you felt this way, Benjamin."

"Well, I know how silly it is to have so many feelings about plates we don't even see every day."

"No, I had no idea you felt this way about *me*. To be sure, you always say such sweet and wonderful things. But to think I could provoke such intensity."

"Didn't you? Don't you? I mean . . . don't you feel that way about me?"

"I . . . I am certainly gratified by your strong sentiments. And I do love you, dearly, truly, I do. But you know . . . your words are like poetry. And poetry, one never really knows . . . Benjamin, I simply had no idea you held such a depth of feeling for me."

"Then, you do not share it? You do not love me?"

"No, Benjamin, I do love you. And in time, I shall come to love you even more. But I have only known you, what, these nine months, and I must own that—"

"You do not love me?"

"I do love you."

"But not as much."

"I'm not sure. Just differently, perhaps."

Benjamin's heart constricted inside him in a burst of true physical anguish, but he kept his voice steady as he said, "I understand."

They placed an order for new plates the next day.

# Twenty Nine

PLANNING A COUNTRY ball when one has a mind tuned towards matrimony is a tricky thing. The menu must be filling without being heavy. The drinks must be liberally supplied, but light. The music must be buoyant, but neither too diverting nor too loud to preclude conversation. Above all else, the guest list must be selected with the tactical prowess of Napoleon.

It was like a convening of the Napoleonic Council when Constance and Elizabeth met to review every family in their vast acquaintance and navigate the perils of selective invitations. That all families in the immediate vicinity and parish must be included was a given. Luckily, none of these families had any remaining daughters (or even sons) to be of any concern. Constance and Elizabeth had certainly seen to that over the last twelve years. This did leave a serious deficit of persons known to dance, and it was well understood that for young people to have any privacy on the dance floor, a large number of dancers were needed. Thus, the two matrons occupied themselves in careful consideration of the families of the surrounding counties.

The Ashcrofts should be invited, as their four stringy boys would make a good stock of dance partners for the three plain-faced daughters and one bespectacled cousin of their neighbors, the Gellings. Because the Gellings were invited, it was understood that the Crawfords must also be invited. Otherwise, there would be no end of strife in that direction. The Crawfords had one boy and one girl, each too handsome for Constance and Elizabeth's comfort, and so, equally handsome counterparts must be sought to distract them.

In the end, some twenty-five families were invited, and Constance and Elizabeth suspected that they would have a party of more than forty dancing-minded youths, plus some parents who didn't mind making themselves a bit ridiculous by joining the troupe. Then there would be some fifty other guests who would occupy the evening in eating, drinking, gossiping, and playing cards—in short, a good-sized country party for a fine summer night. Constance and Elizabeth counted on this number to be sufficient for giving Diana and Hudson their opportunity for romance.

Elizabeth spared no expense in her conception of the menu, and though Constance advised her towards a temperate evening, Elizabeth did nothing halfway. Wine and champagne were ordered by the case, and huge quantities of fish were commissioned by the local monger. Mutton pies and beef medallions had been fashionable the last time Elizabeth visited town some four years before, and these were included on the menu with great pride.

The band was the greatest stumbling block. Invariably, a good band is hard to find. In truth, on such short notice, a good band was entirely out of the question. A decent band was all that could be hoped for, and even that standard proved aspirational. The only band which could be secured on such short notice was a ragtag unit said to be previously encamped with a regiment of officers; the reason for their decampment remained suspiciously unknown. But good music is not essential for good dancing. This was said, and said often, by the two friends in their mutual reassurances.

Onward marched time, and the date of the fête was rapidly approaching. Elizabeth, prone unsurprisingly to dramatics, sent her carriage to the rectory for Constance nearly every day. The Reverend Samuel Astley might have been disturbed by how frequently his wife's attention was called to such a secular matter, but he did not notice. Constance had procured a new stock of philosophical papers at the beginning of their project, and in the final week of planning, Samuel was entirely occupied in their study. Indeed, when his wife reminded him to air out his good coat for the evening, he was more than a little surprised to discover the date of the ball had arrived.

# Thirty

It was only a quarter moon on the night of Elizabeth's ball. This was far from ideal for the many guests traveling long distances across country roads. Arrivals to Eastbey Abbey therefore began a bit later than expected. Unsurprisingly, Constance and the reverend were the first to arrive. To create anticipation for her cousin's supposed beau, Maggie had been instructed that Diana should arrive later than expected. However, because the Langley Hall party and their town coachman had not yet been to Elizabeth's estate, they were detained for nearly twenty minutes at a crossroads as they waited for another coach of partygoers to lead them in the correct direction. This little setback was nothing to a man in pursuit of a beautiful girl, though.

As soon as Hudson entered the great hall of Eastbey Abbey, he spotted Diana ahead of him in the receiving line. Rushing the removal of his boots and slipping into his tasseled dancing shoes, he quickly caught up with her and had the pleasure of escorting her into the dance. When first they met, he greeted her in playful recollection of their banter before the New Glenbury church.

"I say, is that you, Lady Diana Huxley? What a coincidence. I never imagined I'd meet you here."

Diana smiled brightly at his jest, relieved to find a familiar face so soon at such a large event.

"There he goes, never to be seen again," Noah said to Ellis.

"Yes, what a lucky man. I wish my Melissa were here."

"Why? So you might leave me entirely alone?"

"No! So that she might meet Diana. I have talked with Hudson about it a great deal, and we are sure they will be friends."

"I can hear no more of this. Ellis, please, have mercy."

"Oh, I cannot wait until fate thrusts your lady love before you."

"I'm about to thrust you before me on this floor if you don't—"

The ever-watchful Mrs. Bellwood clicked her tongue at them several times, and harmony was restored, or at least, violence avoided.

When the greeters had been greeted and introductions made, Mrs. Bellwood settled herself into the comfortable and familiar seat known to all women of a certain age at a ball: the Mothers' Table. There she stayed all night, giving counsel and sympathy to the other mothers of children at every age. Subjects included: the insufficiency of both an away and at-home education, teething corals and their misplacements, tales of illnesses conquered (with the condemnation of all country doctors), and how fast they do grow up. . . . In short, she passed the evening in an aura of mutual delight, surrounded by the only women in the world who she felt could truly understand her.

Noah and Ellis were quick to part, each feeling that little good could come of their continued company. Noah confidently strode through the card room several times. Yet, try as he might, he could not muster enough of his hero Lord Byron's devil-may-care abandon to actually sit and play cards against this assembly of country gentlemen. Having spent all his life in London, Noah held a special reverence for the country gentleman. Of course, he aspired to one day live comfortably among them, as all city boys do. But, like many city boys, he also held a deep suspicion that the ample leisure time of gentlemen in the countryside was spent in the honing of talents for cards and other idle occupations. He feared that, if given the opportunity, these country gentry would devour Noah's meager purse and plunge him into debt.

Noah had a great fear of debt. His uncle Harold was said to be in debt, and this elicited no small share of contempt from the whole family. Even his mother would instruct her sons to pack away the French figurines from the mantel before any visit from Harold was expected. So, after some literal back and forth, Noah contented himself to stand near the card-room door as he worked up the courage to either enter or abandon his ambitions entirely.

Here Reverend Samuel Astley found him. The reverend, as a rule, did not play games in company. On some quiet evenings, he and his wife would indulge themselves in backgammon. They were always careful to pack up the set entirely and stow it in the bottom drawer of his desk so that the servants might not see it on their cleaning of his study. Still, in complement to his abstinence of play, the reverend made a point to take a long, meaningful look around any card room at a party, to remind the occupants who *else* was watching them from above at that moment. He assured himself that this practice was the full extent his duty in these situations, and, with a dignified sense of purpose, he did it now. Then, spotting the young Noah Bellwood standing near the door looking unoccupied in thought and purpose, he delighted at the opportunity to resume his debate with the stimulating youth.

Noah was grateful for the distraction from his own self-doubt. As a result, he was not nearly as disagreeable as he was sometimes inclined to be at parties. He received the conversation of the Reverend Samuel Astley with gratitude, at first.

Then of course, his disagreeable temperament took over. Noah's suspicion that country men were made of stronger stuff than their city counterparts was confirmed by the old reverend, who was not thrown off by his disparagement. Rather, the reverend persisted in livelier and livelier suppositions and suggestions. Before long, Noah found himself in a true tête-à-tête of philosophic minds. The greatest shock of it all was just how much he was enjoying it.

So it came to pass that the two men were inseparable the whole night. They walked and talked, debated and discussed, ate and ambled across all manner of subjects. Noah was well read for a young man, and the reverend was well read for a clergyman. Around and around they went in fervent conversation until, somehow, they found themselves seated at a card table as partners in whist (all while debating fiercely the merits and demerits of such amusements). The whole of the card room was made very uneasy by this development. It took some several minutes before conversation and play in the room could return to normal.

Ellis, on the other hand, in separating from his brother, found himself the object of much attention by a horde of rather plain-looking sisters: the Gelling daughters. The Ashcroft sons stood sentinel around the Gelling gaggle, casting aspersing looks at the stranger until a timely mention of his darling Melissa scattered the Gellings in search of easier game. It was only then that the Ashcroft party made their introductions.

Owing to Ellis's affable nature, the whole group became fast friends. Soon there was dancing aplenty, and none of the Ashcroft boys begrudged him a partner. Many even offered to set him up with cousins and sisters who might not otherwise have the pleasure of being asked to dance. Ellis found all this to be remarkably charming. It confirmed his suspicion that all country gentlemen exemplified nothing but kindness and hospitality, possessing none of the connivances or pretense of their city counterparts.

Ellis imparted this opinion to Constance. After a few dances, he went in search of refreshment and found the reverend's wife idling by the punch bowl. She was delighted by his impression and only too happy to engage with this young man in conversation again. Their discussion went very much as it had at the Wuster Park dinner. This time, however, Ellis had the full use of his auditory faculties. The only moment of some confusion was when Constance inquired if Ellis had been so good as to follow her advice. Ellis, having never heard that advice, was not sure if he had been fortunate enough to follow it. After a moment of deliberation, though, he answered with a resounding affirmative. Thus, he was cemented in Constance's mind as the most clever, good-natured boy ever to live. She felt certain that no wife would ever do him credit.

Hudson and Diana were inseparable for the entire evening. Diana, resplendent in one of her new London dresses, looked pretty enough to have her portrait made. This compliment Hudson paid her several times. Not normally fond of such flattery, tonight Diana could not help but agree with his assessment. She had appraised herself in the tall cheval glass of her bedroom before departing that night. Her new London dress was well suited to her shape. The wider sash under her bust balanced the scale of her form. The neckline framed her collarbones and made a beautiful column of her neck. In her hair, there nestled twelve velvet violets that Diana knew for a fact cost as much as the three silk roses she had been so reluctant to send home. Hudson was always very finely pressed and dressed. It made perfect sense to Diana that her new *ton* finery would inspire admiration from the sartorially sophisticated young man.

Diana's loveliness earned her no goodwill from the other young ladies in attendance that night. Since the guest list had been designed to exclude any girl prettier than she, it seemed entirely unfair to the other girls that Diana should also be the best dressed. They need not have been so fierce in their jealousy. In truth, Diana's comparative beauty and tall stature made her an intimidating figure to all the young men, with the lone exception of Hudson Birch. Naturally, Diana's own shyness did little to recommend herself to new society.

Since receiving his invitation to Elizabeth's ball, Hudson had been eager to impress Diana with his fashionable London formals and his knowledge of the most modern dances. The second part of his plan was quickly dashed. The ill-assembled band did not seem to be familiar with any of the songs popular in London for the last decade. Instead, they delighted their dancers with old country reels and classic court tunes of times long past. Diana, it seemed, was equally lost, and the two laughed their way up and down the lines, doing their very best to match the other dancers.

They might have fared better if they had divided their ignorance in adopting other dance partners, but Hudson was utterly unwilling to surrender Diana. Mr. Birch suspected that all country gentlemen were naturally the most skilled and ardent lovers. He felt that their easy charm left their city counterparts with no alternative but forfeit, once they set their cap to a girl. So, his strategy was to occupy Diana as completely as he could, in the hopes of keeping a competitor at bay.

This excessive attention was not necessary to secure Diana's felicity, but she did appreciate his steadfast presence, especially given that Maggie, her cousin and chaperone, was nowhere to be found.

If Maggie had been a more attentive chaperone, she might have reminded Diana of her obligation to dance with some other partners out of politeness. She might have reminded her to drink water and take tea to give room for conversation. She might have supervised a moonlit stroll through the garden, giving the young lovers just enough distance to exchange the most sincere compliments. She might have done all of this. Instead, she was walking with Elizabeth and getting, it must be said, quite drunk.

This was Maggie's first ball as a married woman, and the experience was wholly new to her. Instead of circling the room soliciting invitations to dance and holding herself at a distance to be best observed by her rivals and potentials, she was greeted with the option of sitting at the Married Ladies' Table (near, but separate from, the Mothers' Table). There, the conversation dwelt upon the subjects of most concern to women of that station. In the scant half hour Maggie could tolerate such society, the topics remarked upon had been: the rising price of good mutton, the impossibility of getting decent help, the dangerous richness of French cuisine, and the audacity of *some people* never specified. Then, Maggie could take no more, and she went in search of reprieve or distraction.

If Benjamin had been in attendance, none of this would have been a problem. They would have laughed and danced like it was the very first night of their acquaintance. But Benjamin was not in attendance. Despite their expeditious ordering of formal plates in London, a feeling of discomfort and anxiety still pervaded the relationship. On the entire carriage ride from London to Wuster Park, Benjamin had stared fixedly out the window, insensible to all Maggie's enticements of conversation. When Maggie had begun her preparations for Elizabeth's ball, Benjamin insisted that he was still too exhausted from their journey to attend. Try as she might to approve of all that her husband said and did, Maggie felt Benjamin was being unreasonably withdrawn, especially considering the triviality of his outburst regarding the plates. She knew he had been embarrassed, but she didn't understand why he should continue to sulk and suffer over such a passing moment.

Maggie found the punch bowl, and it was there where Elizabeth found her. The older woman invited the younger to take a turn on the walkway that circled the great stone abbey. The two women walked together only a short time before Maggie, at this point already a little tipsy, unburdened her heart to Elizabeth, in search of advice.

She told her all about the trip to London, the search for plates, and the angry outburst which preceded Benjamin's standoffish behavior. Though it was a short narrative spanning only three days, Maggie's telling of it was so elaborate that a transcript would be far too long for any reader to tolerate. Elizabeth listened gravely, many times refilling Maggie's glass with her secreted bottle of champagne. (This she had earlier tucked into one of the topiaries for the purpose of availing herself discreetly under the pretense of taking a bit of "night air.") By the time several orbits of the house had been completed and the entire bottle of "night air" consumed, Maggie's ridiculously thorough description of her situation was also complete.

Elizabeth sighed deeply and commenced in her appraisal and advice.

"Maggie, my dear," she began, "you have had a fight and I am sorry to hear it. Though, it is hardly worth the sorrow you give yourself now. A marriage is a business arrangement, plain and simple. As such, it will persist under whatever terms are comfortable to the partners. You and Benjamin certainly had some warm regard for each other and had, indeed, several months of marital felicity, I'm sure. But you could not have been insensible enough to think that that would *last*.

"No, my dear, you are entering the truth of marriage now. My advice to you is to do your duty to your husband with as little complaint as you can manage. Perhaps when you have given him several children, he will either leave you alone entirely or learn to harbor for you some vague tenderness which will give you free rein to travel as you please. Oh, do not cry, my dear! Such is the state of all happy marriages."

"But my parents," Maggie protested with a pathetic sniffle.

"Oh, what do we ever really know of our parents?"

"I just thought . . ." Maggie trailed off, not now recalling what she had thought.

"You thought that it would be different, I know. You thought like a girl, but you are a woman now. And a woman's world is not so simple or so nice as she must always endeavor to make it seem."

Maggie turned to her companion. "What was your husband like?"

Elizabeth stopped walking and stood a few seconds recalling that she had once had a husband.

"He was old when I met him, and he died shortly thereafter."

"I am so sorry."

"I am not."

With that, the subject was closed to Maggie. But it had stirred reflections in Elizabeth. She had realized for the first time, with no small shock, that next year she would be the same age that her husband had been when they met at this very house some forty years before.

# Thirty-One

Elizabeth had been born a poor relation. At a tender age, she was foisted off on an elderly aunt. As Elizabeth would tell it many years later, in her youth she had been a great beauty. The truth was that in her blooming youth, she was most highly esteemed for her ample bosom. One fact of her narrative not up for debate or alteration over time was that Elizabeth was clever. Though she had never had the benefit of a decent education, she picked things up with remarkable alacrity. This was especially true of languages, though keen account keeping was never a deficit.

She'd met her future husband on a warm summer night, much like the one on which she walked with Maggie now. There was no party in the background, and the night without the benefit of candles had been remarkably dark. She was brought to act as maid to her aunt at a dinner given by Lord Dormer. The old lord was liver-spotted and had more hair in his ears than on his head. Though he was abstracted in conversation and known to be well into the season of senility, he had stared down Elizabeth's dress with the attentive enthusiasm of a foot soldier in the King's Militia.

Elizabeth put two and two together, and (pressing her two together) she made an especial point at bending and leaning towards the gentleman at each service her aunt requested of her. She watched as this old man grew hot under the collar and shifted uncomfortably in his seat. She did not cease her attack until, so stirred was he by her presence, he was left with no choice but to acknowledge her existence. Her aunt had presented her and made some trifling boast about her cleverness with French. When Lord Dormer then produced a remarkably coherent French phrase to test her, she answered in perfect reply. He arched an eyebrow and then intoned, as calmly as he could, that she would be welcome to come and visit him for some French tutelage at her convenience.

The man had not even had the sensibility to wait until their third meeting before groping her soft flesh in his hungry hands. Rather than cry out, slap him, or storm off in indignation, Elizabeth had left his hands as they were, looked him square in the eye, and said, "If you want to do that to me again, you have to marry me."

"Marry you? What reason would I—"

"I can think of two." She cut him off and placed her hands over his own, pushing them further into her pillowy expanse.

It was a risky move, to be sure. Elizabeth had reflected on this in the wisdom of her later years. But it had worked.

Stroking her soft, wide chest like a cat, she coaxed him.

"Say it. Ask me. Do it. You are master of this estate, are you not? Why should you not have me? Why should you not have a pretty, young wife? It's only right, really, that a man of your consequence should enjoy himself."

He had begun to sweat, and she could see from his seat that he was at full attention to her offer.

"Marry me and have me as you want me, every day. Marry me. Say it. You want to. I can feel how much you want to."

She came even closer. Her perfume of lilacs enveloped him. She gently removed his hands from her chest and placed them, firmly, slowly, and tenderly upon his own lap so he might feel, if he was not yet aware, the powerful spirit she had excited in him.

Then, in a moment of divine inspiration, she pulled down the center of her bodice, just an extra inch, and with her hand on the back of his head she guided his old, peeling nose into the tender embrace of her two good reasons. He spoke the magic words. She expelled him.

"Find me a ring. No, better yet, call a servant and tell *them* to find me a ring."

His hand was shaking as he rang the bell on his table. A servant arrived, a ring was pilfered from the late Lady Dormer's jewelry box, and then it was official. She flew home to inform her aunt, who promptly called her a hussy. It was only three weeks later that by special license, the old lord married the young Elizabeth. Thus, she became Lady Elizabeth Dormer.

It will not surprise anyone familiar with the ways of an English village to learn that the new Lady Dormer was not well received. In New Glenbury and the surrounding county, she had no friends of proper station who could visit her in her elevated circumstances. None of her husband's nearby acquaintances would deign to come and pay respects to the most shameful match anyone could ever remember. There was even talk about having the marriage annulled among some of the more indignant staff of Eastbey Abbey who had been counting on inheritances from their childless master. But nothing came of it.

For the first four years of her residency in Eastbey Abbey, Elizabeth made herself agreeable and available to her husband. However, he did not often recall that she was his wife. Instead, he often assumed she was a visitor, and was always ringing the bell and calling for tea to be served, no matter the hour. Elizabeth protested to none of his requests. She did not see a point in correcting him. As he would ramble on in the repetition of some story from his youth, she would simply look away and think to herself about how she would redecorate whatever room they happened to be seated in. She trusted death would come for her husband soon enough.

And, after four dutiful years of this dull and lonely existence, the Lord Dormer suffered a fit of apoplexy which rendered him insensible and bedbound.

Elizabeth hired two nurses and began redecorating. He died about a year later.

For a while then, she went on tour. She took a place in Paris, gambled in Battenberg, and regularly attended the Carnival of Venice. She enjoyed herself abroad and made many friends for whom her money and title were enough to impress. They never minded that her original station was so low. Always though, when she longed for tranquility and solitude, she returned to Eastbey Abbey in New Glenbury. There, most local gentry would still not receive her, and she did not much care for their company besides. Things carried on in this pattern for a good ten years until she was called upon by the new reverend's wife, Constance Astley.

Elizabeth had been just thirty-two and Constance a fresh but sensible twenty-three. Constance had left the rectory that morning thinking that she was to go and pay call to a lonely old widow. Elizabeth remembered fondly her surprise at finding a rich young widow inviting her to take tea instead. The two women had felt an instant mutual regard for one another's intelligence. Though Constance at first considered Elizabeth as a curiosity, this curiosity soon gave way to a tender and true friendship.

That was more than thirty years ago, Elizabeth reflected. In those years, they had seen so much of each other that they were now dearer than sisters. When Elizabeth was laid ill with a cold that took a dangerous turn towards pneumonia, Constance sat by her bed and nursed her for six weeks.

When the last of Constance's miscarriages resulted in Doctor Thompson declaring that she would never bear children, it was Elizabeth who filled the rectory with flowers, and came each day to sit and read with her friend.

Elizabeth's donations to the parish had always been perfunctory, but as her friendship with Constance deepened, they became lavish. She could well afford it, for her bank account drew such interest as to accrue more than she, in all her extravagances, could spend in a year. Though Constance had much simpler tastes than her friend,

Elizabeth was always certain to return from any trip with a fitting gift to keep her companion in comfort. Even the Reverend Samuel Astley owed a great number of his fine library books to Elizabeth's proclivity for gifts. Much as she complained of his inattentive nature, Elizabeth respected her friend's desire that her husband should be happy. So, she added to his happiness when it was convenient.

Admittedly, though she teased Constance endlessly about her attentions to those less fortunate, Elizabeth could not help but admire her friend and all she did for the people in her regard.

Now, staring into the dark summer night and remembering all of this, she looked to the future. It was likely, she supposed, that one day she was going to die, as everyone did. And she earnestly wished, not for the first time, that she might be blessed to die before Constance.

Her logic in this hope was twofold. First, it was stated in her will that every single one of the couples she and Constance had matched was to be left two thousand pounds, and an extra hundred to each living child of the union. She knew that Constance would not approve of such extravagance; Elizabeth only regretted she would not be there to see the look on her face when it became known.

Her other consideration was that she genuinely could not imagine how wretched and lonely her life would be without her friend.

Elizabeth dabbed her eyes with her handkerchief. She was suddenly aware that Maggie had wandered back inside some time ago. She thought of this young girl, so newly married, and wondered if she had been right in her advice. Love may have never entered into her marriage, but she still understood how vital it was to her life.

# Thirty-Two

TWO DAYS AFTER Lady Elizabeth's ball, Diana and Maggie once again rode in the carriage over the soft hills surrounding New Glenbury towards Eastbey Abbey. Diana was remarking about the coming summer's harvest prospects. Maggie found this most agreeable. It was a subject so outside her care or comprehension that she felt entirely free to ignore it, and the leader of the conversation was so knowledgeable that she needed no assistance in keeping up enthusiasm for the subject until they had arrived at Elizabeth's front door.

Elizabeth welcomed them in with a great deal more warmth than she typically showed to house guests. Indeed, Maggie thought, she seemed quite refreshed since the party.

After handing over their bonnets and shawls to a footman, Lady Elizabeth clapped her hands together in giddy anticipation and announced that she had a surprise in store for them that day.

She led them through the entry room, the pink drawing room, the green drawing room, the library, and then all the way back to the small music room at the south end of the old abbey. In contrast to the great hall of Eastbey Abbey, where the festivities of her ball had been held, most of the abbey was composed of small, squat rooms. Each one led directly into the next with no hallway to connect them. A stone-paved courtyard at the center of the building was used by the servants in their errands.

The result of this medieval architecture was that all the rooms were much too small to serve their proper function. This was especially obvious in the music room. The pianoforte took up nearly the entire width of the space, and only a few chairs could be seated comfortably at a distance great enough to avoid the audience being overpowered by the performer. This, combined with Elizabeth's maximal style of decorating (consisting of many pieces of French furniture purchased when the political turmoil of that country made their importation a moral imperative to the aesthetically inclined) gave one the feeling of being accosted by opulence at every turn.

Despite the close quarters of the music room, in two ostentatious chairs sat Constance and a stranger. The stranger was a broad, red-faced man somewhere in his forties who was missing his leg from the knee down. In its place was a carved wooden calf and foot, attached to his thigh with some leather straps and metal joints.

When Diana saw this, she audibly gasped with such little hesitation that Maggie nearly boxed the girl's ears for her social ineptitude.

Rather than be offended, the man gave a sudden start, looked down at his missing limb, and cried out, "Good heavens! Where did it go?!"

Diana looked faint from the shock, but then the man roared into a hearty laugh and said, "I'm only pulling your leg, honey. See, I have just one of my own, so I pull others' when I get the chance."

He laughed again. Constance and Maggie had no idea what to do or say, but Diana and Elizabeth both laughed, too, and seemed at ease. Maggie, in a bid to restore order, introduced herself to the man. He, in turn, introduced himself. This was how Maggie learned that his name was Captain Rex Tanders. He had lost his leg in the service of king and country, and he now made his way through the world as a flute and fife player for army bands, and for bands near to the army in that unofficial capacity that often arises when there is great demand by soldiers for dancing.

He was, in fact, the flute player from Elizabeth's ball. The rest of the band had moved along to other venues, but Captain Tanders, hearing from Elizabeth of Diana's great desire to learn the flute, was eager to stay on and tutor her. Or at least, this was the explanation given to the group to explicate his continued residency in Eastbey Abbey.

This was Diana's first time learning that she was eager to play the flute. To her great credit, she took the news in stride. Captain Tanders then procured from his shabby coat two flutes. After looking each over carefully, he handed the cleaner one to Diana. She held it upright in her hands like a heavy candlestick.

As the lesson looked like it would be slow to commence and the music room was comically small to host more than one conversation at a time, Constance offered Maggie her arm and they left Elizabeth to supervise the lessons.

Away from the door of the music room, as they passed through the succession of small rooms leading to an egress, Constance found time to explain that Captain Tanders was Elizabeth's *special guest*. Elizabeth had had special guests of this nature before, because she was such an ardent patron of the arts. But, Constance also clarified, Maggie should not count on the patronage lasting so very long. Constance assured Maggie that she would see to Diana getting a *proper* flute master when the time was right.

Once this was understood, the conversation then turned to its true purpose for Constance, which was ascertaining what Maggie knew of Diana's sentiments to the handsome Hudson Birch, and learning how the visit with his parents had gone while they were in London.

Maggie recounted the unfortunate and confusing incident of the elder Mr. Birch snatching the letter and dismissing the messenger with a halfpenny. Then Maggie tempered this disappointing report with the assurance that Diana really did like Hudson and that Hudson had shown every indication of liking her right back.

"Perhaps we should not force them together so often. I don't know, Constance. I begin to think that this plan is ill-fated. Such a short courtship and with them both being so young—I'm not sure they will ever be able to love each other the right way."

Constance asked Maggie to clarify what the "right way" of loving someone was.

That was how Maggie came to tell Constance of her trouble with Benjamin. She recounted his plate-related outburst, of course. But it was his continued aloofness since their return from London that she dwelt upon with numerous examples. He did not wait for her at the top of the stairs before dinner. He did not rush to her side each day when he returned from the mill. He did not extoll the extent of her beauty as she brushed her hair for bed each night.

Constance did not seem surprised by the parts of the narrative Maggie had shared with Elizabeth the night of the ball. In fact, she seemed as familiar with the chronicle as if it had been recounted to her already, because it had been. The news of Benjamin's continued aloofness was new, though, and privately it puzzled Constance. He must be a very sulky man, Constance considered, if he was to continue to give himself trouble over such a trifle. For Maggie's benefit, Constance was eager to offer her advice. It was the advice she always gave when consulted about marital strife. The reverend's wife's recommendation would be best summarized thus: being useful is the first step to being happy, because you can't be sad if you're busy. This counsel was of no comfort to Maggie, and she was in a distracted, ill humor for the rest of the visit.

Maggie's displeasure was easily disguised as a visceral reaction to the sputtering shrill squeaks of the new flute player, which remained in earshot despite the growing distance. When Maggie, blaming a headache, begged leave to take Diana home before tea, it was readily assented to by the other women, who affirmed that they also had headaches.

On the carriage ride back to Wuster Park, Diana surprised Maggie with a strange question.

"Do you think Lady Dormer will marry Captain Tanders?"

Maggie had to ask her to repeat the question. It seemed so strange that Diana would consider such a thing.

Diana then explained that, during her lesson, she noticed how fond Elizabeth seemed of the flute player. Captain Tanders had seemed very fond of Elizabeth as well, pinching her cheek when he thought Diana wasn't looking.

Maggie had to stifle a laugh at this before explaining that it was highly unlikely that a wealthy woman like Elizabeth would ever wed someone who could offer her so little as a one-legged flute player from an unofficial army band.

"If they are in love . . ." Diana countered.

"I very much doubt they are in love, Diana. Their social stations are near opposites. I'm sure they're just . . . flirting with each other for fun."

She thought about ending the explanation there and hoping the young girl would draw her own correct conclusions. Upon greater reflection, she felt the need to direct those conclusions a bit further.

"But idle flirting is not a thing for young ladies," Maggie continued. "Do you understand? You cannot toy with the emotions of a man until your place in the world is very much settled. Or, rather, do not toy with anyone's emotions ever. Elizabeth is a very . . . Well, she lives her own way and is rich and respected enough to not require any more riches or respect."

Diana took all of this in. She had not considered the possibility of flirting for fun, but it made perfect sense. Lady Elizabeth was rich and wise; Captain Tanders was charming. Her cousin Maggie's reaction to the suggestion that they might wed confirmed what Diana had hoped was true: there could be no serious intention behind Hudson's attentions to her at Lady Elizabeth's ball. He had just been flirting for fun. It was not serious. He had just been flirting for fun. She nodded to herself as she solidified this notion in her consciousness. Just flirting for fun, not serious. His tender looks, his sincere smile, his ceaseless attentions were all just for fun.

It *had* been fun. Diana had hardly known herself in those unguarded moments when he made her feel she could do no wrong. It had all been for fun. Though there was a touch of sadness at this understanding, mostly there was relief. Diana knew that nothing serious could ever arise between herself and Hudson. He was too kind and too naive for her. He could never be made to understand her family, and in his ignorance, he would be ruined by them. Diana would not do that to a boy she admired so much, and she admired Hudson *so much.*

Diana returned from her brief reverie with a sudden curiosity.

"Cousin Maggie, do you like being married? I mean, do you like *all the parts* of being married?"

Maggie knew exactly what she meant, having asked her sister something very similar after Caroline's wedding.

Rather than answer right away, Maggie countered, "What do you know about a married woman's life?"

Now Diana grew shy. "Oh, nothing so much. Only I know about horses. And babies. You know . . . how new horses are . . . you know." Then she blushed violently, regretting her question.

Maggie had never given much thought to how she would answer this question about marital pleasures. She reflected on what her sister said to her when she had asked it: "No" was the simple and final reply that Caroline had made, and no further questions had been considered.

Maggie wished that she had been given clearer expectations for her own married life than this brief reply. She resolved to do better for her cousin.

"Well, Diana," she said, "how much you enjoy *married life* is dependent a great deal on whom you marry. If you marry correctly—" But here she paused, remembering the exact correctness of Caroline's courtship and engagement. "That is, if you marry wisely, you are more likely to have a good married life."

"Yes, but . . . does it always . . ." Diana could not bring herself to finish the sentence.

Maggie ended the conversation with a simple, "We'll talk more about this when the timing is right. Don't concern yourself with such things now."

They rode in silence the rest of the way. While Diana was lost in her own reflections, Maggie was thinking about a ride in the same carriage that she and Benjamin had enjoyed *as husband and wife*.

So overpowering were her memories of their frenzied passion that when Benjamin greeted Maggie at the door upon her return to Wuster Park, she blushed. However, Benjamin could not discern that Maggie had been thinking of their time together with the curtains drawn tight in the bouncing conveyance. Rather, he attributed her blushes to the continued discomfort she seemed to feel in his presence since his angry outburst about the plates. To avoid mortifying her further, he decided not to mention her reddened cheeks, even when they shared several minutes alone at the table waiting for Diana to rejoin their party.

Instead, he asked about their visit and even politely chortled at Maggie's retelling of Captain Tanders' leg-pulling joke. The rest of the repast was spent focused on Diana. Benjamin asked her a number of questions about how she liked the flute, what songs the captain was intending to teach her, and what Lady Dormer had said about her playing. Diana answered all of these easily enough, and Maggie was thankful that her once silent cousin had gained enough confidence to take the conversational pressure off of her. She spent the time vacillating between her hurt feelings at Benjamin's continued aloofness and the persistent intrusive memories that Diana's carriage-ride question had stirred in her.

# Thirty-Three

Life in a country house is apt to fall into a hypnotic rhythm as days pass in rapid succession amidst a feeling of time halted. So passed the days at Wuster Park. Collectively, the inhabitants performed the gentle pantomime of rising, dressing, eating, walking, visiting, and other regular occupations before each night ushered in the fitful sleep of sweltering summer nights.

Diana and Maggie spent most of their days in the company of Constance and Elizabeth, in the pursuit of some lightly edifying occupation. Occasionally, they paid calls to other neighbors. Once a week they would take baskets of food prepared by Mrs. Rollins over to the cottages on the far reaches of Wuster Park, and most weeks included at least one outing with the Langley Hall party. At the dinner table, the household of Wuster Park would primarily discuss Diana's progress with various projects and any other topical neighborhood gossip. Each night, Benjamin and Maggie would retire to their chamber and exchange carefully worded pleasantries.

Since Benjamin's outburst about the plates, Maggie had been quick to forgive and forget, putting the whole episode down as a simple miscommunication. Try as she would to resume the romantic discourse of their relations, Benjamin continued to hold himself in reserve with her. No longer did he make grand, rambling declarations about her beauty or charm. No longer did he seize her passionately behind closed doors and cover her neck and collarbones in feverish kisses. No longer did he draw her close to him in the stillness of night.

This persistent withholding was for Maggie an unrelenting mortification and confusion. It was made all the worse by the casual dismissals of her concerns by Constance and Elizabeth. Try as she would to content herself with the new order, she still pleaded to them every so often for assistance in setting the situation right. What the older women privately thought of their younger friend's position was never readily shared. Instead, they deferred and dismissed her concerns with reassurances that all was exactly as it should be in any happy marriage.

Benjamin's attitude during this time was bent purposefully towards indifference. He tried not to feel. It was his excess of feelings that had stirred him to such an outburst about the plates, and it was obvious that his depth of feeling for Maggie was not returned. In his logic, further feelings would only lead to further conflict. His father had been an angry, loud man. To his wife he was constantly raging, pacing the floor of her darkened sickroom ranting about inconveniences and slights both real and imagined. Benjamin had sworn to himself that he would never devolve into a domineering patriarch, but his eruption of temper over something as simple as plates gave him great doubt about his self-control.

Distance, he felt, was the only preservation from the instability that passion wrought upon his soul. So, he tried not to see the pleading looks Maggie gave him in their rare moments alone. He tried not to think of her when she was away from him. There came a certain calmness with a quiet mind. So, he courted this calmness with an active avoidance of consideration.

But still, he felt it—a slight sadness soaking into the edges of his life, like rainwater through the seams of his great wool coat.

Maggie suffered mostly in confusion. She could not reconcile the certainty that Benjamin was upset with her with his insistence that no problem existed between them. In the very few times she had ever witnessed a disagreement between her parents, the cause had always been discovered to be a misunderstanding. The solution had always been the calm and careful discussion of the subject until clarity concluded the conflict. As Benjamin would not engage in such discussions, a solution to their situation felt impossible.

On the one unfortunate visit Maggie had paid to her sister Caroline at her husband's country house in the north, she had also seen their version of marital strife. Stony silences were punctuated by explosive shouting arguments that rang through the whole house. At these outbursts, the staff would flee to the kitchen lest the angry pair should storm in on them in their brutal campaigns around the main floor. Sometimes, Maggie imagined that even this style of argument might be better than the uncertainty that hung between her and Benjamin now.

But Benjamin was not cold and silent with her as Caroline's husband had been to Caroline. Benjamin was polite to her in conversations at meals and often read aloud to her and Diana in the evenings. Always, his voice was pleasant, if a little detached, and he continued to behave in such a way that Maggie began to doubt if he was even upset with her at all. She wondered, was it possible that she misunderstood their situation? Was it possible that she misremembered what their relationship had been before? The longer this condition persisted, the more unclear it was to Maggie how to alter it. So, she focused instead on what she felt she could understand: Diana.

Diana sensed that something was off between her hosts. When she first arrived to Wuster Park, Benjamin was so ostentatiously enamored with his wife that he was often insensible to the notice of any other person. In those days, he hung on each of Maggie's words. Now he nodded inattentively and asked only the vaguest of questions at their shared meals. Diana wondered if perhaps she was to blame for this disharmony. She had run from the room when Benjamin raised his voice. Perhaps such an action had offended him or made him displeased with her company. She tried her best to give no cause for further offense and make herself as small as possible in all shared spaces.

Outside of Wuster Park, the girl found greater comfort. Captain Tanders continued his lessons with Diana regularly, and her musical progress was not disappointing. Instead of teaching the girl to read any notations, he had her watch and then replicate the finger patterns and rhythm of his playing over and over. By fits and starts, she was able to string these bursts of music together into a pattern that very nearly resembled a song. It was slow work, and the sound was anything but pleasing, but it was progress towards an important accomplishment. All her female friends hoped that before too long, Diana would be able to display her talent for Mr. Birch and get one step closer to winning his hand and heart.

# Thirty-Four

"Ah Diana, what a sweet girl she has become," remarked Constance to Elizabeth and Maggie.

The three women were watching Diana and Captain Tanders practice the flute in the garden outside. It had been too hot and bright to expect anyone to sit, stand, or play comfortably in the south-facing music room of the abbey. So an al fresco instruction had been agreed upon. This was very agreeable to the older ladies, as they did not have to hear so closely the shrill sound of the woodwind section.

"I know just what you mean," said Elizabeth. "She's looking much rosier than when you first brought her here, Maggie. And her new dresses are quite smart. Tell me, has she made much progress on the white-work muslin dress? I've a mind to get up a party for a picnic. Though if Mr. Birch sees her too often in her blue or sprigged muslin dresses, he will think she has no others. Already, I think she has worn each twice in meeting him."

"I think he's well past caring what she wears," Constance retorted.

"Nonsense, he is from London," Elizabeth replied. "The girls in his set are never seen in the same dress twice. It is quite known. He will think her very provincial."

Constance, with her greater sensitivity and perception said, "I believe her provincialism is one of the chief attractions Diana holds for him. When I followed them on their walk up Coolderns Crest last week, I overheard him asking her a number of questions about *birds*."

"She has a great deal of natural knowledge," Maggie affirmed.

Elizabeth scowled. "Yes, well, all of that is fine while they are in the country. But you must consider that Mr. Birch will be looking for a wife he can take with him back to his home *in town*. So, I ask you again, Maggie, how goes her white work on the new muslin dress?"

"It is nearly complete, as long as we don't add any other designs to the ones marked."

"Yes, very good. I think I'll arrange for a picnic next week. If she hasn't finished it by then, we can get Constance to fill in the rest."

It was at that moment, by happy providence, that the women watched as Diana played straight through the entire song that Captain Tanders had been trying to teach her. It was a sad Scottish ballad, chosen because it would not suffer from being played slowly. At its low and slow conclusion, all three women exchanged looks of great satisfaction. The plan was wordlessly settled between them: Diana would exhibit her musical abilities as well as her new muslin gown at the upcoming picnic.

# Thirty-Five

DURING THIS SLOW stretch of time between Elizabeth's ball and the upcoming picnic, Hudson decided to read the two letters that had arrived from his parents after Diana's visit to London. He expected that the letters would contain his parents' pronouncements on Diana and either their approval or disapproval of her as a person. As eagerly as Hudson longed to know their thoughts, he was equally anxious to avoid them—for, as long as he had neither their approval nor disapproval, he could continue his admiration unchecked.

But upon reading his mother's letter first, it seemed obvious to him that she had not actually met Diana. The whole letter was instead a repeat of a lecture Mrs. Birch was fond of delivering about the dangers of governesses and parlor maids. With Diana being a daughter of a baron, there could be no possibility that the letter was a reference to her. At least, that was what he thought upon his first reading.

Then he read his father's letter, and the meaning of both became clear. His father explained that they had met the "nice tall girl" very briefly and had found her to be very pretty. Then his letter took a long, meandering detour through some recollections of his own infatuation with a tall, dark-haired woman from his youth. That story concluded with his great regret at having not asked the tall girl to dance. Then the letter itself concluded with the confession that, owing to some unspecified mistake, the Birches had not invited Hudson's tall girl into their home. In fact, Mr. Birch confessed, they knew nothing about her, not even her name.

Hudson was mortified by this revelation. At Lady Dormer's ball, when he'd asked Diana what she thought of her visit to his parents' house, she had been vague, but pleasant. She had made no mention of the terrible snub they had given her. At first, Hudson could only reason that her blithe toleration of this offense was due to her exceptional breeding. Then he wondered if it was perhaps owed to her disinterest in his family as a whole. Perhaps, he thought, she was relieved to not have to spend time with people so far below her station. It was with this dejection that he carried himself outside for a solitary walk.

Hudson was not fond of solitary walks. He was not fond of solitude at all, really. To combine the numbing solitude with the stimulating barrage of flora and fauna out of doors was taxing on his nerves. Still, he forced himself to go out alone that afternoon in some strange act of penitence for the failure of his family to further his progress with the object of his affection.

He started his journey heading south from Langley Hall. The property that surrounded Langley might once have been designed for enjoyment, but years of neglect and mismanagement had obscured any original paths of pleasure. What remained were functional carriage roads and diagonal footpaths used by servants and villagers in their journeys across the countryside. Turning west, Hudson took one of those footpaths, not knowing where it might lead.

It led eventually to a break in the low stone wall that encircled the grounds of Wuster Park. Obviously, it was a shortcut between the two properties, but Hudson had not even known that the two estates shared a boundary. For a while, he stared at the dip in the rockwork. He wondered if it was proper for him to step over it and enjoy the park grounds at his leisure. He had toured the grounds of Wuster a few times in the company of Diana, her cousin, and his friends. But he resolved not to trespass. Instead, he began to walk along the boundary wall, making a new trail between them, or so he fancied.

He did not plan on encountering anyone. So, it was with more than mild mortification that he discovered the object of his persistent thoughts before him, appearing just on the other side of the stone wall.

Diana did not see him at first, but he saw her. She was wearing a blue muslin dress that seemed to glow in light dappled by the leafy trees overhead. She held her bonnet in her hand, and her hair was only half secured. She was kicking at the underbrush, turning over stones and logs with her feet. She seemed wholly concentrated on this strange project. Suddenly, the sound of some screeching bird overhead caused her to look up. And there was Hudson, standing just on the other side of the stone wall, staring at her in silent admiration.

Startled by this sudden meeting, she let out a small yelp before laughing. Then, in an assumed baritone and London accent, she parroted Hudson's familiar greeting of her:

"I say, is that you, Lady Diana Huxley? What a coincidence. I never imagined I'd meet you here."

It was Hudson's turn to laugh and reply, adopting an exaggerated feminine tone, "Why, Mr. Birch, you do so forget yourself! We have been acquainted for some time!"

The two giggled together like children sharing a secret. Diana motioned that Hudson should join her on the other side of the stone boundary wall.

"Mr. Birch, what are you doing here? You've not come all this way just to laugh at me."

Rather than explain his full reasoning, he said simply, "I got lost."

This was true in a few ways.

Diana's ease in his company was flustering. Hudson was keenly aware that they had never really been so alone. Hudson then realized he had never been so alone with any girl before. He blushed just with the thought of it. But if Diana was worried about such things, she gave no signal. She just continued to walk with her sheepish companion by her side.

At last, Hudson mustered the courage to speak. Unfortunately, the only subject that occurred to him was the one he least wished to discuss.

"I say, I have just read some letters from my family—"

"Are they well, I hope?"

"Oh yes. But no, I say, I mean . . . well I have heard what happened when you came to call on them and well, I say, I'm terribly sorry. They're not, you know . . . it's not that they don't . . . well, but then, you know."

"You mean about the letter? Did I not bring it soon enough? We had been in London more than a week when we delivered it. I'm sorry I did not think to ask if it was urgent."

"No, no. I say. Only, I had hoped that they would invite you inside."

"Perhaps they were busy."

"Yes, perhaps. I would have liked you to meet them, you know."

"Oh. I would have liked that too. But, perhaps it's for the best."

This last little sentence wrapped itself around Hudson's heart like a wet wool blanket. Then, Diana continued. She spoke, not while looking at him, but while looking at the ground ahead as she walked carefully through the leafy underbrush.

"I am so new to town customs and things. I'm sure I would have made a mess of it. I'm always forgetting the right times to say and do the things that everyone else finds so easy. With your parents being so used to the ways of London, I'm sure they would have thought me very foolish."

"No, certainly not. You do not think I am a fool just because I've gotten lost in the woods, do you?"

He had started this question in jest, but by its conclusion he discovered himself quite sincere. Did she think him a fool?

"Oh no, not at all. You are new to the countryside, that's all."

"So, it is the same for you and town, I'm sure."

Diana smiled with some tint of sadness.

"Ah, but it's more than just town customs. It's all very different, even here. I am forever making some mistake or other. Just ask my cousin."

"I cannot think of a single mistake I have seen you make."

"No? Perhaps because you have been helping me make them."

Now she looked at him and smiled. "Tell me, did you know it was wrong to dance all the dances with me at Elizabeth's ball?"

"Wrong?"

"Yes, I am told it was impolite."

"Well, I say . . . I say . . . I suppose I did know that it was. . . . But who else would you have danced with?"

"Yes, that's exactly what I said!"

"I say, silly rules like that are just meant to be broken so that fussy old people have something to complain about."

"All the rules seem silly to me. It's hard to know what can and cannot be broken without—oh, but look!"

Without concluding her thoughts, she dropped low into a squat and pushed back some green leaves. Hudson knelt beside her. It was with great effort that he kept his eyes on the small red berries that were the object of her attention, and not the cascade of dark hair that tumbled across her collarbones.

"What are they?" he asked.

"What do they look like?"

"Well, they look like strawberries, but they're too small."

"They're wild strawberries. First of the season."

She plucked one of the little red seedy gems and popped it into her mouth.

"They're almost ripe. Try one."

Hudson had to suppress every one of his urban instincts which warned against eating anything and everything one found in the woods. He bravely reached out and selected his own sample. He placed it gingerly in his mouth, apprehensive to the last moment until the sweet juice of the berry soothed his soul. Then he looked at Diana in wonderment.

"It's sweet. But so small. I say, can we eat more of them?"

"I don't see why not."

She pushed back more leaves, showing Hudson how to recognize the little plant. It was too shady in this part of the woods for many of the wild strawberries to be ready. After finding that the general population tended more sour than sweet, the two foragers resolved to leave them be for now. They continued on their walk.

Without much of an introduction, Hudson again launched into conversation.

"I know what you mean though about the rules and such. There are so very many, it is hard to know exactly, you know."

"Yes, but you grew up around them. You have lived among people who know them—"

"Are things really so different up north in your home?"

"Yes. I suppose they are."

"I think it must be nice. It must be hard for you to be away so long. Why did you come down?"

"Oh, I . . . I needed a change. It's not always so nice."

"That's why I came here too. That, and to learn to shoot."

"And do you like it here? Do you like the country compared to all of London?"

Hudson answered honestly, "I like it more and more each day."

Diana heard the words and could not help but smile. Who would not be enchanted with this place, she thought. The mild, groomed nature was just what a boy like Hudson should have.

He sensed her smile without daring to look at it directly. He felt himself blushing.

A glimpse of a stone folly in the distance recalled him to himself. He realized with no small embarrassment that he had been imposing terribly on Diana's character by walking with her in such solitude. She was probably too polite to say anything, but he felt surely that she must be anxious for his departure before they ran the risk of discovery.

"I have enjoyed our walk today, Miss Huxley. Thank you ever so much, I say. And now, I will depart."

He bowed low. In the time it took for him to rise, Diana schooled her expression of disappointment to one resembling a placid acceptance. Not knowing what to say, she extended her hand in the most formal of ways. Hudson took it. Then, in a moment of bold spontaneity, he held it to his lips and kissed it. The warmth and tenderness of his lips on her skin sent tingles up her arm, and she flushed pink.

When he opened his eyes, Diana was gazing upon him in a look of inscrutable shock. He turned abruptly, walked stiffly to the low stone wall they had been skirting, and then upon crossing it, took off at a run, crashing through the forest as if pursued by a bear.

Diana watched him go with a tender regret. She had enjoyed their quiet moment together alone in the woods. It reminded her of the long rambles she and Charlie McFaden used to take across the peaks and crags around Yansworth. She realized now, with sudden sentiment, that she missed those walks. She missed them more than anything else about her life back north.

# Thirty-Six

Elizabeth's picnic was far from the first country picnic the Langley Hall residents had been invited to attend. Several times now, they had been asked by their neighbors to go outdoors to partake in some walk or enjoy some view with the promise of refreshments at the end.

The plans for such activities were usually arranged on the walk home from church on Sundays. Hudson made a point of always accompanying Diana on this ritual of rural promenade. Offering her his arm, he would greet her with the same phrase of their first Sunday meeting and she would reply with some clever variation of her original rebuttal.

Hudson was not at all shy of society suspecting his preference. While some suitors might have held their displays of enthusiasm in reserve, it was plain to anyone in observance that he was more than partial to the baron's daughter for company. As Diana's circle of friends were eager to encourage the connection, they found plenty of local excursions for the group to enjoy together throughout the week.

Very often, the objective of their activity was the arrival at a particularly scenic view. Picturesque trees or riverbeds offered some enticement as well. Naturally, the true activity was always the journey.

After a cramped carriage ride wherein Mrs. Bellwood would sleep, the group would set out on their mild adventure. The young people always led the way. Invariably, Hudson and Diana walked behind Noah and Ellis while the chaperones took up the rear. Hudson savored these moments of Diana's undivided attention. She never seemed more at ease than when outdoors, and she was always pointing out some otherwise invisible feature of natural wonderment. Without her enthusiasm, it's quite possible that the three London men would have found such excursions to be dull or taxing. But Diana's appreciation was infectious. She was adept at manufacturing amusements for the group.

At a visit to Stonbridge Lake, she taught everyone how to skip stones. Even Maggie was new to such a pursuit, though Constance was surprisingly well practiced in the art. On a walk through the Redworth Woods, Diana pointed out the ground nests of the tree pipits and soon there was a contest to see who might spot the most. She had been cautioned by her cousin not to volunteer the names of every tree or plant they passed. Though, when asked, she almost always knew the answer.

Hudson and his friends couldn't help but be impressed by Diana's compendia of flora and fauna. Though, perhaps because of their limited exposure to rural society, they assumed all country citizens to be equally informed. Still, Diana's presence was a welcome one, even to sulky Noah. It was agreed by all the boys that she was good company and days spent with her were invariably jolly.

When the invitation to Elizabeth's picnic arrived, the Langley Hall party imagined it would be very much the same as the other outings. They were wrong.

# Thirty-Seven

Elizabeth was not a lover of nature. Furthermore, she had no patience for long walks. Her idea of a perfect picnic, therefore, was within her own garden grounds, right outside the windows of Eastbey Abbey. Designed in the exacting and geometric French style and maintained by a small cavalcade of French gardeners, these formal garden grounds were as beautiful as they were impressive, and there was much to recommend them to the enjoyment of all.

Elizabeth's picnic was to be held on a Thursday. Much to Benjamin's amusement, it was announced by formal invitation. The cream-colored dispatch was delivered to him at breakfast that Monday morning. Maggie was quick to tell Benjamin that he did not need to go if he did not wish to be away from the mill that day. His sour attitude still persisted, and Maggie felt sure that he would prefer to stay home. Benjamin countered that it had been too long since he had enjoyed the society of his neighbors. He tempered this enthusiasm with the admission that the summer heat made sitting in the mill office and sorting papers a rather stifling experience. He therefore assured Maggie and Diana that he would attend.

Maggie was tempted to wonder if his heart might be softening at last. But she dared not indulge this conjecture. It was true that he had lingered a bit longer in recent days in the drawing room after

Diana excused herself to bed. It was true that he had been more attentive in his questions to Maggie about her day's activities. But Maggie did not dare to hope that things might return to the way they had been before. She had worked so hard to resign herself to the way things were now. It seemed very foolish to try to take comfort in something as small as the acceptance of an invitation to a neighbor's casual picnic.

But this was not to be a casual picnic. Eager to impress in her entertaining, Elizabeth once again exerted herself in the organization of a grand event. Though the attendance was limited only to the three families of her intimate acquaintance, she insisted on the erection of a large canvas tent. On the morning of the picnic, many rugs, cushions, and seats from the abbey were relocated to underneath that canvas tent. There they were arranged to great advantage. The effect produced was of a rather Eastern flair. It encouraged lounging and sprawling. The tent was also supplied with ample refreshments organized across a long table, where two footmen stood ready to fan flies and lift lids for the guests.

For the day's amusements, Elizabeth had an archery range erected. She had the hedge maze freshly clipped and a bowl of hothouse strawberries placed at its center. She had her gondola (an ill-advised and extravagant purchase from her wild Continental adventures of yore) removed from its little boathouse at the south end of her decorative pond and made ready with cushions and flowers for all to enjoy. She even procured a fresh suit of bright-green material for Captain Tanders, who was to play music for the party and play a key role in Diana's anticipated success.

The Reverend Samuel Astley and his wife arrived a whole hour earlier than the other guests, as requested. The reverend's general unawareness was penetrated, and he remarked on the splendor of the sight before him. This rare acknowledgement of her exertions by her friend's husband put Elizabeth in a most delighted humor. She took the time to guide him through the hedge maze personally, so he might be the first to enjoy the strawberries concealed in its center.

When the Bellwoods and Birch party arrived next, the boys took instantly to the archery range. Mrs. Bellwood, in a moment of unanticipated confidence, mustered the courage to request a tour of Eastbey Abbey. Elizabeth was all too happy to oblige, thinking she might use the opportunity to learn as much as she could about the history and standing of the Birch family. Instead, she found too much delight in the sound of her own voice to make room for any other on her expedition.

What Mrs. Bellwood would say of the picnic that day would be very little, for she dozed contentedly in one of the comfortable chairs under the canvas tent after her tour of the abbey. Of Eastbey Abbey though, she could forever extol the magnificence. Never had she seen so *many* rooms, all in such elaboration of decoration. Tassels and braid existed in such abundance, it seemed likely they had gone to seed and were spreading about the estate like buttercups across a meadow. Venetian glass and china vases jostled shoulder to shoulder like an opening-night theater crowd atop mantels and sideboards. Rather than being abraded by the stark contrast between the dark, close, and heavy medieval architecture and the bright, exuberant, excessive decoration, Mrs. Bellwood felt this combination to be the pinnacle of elegance—for it spoke so clearly of both an ancient history and a present fortune that it matched her ideal for just what a castle should be. Never mind that it was an abbey.

A keener eye might have perceived that such an abundance of rooms was a result of Elizabeth's lack of patience for any serious remodeling which (at no prohibitive expense) might have combined some of the smaller rooms, once cloisters for those of the cloth, into fewer rooms of reasonable size. Being contented to use the great hall for dancing and the former chapel for a dining room, Elizabeth saw no need to rob herself of any opportunity to decorate. She explained all of this to Mrs. Bellwood in a most confiding tone on their tour. This conversation, had with a true *lady*, was one Mrs. Bellwood would find excuses to mention often and always for the rest of her days.

As the Bellwood boys found delight in the archery range, their instructions in the finer points of that sport came from an unlikely source: Constance. The reverend's wife explained that archery had been a very fashionable sport when she was younger. It seemed that she had taken a great deal of pride in her ability to outshoot many young men from fine families whose names meant nothing to the Bellwood boys, though they nodded with the recognition that at one time they must have meant something to someone.

Hudson found joy in little else but Diana. From the moment she alighted from Benjamin's barouche, he was by her side. He fetched her lemonade and a plate of small sandwiches. Then he made such a show of imparting all the details of the day's amusements, one would have thought that this was his picnic, planned for her sole enjoyment.

Captain Tanders kept the atmosphere lively with the exotic sounds of a Spanish guitar. He played no tune in particular, but strummed and plucked gently while sprawled rather coolly among a heap of pillows under the canvas tent. A private note to Maggie had instructed them *not* to bring Diana's flute. After everyone had been given ample time to enjoy the activities presented for them, it became obvious why.

Captain Tanders removed his flute from its small case and began to play a lively tune, at which time Elizabeth asked Benjamin to favor her with a dance. This odd pairing drew a significant amount of attention and applause at the conclusion of the number.

Then, as if the thought had only just occurred to her, Lady Elizabeth said very brightly, "Diana, do you not play the flute? Won't you favor us with a song?"

Diana looked as mortified as if she had been asked to disrobe and display her corset and underskirts. But looking around, she only saw vigorous nods from her female companions. She shyly approached Captain Tanders and took his flute. With trembling hands, but a good memory, she played her little song to a tolerable degree of proficiency that might have been excused by the instrument being a borrowed one and the performance being impromptu. Its effect was everything the women could have hoped. Mr. Birch was amazed.

Over and over, he declared her to be "A songbird! A lark!"

Upon the conclusion of his rapturous applause, Hudson begged Diana to play another song. Before Diana could reply that she knew no other song and was only very lately acquainted with this one, Captain Tanders took the flute from her hands.

Gravely and with practiced enunciation, he said, "I can't be sharing this with you any longer, miss, or I won't expect the mistress to pay me for my services. Though you do such credit to the instrument, it's clear you have skill and talent enough to outshine me."

This last sentence, Maggie felt, was certainly straight from the brain of Elizabeth. She admired that the captain was able to deliver such a line without laughing. It seemed the talents of this consummate performer were many and, Maggie imagined, well used by Elizabeth.

As the captain resumed his playing of the guitar, Constance made her way to Elizabeth. During Diana's performance, Constance had been close at hand to the Bellwood boys. There, she had overheard Mr. Birch as he whispered to Ellis that Diana had the most beautiful long arms he had ever seen. To compliment a girl on her lovely arms was surely a sentiment of the warmest regard. Diana's new white-worked dress was cut very prettily with a wide, open neck that showed her *womanly virtues* to great effect. To say, then, that her arms (a pair of appendages that nearly everyone possessed) were lovely was to say, the ladies conjectured, that he admired her so thoroughly, even her ordinary features were rendered magnificent.

As Constance and Elizabeth were excitedly discussing this most auspicious sign, Benjamin turned to Maggie and asked if she might like to join him for a wander in the hedge maze. The look of surprise on her face at this request must have startled him. He quickly said that it was only a suggestion and she might also stay and feel no obligation. Before he could hedge his offer further from its purpose, Maggie took him by the elbow and steered them together to the entrance of the maze.

Inside the cool closeness of the narrow boxwood canyons, Benjamin and Maggie began to snake their way slowly to the center.

Along the way, they made a few false turns and found themselves bumping into one another with sudden stops and pivots. This physical confinement and repeated corporeal confrontation is, of course, the entire purpose for which a hedge maze is designed. After a first few stiff bumbles and polite apologies, the couple soon found tentative laughter at the dead ends and hard turns of their captivity. Quietly, Maggie hoped they might not reach the middle for a long time. The proximity of her husband and their slow thawing of spirits seemed a prelude to some warm reconciliation.

Benjamin felt it, too. In the weeks since they had returned from London, his remaining attitude of aloofness seemed more and more a product of his own stubbornness and less a result of some strong warranting logic. Now, in the confines of the hedge maze, he could smell Maggie's perfume of lavender and rose trailing behind her. Under that scent, in moments when she came near to him, he inhaled the powdery fragrance of her skin and hair unadorned. He felt a powerful pull to be ever nearer to her.

At the zenith of their mutual desire to find themselves forever confined to the hedge maze, they suddenly reached the open clearing at its center. There they found a sundial whose accuracy was interrupted by a heaping bowl of strawberries enshrined in a tall cloche made of fine white net.

Without words, only some reluctant laughter, the pair approached the sundial, and Maggie lifted the cloche for Benjamin. From the bowl he withdrew a perfect red strawberry, warm from the sun. His hand extended towards Maggie's mouth, the corners of which curved upward in an anticipatory expression.

He placed the strawberry between her lips. He held its green top as she bit into the soft, sweet, seedy flesh. They locked eyes. A moment longer and they would have fallen passionately into one another's arms in blissful reconciliation. But at that exact instant, when all the world around them had fallen silent and they were holding their breath for what came next, they heard two distinct noises: a splash, and a scream.

# Thirty-Eight

What had happened was this:

Feeling that there was no better time to show off the loveliness of Diana's arms to her admirer, Elizabeth suggested to Constance that the girl might like to row the gondola out on the lake with Mr. Birch as her passenger. Constance wisely countered that the two awkward youths would perhaps get along better in their courtship without too many opportunities to share unsupervised conversation. Though Mr. Birch seemed very eager to hear Diana name and describe all the beasts of the wood and plants of the field, extending beyond these subjects had never proved successful for Diana. Thus, it was decided that Diana would row Elizabeth out on the gondola so she might be seen to advantage by her beau.

Wasting no time after the plan was settled, Elizabeth summoned Diana from the archery range. She had been showing some natural skill in that sport and was sad to leave it. Upon second call, she made her way to the small dock in the marshy reeds of Elizabeth's decorative pond. There the women, young and old, took their places on the gondola. Elizabeth reclined magnificently, while Diana took the long *remo* in her hands. Then, with great demonstration of her lovely arms, she began to poke and prod the bottom of the murky water to propel them forward.

As the exotic black lacquered boat was drifting lazily to the center of the pond, Elizabeth settled into the lush upholstery of the seat. She felt the sun on her skin. She remembered Venice, and the sounds of the gondoliers calling round the corners. She remembered how footsteps of pedestrians on bridges echoed off the water and up the canyon walls of the stone city. She remembered the young French officer, notably far from his regiment in those early war years. She remembered how he had spun stories in her ear as his hands strummed her corset lacings the way Captain Tanders strummed his Spanish guitar. Given more time, she might have next wondered if that young French officer made it through the war alive. Before her thoughts could take that melancholy turn, a shout from the shore caused her to sit upright and turn her body sharply to the side.

The shout had come from Mr. Birch. He had pierced an apple straight through with an arrow in a magnificent shot made more by good luck than good skill. He was calling loudly to Diana to see this great feat. Diana naturally turned to face him on the shore, somewhat behind her. Her sudden movement, combined with Elizabeth's sudden shift in the boat, caused the gondola to pitch strongly to one side. As a result, Diana and her new white-work muslin dress were tossed into the pond.

This was the splash that Maggie and Benjamin heard from their moment of near reconciliation in the hedge maze. The scream they heard was from Mr. Birch.

When Diana fell into the pond, Hudson had not a moment to think. Well, he did, actually. But he used that time instead to let out a long, piercing scream of the utmost alarm. Then, the moment of thinking abandoned, he charged—boots and all—into the water to rescue his dear Diana.

His dear Diana watched him stampede into the reedy edge of the pond as she stood, up to her shoulders in the murky lake. Her confused amusement soon changed to genuine concern and then ardent alarm. Hudson's position had become infinitely more perilous than her own.

By charging into the lake without pause, Hudson had shown great courage. But he also betrayed a deficit of practical knowledge regarding bodies of water. His boots, which he might have removed, were soon stuck in the silt-sticky bottom of the pond. This arrested the movement of his lower half, but his upper body continued to fight forward. The result was that he was entrenched in water only waist deep, but splashing forward in vain. His unrelenting charge paired with his entirely entrapped feet and calves pitched his body forward at such an angle that he was very soon in danger of drowning. He had no way to right himself. His upper half was now in water too deep to reach the bottom of, and his lower half was stuck at such an angle as to make freeing it very difficult.

On the shore, a scene of abrupt chaos broke out. Ellis and Noah rushed to the edge of the pond. There they yelled for Hudson to come back, or stand up, or kick his legs, and lots of other advice they could give a friend who knew as little about swimming as they did. Constance commanded all the staff in sight to go in after the boy. But her French was very bad. Her wild gesticulations were certainly enough to communicate her demands, but none in Lady Dormer's household felt eager to ruin one of their uniforms to save a young man who really ought to have known how to swim before running headlong into a lake. The Reverend Samuel Astley was looking for a rope. There were many ropes securing the canvas tent, but each of them seemed to have a purpose essential for the structure of the shelter. Samuel had no idea which one he should select.

Seeing Hudson struggling to right himself and flapping face-down in the water, Diana swam a few quick strokes until she was right in front of him. So great was his panic that he did not notice her presence until she had her arms under his own and was heaving him backwards and back up on his feet. Spluttering and covered in mud, he stood in mute shock as she knelt before him in the reeds. Plunging her hands down his calves, she scooped the mud under his feet, breaking the lake's hold on his boots. When his feet were free, she put her shoulder under his arm and half-dragged the young man out of the water. Having reached the shore, they both flopped, panting, on the sunny grass.

There were a few moments then, perhaps just a few fleeting seconds dilated by panic and emotion, in which Diana and Hudson lay upon the warm grass looking at each other. Hudson beheld his rescuer. Her white muslin dress was made the color of cream by the murky lake, and it clung to her every contour. Even in his near drowned state, he could not help but recognize the eroticism of the image. Her hair was made even darker by the water. It fell, undone and clinging, against her neck and cheek. He looked at his dear Diana, his deliverance from death, this great goddess of a woman looking like a marble statue come to life, and his mind was blank to all else. And what did she do?

She laughed at him. Bright and full, she tossed her head back and he beheld the full radiance of her smile. Her laugh was an ecstasy to his ears. She laughed at him. As her laughter echoed in his heart, nothing else existed.

Then the crowd of friends dashed to their sides. Pulling the pair apart, they rushed to attend to their needs and get them out of their wet clothes. It was at this moment that Benjamin and Maggie burst free from the hedge maze. Unable to predict what catastrophe might await them, they had journeyed most frantically back through the maze. As Constance shepherded the wet Diana inside and Captain Tanders inspected the bedraggled Hudson for signs of aquatic inhalation, Noah and Ellis explained to Maggie and Benjamin in simultaneous voices what had transpired.

The Reverend Samuel Astley, at long last, found his much-sought spare rope. After tying a heavy knot at one end, he stood by the edge of the pond and hurled it to Elizabeth, who remained trapped in the gondola without a guide. When she caught it, he led her boat, like a shy pony, back to the dock. There he held out his hand and helped her from it without any fuss. She was surprised by how profoundly the action struck her, despite all the surrounding chaos. This simple attention of Samuel's was more endearing to Elizabeth than anything else she had ever witnessed him do in their thirty years of acquaintance.

# Thirty Nine

Inside the house, Constance was harassing Elizabeth's lady's maid. At first, Heloise pretended not to understand Constance's request for a set of her own clothing. The reverend's wife would not be deterred. She only increased her volume and obstinacy in the face of stoic protest. However, when Heloise saw that Diana was beginning to shiver (even though she was wrapped in a large blanket), she relented. Heloise returned to Elizabeth's dressing room with her second-best Sunday dress. Heloise would have preferred that Diana should wear one of madame's dresses. But even in her reluctance to relinquish the needed articles of her meager wardrobe, she recognized that Elizabeth's stout stature would make an impossible fit for the tall, lithe, and drenched Diana.

Captain Tanders brought Hudson to his own room to change out of his wet clothes. Hudson, not realizing that Captain Tanders was *not* staying in the servants' quarters, was vastly impressed by the great comfort in which Lady Dormer kept her staff. Left on his own for a few minutes, he made a full tour of the room, leaving muddy footprints all over the fine rug. When Captain Tanders returned, it was with a spare set of footman's liveries.

The captain helped the young man out of his wet clothes and into the dry, slightly old-fashioned uniform. This was accomplished easily and quickly, but the result was far from what Captain Tanders had hoped.

Rather than perk up at the return to a dry and comfortable state, Hudson heaved one deep sigh and collapsed in the armchair by the small fireplace, his head in his hands. Captain Tanders realized with some mild mortification that the boy was crying.

"There, there now, son. You've had a fright but you're all right now," the captain said as he clapped his hand against Hudson's shoulder.

The youth showed no signs of abating his emotion. Captain Tanders tried again.

"You're taking it too hard. This will all be a happy memory sooner than you think."

Hudson lifted his face towards the captain.

"I don't expect you to understand. But, I say, don't you understand? She'll never have me now. Never."

As it happened, Captain Tanders understood perfectly. Elizabeth had explained to him in great detail her efforts to unite Mr. Birch and Lady Huxley. So it was Hudson's good fortune that the captain was especially well equipped to offer counsel.

He pulled up the opposing armchair. Before settling in, he secured two glasses and a decanter of port wine. He filled both glasses. After a long, slow sip, he kindly nodded to the young man and asked him to unburden himself. It took very little prompting. Captain Tanders was Hudson's picture of experienced, masculine virtue. As such, he was inclined to trust him with the confidence of a friend, father, and commander.

"She has saved me now twice! Twice, I say! First there was the bee at the dinner, which I know is not such, you know, an obvious danger. Though men do die from bees and, I say, I very well might have. . . . So she saved me from the bee and now, now she has saved me from drowning."

"One might suppose it's because she cares about you."

"Oh, she cares, sure. But a man can't propose marriage to a girl whom he owes his life twice over. She'd be forever thinking . . . I say, she'd either think me a great idiot, or she'd think I was only asking her because I was obliged. She's already, you know, a baron's daughter. And my father is just a merchant. I lived in a two-room flat until I was eight years old. With that and the fact I keep near dying every time I see her . . . Well, I say, I just don't see how she could ever want to marry me."

"Oh, but you've got plenty to offer a girl."

"It won't matter. She'll never take me seriously. It's hopeless. I say, I'm just not cut out for a girl as fine as she."

Hudson said this last sentence with such palpable heartbreak that the captain felt sure the boy would quit the country altogether if some strong encouragement was not given and given quickly.

"Now, Mr. Birch, this is no way to behave." The captain adopted his military tone, and indeed, Hudson sat up straighter just at the first syllables. "You are nowhere close to being beat and you'd be a fool to surrender. Are you a fool? Or are you a man?

"You are a man. And a man like you is not going to let a little splash in a lake, a most gallant splash at that—why, if it was not for all that mud, you would have reached the girl and been the one dragging her up on shore like a hero! You are not going to let a little water keep you from the girl you love. No! You're going to go after her and you're going to get her, by George! You're going to get her and make her your wife."

Far from the resolute look of impassioned confidence that Captain Tanders had hoped to inspire, Hudson's face took on a dreamy disposition, and he answered softly as if speaking to himself.

"I say, it's a funny thing, though. When she . . . when she's so . . . calm and cool and easy when everything else is going wrong. I say . . . those moments. Those moments are when I feel I *almost* have the courage to ask her. Baron father or not. Bees or not. I just . . ."

"Listen, no more talk about this bee business. Men don't die from bee stings. I mean, they do, but hardly ever."

Captain Tanders wasn't sure if Hudson heard him; the boy had a far-off stare directed at the empty fireplace.

~

The party outside was consumed in reiterating over and over the sudden shock, surprise, horror, and amazement that had befallen each of them as the events had occurred. Until each witness had given vent to their own experience of the shocking occurrence, little else could be done. All the while, inside, Diana and Hudson were being helped out of their clothes and into fresh dry things. Though the day was very warm, it was agreed that such weather could still not be trusted. To stay in wet clothing for even a moment longer than was necessary was pronounced unthinkably risky.

At last, Diana emerged from Elizabeth's dressing room in Heloise's dress. In the inner stone courtyard of the abbey, she met Hudson in his borrowed footman's liveries. They exchanged shy smiles. Diana stood much taller than Heloise, so her dress was supplemented by a long underskirt borrowed from Elizabeth. Her wet hair was pulled back in a severe bun like those worn by kitchen staff.

For his part, Hudson looked rather ridiculous in the old-fashioned formal liveries of Eastbey Abbey. Large brass buttons and copious gold braid adorned his dark-green coat and breeches. He had no shoes. The swollen wet leather of his boots could not be made to button. So he stood in his stocking feet on the stone floor. In this condition, he did not have the confidence to make his oft-repeated greeting.

"We look quite a sight," he ventured.

Diana nodded and smiled her agreement.

"I mean, I say, can you imagine if this is what we wore every day? If this was, you know, a normal way for us to be? You a lady's maid and I a footman? I can't even begin . . ." and he chuckled at the absurdity of such a thought.

Diana smiled, but in that smile there was an unmasked sadness. Hudson paused. He felt in that moment that the debt he owed this beautiful girl was insurmountable. He felt that she, who had now saved his life possibly twice (for no matter what Captain Tanders said, he was sure he would have been mortally wounded by a bee sting), who was so lovely, so sweet in disposition, so wise in all the ways of the country, and the daughter of a baron to boot . . . He resolved in that moment that he would not be beaten. He would not give up. He resolved to offer her his hand in marriage and pledge to her his life. But as he could not do such a thing in an old servant's livery, he was determined to do it when the right occasion presented itself.

The carriages had been called, of course, and everyone soon departed Eastbey Abbey. This left Captain Tanders and Elizabeth to eat the rest of the prepared food and to drink the champagne that had yet to be served. They did so with relish. Before long, they were having a good laugh about the follies of youth, which both professed great relief to be free from yet took great joy in recounting.

# Forty

Mrs. Rollins was just in the process of scraping a spider's web out of the corner of a tall window when the Howard coach returned. Shocked at how quickly the afternoon had slipped away from her, she was relieved that the clock on the mantel proclaimed the Howards were ahead of schedule.

When the circumstances of their early return had been explained, Mrs. Rollins did what she did best. She took charge. A bath was called for. Diana's damp dress and underthings were turned over for cleaning. A strong fire was built in Diana's bedroom. Soup was commissioned from the kitchen.

As these tasks were on their way to completion, Mrs. Rollins shepherded Diana up to her room. There the housekeeper helped her into her nightclothes, swaddled her in a blanket, and planted her in the chair close to the roaring fire. Only when her charge had been thus immobilized did she venture from the bedroom in search of the final ingredient to Diana's recovery: brandy.

When Mrs. Rollins returned to the room, she found Tally and Diana engaged in a debate. Tally the maid was attempting to spoon-feed Diana the procured soup. Diana was protesting that such attentions were not necessary. She insisted that all she really needed was help freeing her arms from the tight swaddle of the blanket which kept them pinned to her sides. Mrs. Rollins shooed the under maid from the room and then readjusted Diana's wrappings with a greater emphasis on mobility.

"I don't need everyone making such a fuss, Mrs. Rollins. I only fell into a lake."

"I know, Miss Diana, but you mustn't blame them for wanting to be useful and take care of you."

"I can take care of myself."

"I know you can. But they don't. You must resign yourself to being a little helpless if you're ever to be comfortable here."

Diana cast her eyes away. "It's not easy."

Mrs. Rollins poured a glass of brandy.

"Drink this. When your bath is ready I'll send the maids away so you can have some quiet time."

Two glasses of brandy later, immersed up to her ears in the warm water of the huge tub, Diana was staring at her hands. Her nails were longer now than they had ever been—little white crescent moons that crowned each finger. The calluses of her palms and fingers had softened. These hands, her own hands, looked utterly foreign to her.

Turning these unfamiliar hands over in the water, she examined the small white scar that marked the base of her thumb. When she'd arrived at Wuster park, the wound had still been fresh, tender, and red. It had only been a few months, and yet the cut had healed without her conscious perception. She had forgotten to be aware of the pain. It was as if it never happened. Diana was not sure if she felt relieved or depressed by the insignificance of it all.

A splinter. She was here in the Wuster Park bathtub because of a splinter. She was here at Wuster Park, living a life different in every way from the one she had known, because a tiny sliver of wood had lodged itself in her hand.

~

That winter, the rats had grown bold in their desperation. Diana could not help but respect their tenacity. Though she had made her family's meager foodstuffs utterly inaccessible, still the rats remained. Though Caldflett was hardly warmer than the heath outside, she supposed to a rat it represented some domestic comfort. Now, if little Nina was to be understood, there was one hiding under their shared bed.

What Diana should have done was fetch the broom to sweep it out and shoo it to a corner or under the empty oak cabinet. But Diana had already removed her boots, and she and Nina had an agreement about keeping one's feet clean before climbing into bed. Instead, Diana braved the possibility of a bite and swept her hand under the low bed frame. She heard the rat scuttle out of reach, but not out from its hiding spot. She squatted low and swiped at it again. It was not her sweeping hand that startled the rat from his hiding spot, but the sharp cry and loud hiss that escaped her unbidden as the flesh of her palm snagged against a jagged edge of the rough wooden floor.

Nina instinctively reached for her sister at the sound of her distress. She clutched Diana's arm tightly. Diana soothed her before she soothed herself.

"Hush now, don't worry so. It's just a splinter. It only surprised me. That's all. I'm fine. The rat is gone. Now move over, I want to get some sleep."

The next morning, Diana inspected her palm. Red and swollen, it greeted her with stabbing pain and a low, burning sensation that filled her with dread. Seeing how difficult it was to perform her morning chores of building the fire and making the breakfast with this injury, she knew it would need to be tended to right away.

When she brought her mother breakfast, she announced that she would need to take a journey to the spring. The apothecary had been to Caldflett the week before, and so her mother only nodded placidly, glassy-eyed and unconcerned. Diana instructed Nan to serve the remaining breakfast porridge at noontime, and then she set out.

The spring water was cold and clear. It flowed in steady abundance up into a carved basin of dark stone before cascading over the sides, rippling the moss and collecting itself into a small rivulet that would wind its way down the mountains to the river, finally to the dark lake that served as reservoir for Yansworth village.

It bore the silence of a once sacred space. No birds could be heard to call there, and even the roaring wind seemed to abate. Everyone in Yansworth knew that this had once been considered a place of great significance. By whom and for what, fewer knew. Still, it retained the reputation of healing properties. It was a pilgrimage destination for mothers with sick babies, boys with broken arms, and old women with gnarled, stiff knuckles.

She arrived at the spring well after the midday meal would have been served. Standing beside the basin, she unwrapped her hand, now throbbing with heat and beginning to itch. In the full daylight it looked even worse. Diana was glad to have made the decision to come. She plunged her hand into the water. The reflexive clenching of her fist lit up the pain in her hand and she shut her eyes tight. She waited.

Just as the burning and throbbing were beginning to subside, she heard the slow footfalls of a horse. Diana looked round to see a familiar face. Charlie McFaden was riding his horse, Jupiter, to stand beside her at the spring. She smiled and waved with her uninjured hand. He returned her greeting with a pleasant nod. When dismounted, Charlie dropped Jupiter's lead. The horse, knowing its freedom, wandered and snuffled at the grass nearby.

"Can I see?"

"It's nothing. Just a splinter. So stupid."

"Let me look."

Charlie lifted her hand out of the cold basin. He pressed at the base of her thumb in gentle appraisal.

"Good thing you came. This looks like it could easily take a turn."

"I thought so too." Diana smiled despite the pain. She liked to know that Charlie agreed with her assessment.

"Why are you here?" she asked.

"Rolled my ankle."

"I don't know that the spring water could do much for that."

"No, but the cold will take the swelling down so I can wrap it up tight. How long did it take you to walk here?"

"I left just after morning chores. How long did it take you?"

"I left just before midday meal. Have you eaten?"

He did not wait for her reply to unhouse a loaf of bread from his sling. He tore off a hunk and handed it to her. She took it without answering.

Diana loved nothing in this world more than Mrs. McFaden's bread. She could taste that this loaf was a day old, but under the chewy exterior, the center was soft and ever so slightly sweet. It was her one selfish indulgence. For when Mrs. McFaden sent her home each Thursday with spare vegetables from her garden, she always included a loaf of bread. Diana knew that she was supposed to share it with her family. But every long walk home she ate the entire thing. Tasting it now, she blushed with her secret guilt.

"What are you thinking about?" Charlie asked. He had watched the emotions play over her face like one watches gathering clouds atop distant mountains.

"Bread," Diana answered honestly.

Charlie was smiling. It was nice to see Diana on an off day—not an infrequent occurrence, since Charlie often found reasons to head into Yansworth on Tuesday. Not every Tuesday, of course. He did not like to make his father repeat his vague and warning refrain: "She's a baron's daughter, Charlie." Such words carried implications he was not fond of considering. But he was fond of considering Diana, baron's daughter or not.

Diana and Charlie settled into the comfortable silence of close friendship. Diana returned her hand to the basin while Charlie sat and tenderly unlaced his boot. When his foot was free, he rolled up his trouser leg. Diana could see the bruising and swelling that was already blooming around his ankle.

"How do you plan to get your foot up here?" Diana gestured to the carved basin that stood conveniently at hand height.

"I'll just put it in the stream here. It's the cold I'm after, not the magic." He chuckled, but then his eyes became serious. "Diana, can I look at your hand again?"

Diana went to his side. He spread her palm wide and inspected it closely.

"I think you've still got a piece in there. It won't heal right if we don't get it out. This will hurt."

Charlie mashed the meat of her hand between his two strong thumbs. The dullness of the numbing water gave way to an awful pain. Diana let out a sharp yelp.

"I'm sorry. I'm going to do it again."

He did. It hurt twice as bad. Tears stung Diana's eyes.

"Stop stop stop." She pulled her hand away from him and took two steps back.

"Now Diana, I'm sorry. But I think . . ."

He did not say what he thought, and in his silence Diana felt her own uncertainty assert itself. If there was a piece of splinter still in her palm, she would not heal. If she did not heal then she could not work. If she could not work, nothing would get done. If nothing got done, her whole family would probably starve. And then her mother would be very angry. Diana did not want to make her mother angry.

"What do we have to do? Tell me plainly."

"Well, if you were a sheep—"

"If I were a sheep?"

"If you were a sheep and you had a thorn in your leg I would have to . . ."

Here Charlie faltered again. Diana could guess where this was going and she didn't like it.

"But I am not a sheep."

"We have to cut it out, Diana. I'm sorry. Go put it back in the basin. Keep it there 'til you can't feel it anymore."

Diana did as she was told. She shuddered, but not from the cold.

In the time that Diana was numbing her hand in the basin, Charlie wrapped his swollen ankle and replaced his boot. Then he whistled for Jupiter, who reluctantly ambled over to his rider's side. Fishing from the horse's saddlebag his knife and a whetstone, Charlie began to sharpen the blade. For a long time there was only the sound of the knife on stone and the bubbling spring.

Finally, Diana broke the spell.

"Let's do it now. My hand is almost blue with cold."

She presented her appendage to her friend.

"Don't look." Charlie said.

"I'm not afraid. I know what you're going to do."

"I know. But if you watch, I'll be nervous. I need to be quick."

"Be quick then."

He was. It was over in just a few moments. The sliver of wood was removed and the flesh of her palm was slowly pooling with blood.

"Put it back in the basin."

Diana rushed to do so. The relief of the cool water was unfathomable. Instant calm flooded through her, and Diana felt there must be some magic there after all. Soon Charlie was by her side. He had some linen, also from his saddlebag. Diana often teased Charlie that his saddlebag contained something for every occasion. Without repeating this, they both smiled at the shared remembrance of this recurring joke. When the basin's pool had diluted the blood to only a tint of pink, Charlie gingerly lifted Diana's hand into his own. There he deftly wrapped the cut in the linen bandage and secured the edges.

"Thank you," Diana sighed.

Then, she leaned forward.

Resting both palms against his chest, she laid her head tenderly against the curve of his neck. Though they had never united in such an embrace, it felt natural, inevitable, gravitational. They stood together, gently swaying in a dreamy calm for a long time. Charlie's hands found the small of her back. The heat of his broad palms penetrated her dress. She could feel the flutter of his pulse under the tawny skin of his neck. He smelled like horses, hay, and salt. Neither of them wanted the moment to end. And so they stood, bodies aligned, in absolute peace and silence.

They must have stood for a very long time, for when they pulled apart, a small line of blood had seeped through Diana's bandage onto Charlie's shirt. Without a word, Charlie fetched another strip of linen from his bag, returned, and redoubled the bandage on Diana's hand. He hoped that they might once again fall into an embrace. But Diana held herself apart, eyes downcast. When he finished the wrapping, he refused to release her hand. Instead, he drew her closer to him and lifted her chin so she might meet his eyes.

"Diana, I love you."

It would not be right to say that he kissed her or that she kissed him. They kissed each other. They kissed each other with an unspoken passion years in the making. They kissed each other with the thrill of discovery and adventure. They kissed each other feverishly, slowly, tenderly, playfully, warmly, and all the other ways that two people can kiss each other. He held her head, his thumb in front of one ear. She grasped at his shirt, untucking it from his breeches as she pulled him closer to her. They tumbled, as all young lovers must, into the grass. He ran his hand along the length of her, from knee to nape. She felt his back, his shoulders, his arms.

In one long moment, they pulled apart and surveyed each other to ascertain if such events were in fact unfolding in their shared experiences. This confirmed, they resumed.

The rarity of this shared solitude urged them onward in their exploration. Desire was their guide.

When the sun was low in the sky, they recalled the existence of the world outside their own shared passion. Diana was in a panic. If she left right away, she would get home well after dark. Charlie saw the alarm in her eyes as she made this swift mental calculation.

"Let me take you on Jupiter. We'll go fast."

Diana could not afford to decline his offer. They mounted the horse and set off in the direction of Caldflett Castle. Jupiter did make quick work of the journey, but wrapped in Charlie's arms, their bodies bouncing together in the saddle, Diana wished the journey might have lasted an eternity. It was too late when she noticed the small silhouette of her sister, Nan, atop the ridge. The moment she spied her, she knew that everything was about to go wrong.

Nan quickly turned and began to run back in the direction of the castle. Charlie felt Diana go stiff with anxiety. She answered him before he asked.

"My sister has seen us. She's going to tell my mother. Let me down."

"She won't know anything except that I helped you get back here."

"Nan won't, but my mother . . . I have to go, Charlie. Let me down."

Charlie reined Jupiter to a stop, and he dismounted so Diana could make her way off the saddle unimpeded. As she turned to go, he caught her unbandaged hand in his own. He wanted to say he was sorry.

"Thank you," he said instead.

She paused. Her earnest eyes met his.

"Thank you," she replied.

Then she ran up the hill to Caldflett Castle.

Caldflett Castle was an eerie calm when Diana pushed open the door. There was no fire burning in the hearth, and the dishes from that morning's meal had not been cleared or cleaned. Instinctively, Diana began to gather them. Before she could transfer the pile to the washtub, she heard her mother's voice calling her to the other room. With stoic apprehension, she obeyed the summons.

Twelve days later, leaving behind everything except the dress on her back and the boots on her feet, she left Caldflett Castle for New Glenbury by the post carriage.

Now, she was here in this bathtub, looking at the small scar that was the only proof she would ever have that Charlie McFaden had loved her.

<h1 style="text-align:center">Forty-One</h1>

THAT NIGHT, AFTER Diana had been properly doted upon by the insistent Mrs. Rollins and sent to bed early, Maggie joined Benjamin in the library. A small fire had been lit there, and the couple now congregated around it.

"I thought, all in all," said Benjamin, "it was a rather nice picnic."

"Oh yes, excepting the near-drowning incident, it was lovely."

Benjamin laughed, genuinely laughed, at his wife's sly appreciation of the folly of the day.

Then, when a moment of silence fell, Maggie ventured, "And Elizabeth's gardens are very grand."

"Very grand indeed, and all so close together."

"Yes, I think she told me once that because she could not decide which of the French styles she likes best, she had one of each made. I take from her stories that she spent some happy times in French gardens."

Maggie raised her eyebrows teasingly at Benjamin, and he returned her knowing look with one of his own. Then another moment of quiet befell the conversation.

Just when Maggie thought she could stand the silence no longer, her husband broke it, but only to say, "Well, I think I shall turn in for the night. Goodnight, Maggie."

And he quitted the room politely, insensible to the look of devastation he left behind on his wife's face.

For nearly an hour, Maggie sat and brooded by the dying fire, watching the embers turn to ashes and the light of the candles eclipse the glow of the hearth. Though it was well into summer now, she felt the room had a chill; she hesitated to quit it and find the reception in her shared bedroom even colder. But quit it she must. As Mrs. Rollins came in to snuff out the candles and lock up all the windows and doors for the night, Maggie gathered herself and departed to her bedchamber.

Within her own small dressing room, separated from the main chamber by a discreet door, Maggie became sensible to an inkling of an idea. Brushing her soft brown hair and remarking to herself in the looking glass how long it was getting, she let her gaze wander across face and figure to see if they, too, had changed in the passing of time.

She would be twenty-nine in a few months, and she observed with equal parts satisfaction and surprise that she still looked fresh and familiar to herself. Her sister, Caroline, had once confessed how worn down she felt after her marriage. Maggie did not feel worn down. Though, she recollected that she had not had much in the way of *marital demands* these long few weeks.

In a fuller consciousness of her intentions, Maggie completed the rest of her evening toilette. Then she supplemented the process with the addition of a few drops of her French perfume to wrists, neck, and décolletage. She left her cotton nightdress on its stand and selected instead a pink silk robe from her wardrobe. It was a bold luxury that she had ordered for her wedding wardrobe. She had not yet had a chance to enjoy the cool feeling of the fine silk or the gentle texture of the delicate lace that adorned its edges.

Looking again at herself in the long glass, she nodded with satisfaction and the anticipation of a satisfaction even greater . . .

~

Maggie and Benjamin lay together some time later, warm and content with all the blankets and pillows strewn about the floor of their chamber. Together they mourned for the time they had lost to their misunderstanding (for Benjamin refused to call it a quarrel), and they rejoiced in the new appreciation they had for their mutual affection. Benjamin explained his anxiety arising from his outburst, and the great pains he had taken to quell his passions to protect her from the angry, abrasive spouse he might become. Maggie reassured him that his fit of plate-related passion was a far cry from the displays of temper he feared it portended.

They passed much of the night talking, professing their love, and making such grand plans for the future as would take ten lifetimes to complete. Maggie recounted the "bad advice" which Constance and Elizabeth had both imparted. Together, they felt the winsome pity that only the young and untested can feel for the old and wise. They even spoke at some length on Diana and Hudson, their obvious adoration for each other, and their utter ineptitude at expressing it.

"I am glad," Maggie said, "that I waited so long to form an attachment. Young people barely know how to speak to each other. I cannot imagine what our courtship would have been if I had been my blunt and awkward self at nineteen when we met."

"Oh and I, at nineteen—you would not have even favored me with a dance, I'm sure. I couldn't put two words together without first meditating upon them for five minutes. Truly, we are lucky to have seen so much of the world to be able to really appreciate what we have found in each other."

No one in the house of Wuster Park noticed much of a difference in the restored happiness of the couple, except Mrs. Rollins and Diana. To them it was obvious that a warm reconciliation had thawed the weeks of coldness and the couple had a renewed rapturous regard for their romance.

Maggie made the polite gesture of inviting Diana to join the happy couple for a countryside ride in the barouche. Diana courteously declined. Her disinclination was met with no rebuttal or enticements. Maggie was too happy to have a carriage ride alone with her husband on such a fine summer day.

And oh, it was a fine summer day. The ox-eye daisies and the purple clover appeared in profusion. Opening roses and blooming honeysuckle perfumed the air. A day like this was made for lovers to enjoy together. Benjamin and Maggie could have driven endlessly through country lanes were it not for that pesky progression of time which has such a nasty habit of turning day into night. But then, as the sun began to fall from its zenith, Maggie and Benjamin were re-called to the certain favorable advantages of night. It was agreed then that they should return to Wuster Park directly and fulfill the obliga-tions of dinner to make way for the distinct pleasures of an evening spent together.

When Diana did not appear at dinner, claiming a headache, Maggie relished the opportunity to dine alone with Benjamin. Though she would not admit it to him, she wondered privately if it had been unwise to bring Diana into their household so soon after being married. This evening spent tête-à-tête was more delightful to her than any Maggie could recall having passed in that house. It panged her to feel that this seclusion was to be so short-lived.

As the couple took their after-dinner repast in the drawing room, Benjamin reminded Maggie that very soon the drapers and paperhangers of their recent London redecoration orders would be arriving. Then the pair had a delightful time of thinking over all their fine and elegant choices in such matters.

It need not be said how eagerly the couple retired to their shared bedroom that night. It need not be said how they smiled upon each other as they undressed. It need not be said how little time they lost to conversation as they united in an embrace. It need not be said how much sleep they lost to conversation when their more pressing mat-ters had been resolved.

It need not be said, but let it be said: they were happy, happier than either of them imagined they could be.

# Forty-Two

Constance and Elizabeth were happy, too, though not in the same way. Captain Tanders had recounted his conversation with Mr. Birch to Elizabeth, who recounted it to Constance. The friends had been delighted to hear that Hudson was indeed meditating on matrimony. This confirmation that their quest was progressing as planned made them both feel confident in the continued necessity of their efforts on behalf of the unaware young people at the heart of the matter.

They used Mr. Birch's thorough moistening in Elizabeth's pond as an excuse to visit Langley Hall to be assured of his good health. Hearing the blasts of gunshots and shouts of mirth ringing through the woods on their drive up to the hall, the women were assured on this point before they had even been announced. Still, they summoned Mrs. Bellwood from her midday reverie. Through a series of leading questions to the matron, they managed to learn a great deal about Mr. Birch's father, mother, prospects, and personality.

Mrs. Bellwood had been friends and neighbors of the Birch family for more than ten years. Because she was of that newly moneyed set which had no inherited shame or long memory for the embarrassments of their predecessors, she spoke openly, easily, and with great authority about all the particulars of the Birch family. She readily shared her knowledge about their income, whom and how much they paid for their washing and candles each week, and all she knew of their matrimonial aspirations for their only son.

From this conversation, it was discovered that Mrs. Bellwood was entirely oblivious of the fondness between Hudson and Diana. How Mrs. Bellwood had spent the summer so far unaware of the growing attachment between the young people was a mystery. She was soon made aware by the illuminations of Constance and Elizabeth.

Mrs. Bellwood professed herself certain that *any* daughter of *any* baron would be more than acceptable to the Birch family.

Privately, Elizabeth and Constance thought this lack of discernment less than agreeable. This was communicated only by a knowing glance between them. But for Diana's sake, at least, they were pleased. Before departing they also suggested, ever so tactfully of course, that Mrs. Bellwood might just mention in her next letter to the Birch family some of the details about *Lady* Diana Huxley. They explained, somewhat vaguely, that the meeting Diana had shared with the Birch family in London had not been really sufficient to make all her charms known to them. Having more specific knowledge, they rationalized, might assure Hudson's mother and father that Mrs. Bellwood was making excellent connections for their family.

The idea of a letter was novel and agreeable to Mrs. Bellwood. She had not penned a single line to the Birches for the whole of the summer. So, when her unexpected guests departed, that dear, sweet, sleepy mother promptly sat down at the desk in the musty little library at Langley Hall and began to write.

The letter was posted the next day. The result was an immediate and enthusiastic letter of encouragement to Hudson from Mrs. Birch. She assured her son on behalf of both herself and her husband (who was now *very certain* that he had liked this nice tall girl immensely) that they were pleased by his selection of bride and they felt certain from their brief acquaintance that Lady Diana Huxley had possessed a very regal bearing befitting her background, which was obvious even at a moment's glance.

Mrs. Birch's letter to Hudson arrived as soon as post horses could convey it. In reading it, he felt as though his mother had been able to read his very mind. He could not fathom how she had known about his new resolve to wed his dear Diana. Though in truth, her letter said plainly that it was Mrs. Bellwood's correspondence that had supplied her information.

Now that Hudson had his parents' approval at his engagement, he was only left with the not-so-small matter of getting the approval of Diana herself.

Hudson did not trouble himself to seek the approval of his friends. Ellis was already campaigning for a double wedding, and Noah was unlikely to consent to anyone's matrimonial plans. Hudson did find it useful to talk over the subject with his two confidants. Subsequently, the three youths began to compile what little they knew about securing a girl's hand and heart.

Hudson's first proposed proposal was a letter. To him, a letter seemed very sensible. It had the benefit of being long considered in its composition, without having to be memorized like the grand declaration of an in-person application. However, this epistolary idea met with severe disapproval from both his companions.

"Propose to her by letter? You are not five miles from her door! She will think you're afraid of her. And when she accepts, she will be forever lording it over you," Noah expatiated.

"I say! You think she will accept my offer, then?"

"Of course!" Ellis cried in jovial assurance.

"She would be a very pretty fool to turn you down," Noah consented.

"What do you mean? She is a baron's daughter. She could have anyone!"

"Ah, but you are very rich, and her family is not."

"Not rich? I say! What do you call Wuster Park, Noah?! A cottage?"

"I call it her cousin's estate, in which she is a guest," Noah replied. "Think back, Hudson. Do you not remember her dress when we first met her riding out on that little bay mare? Thick country cotton and very out of date."

Noah had an eye for the tells of genteel poverty, as many untitled young men who like to think themselves superior to others develop in defense of their own self-worth.

"But all her dresses now are fine." Hudson countered.

"Probably borrowed from her cousin. And she is one of what, five siblings? Even if only half of them are girls . . ."

"She has three sisters."

"Then her father has four girls to settle upon. I doubt you'd get much of anything from the old baron excepting a handshake."

"But that doesn't matter at all," Ellis cut in, "because you love her, and she obviously loves you! And a baron for a father-in-law is not nothing. Even if all he should do is shake your hand, that's more than Noah and I can get from a baron."

"True. Very true. But I am not convinced, Noah. I say, perhaps the girl likes wearing old clothes when she rides because she doesn't want to spoil her good dresses. That's just sensible. And a baron, even with four daughters, cannot be without . . . Well, and so what if she hasn't a penny? I don't want to spend my life wedded to a shrew just to have a few more acres outside my window. I think I have to try. For I do love her."

Still, the question of *how* to ask her remained painfully unanswered.

# Forty-Three

THIS QUESTION OF Hudson's proposal was also pressing upon Maggie, Elizabeth, and Constance while Diana was out in the garden making a runny watercolor of the landscape.

"So, Captain Tanders says he requires a crisis to compel him to make an offer. That should be simple enough. Inevitable, really," Constance intoned.

"No, quite the opposite. Another crisis and he'll quit her and the county entirely. Captain Tanders said the boy looked bereft at the idea that he was in her debt for his life twice over now," Elizabeth corrected.

"What was the first incident?" Maggie asked.

Elizabeth reminded her of the bee fiasco.

"And he thinks he might have *died*?"

"Town boys have a very exaggerated understanding of the dangers of rural life," Constance sagely replied.

The women sat and sipped their tea in stately consideration befitting a council of diplomats.

Finally, Maggie concluded, "A small crisis would be something that could work to our advantage in both directions. If he should rescue her from it, he would feel they are equal. If she rescues him again, he seems equally likely to propose out of admiration. So, we need

210

only to manufacture a small crisis."

"The problem with manufacturing a crisis, is one can never be sure that it will be small," Constance replied, looking pointedly at Elizabeth.

Elizabeth gave no answer, but the two older women exchanged such a long, lingering look of mutual remonstrance that Maggie could not resist in asking an explanation. Constance answered.

"Well my dear, we have long promised not to speak of it. But since you have asked . . ."

"And you should not under any circumstances tell anyone about this," Elizabeth enjoined.

"No. We share it only as a parable of caution."

"Yes, exactly Constance, a parable of caution. A secret parable, mind you."

Then the ladies took turns, very solemnly at first, but soon giving way to fits and bursts of giggles, in the slow recount of one of their first forays into matchmaking—a story that concluded with a series of unlikely coincidences which resulted in the burning down of an entire cottage and barn.

"No one was injured, of course!" Constance was quick in clarifying.

"Excepting the few goats tied up in the barn."

"Yes, excepting the goats."

"And it *did* work!"

"Though not as we thought it would."

"But they *were* married."

"And they got to live in a nice *new* cottage with nice *new* goats."

"So really, it wasn't all that bad."

The two old friends smiled at each other now with sheepish blushes at the memory of their folly and fun.

Constance said to Elizabeth, "You know, I recall how you said we would laugh about this one day. I did not believe you then. Lo, here we are."

"I have always been wiser than you give me credit, Constance."

"Very true, Elizabeth. But let it be a lesson to you, Maggie, just as it has been to us—make no trouble in matchmaking! There will be enough of it already. And trouble, once made, cannot be unmade."

"Then I suppose," Maggie conceded, "that we must wait for the next small crisis to occur on its own."

And this plan of the unplanned was solidified with competent nods of knowing ladies all around.

# Forty-Four

THE NEXT SOCIAL event of the summer season occurred thanks to the encouragement of a most unlikely person: Noah Bellwood. The sullen youth, forever lamenting his lack of Byronic abandon, had resolved to improve himself. It was confidence he felt sure that he was lacking, but not just any confidence. Specifically, he desired more confidence at cards. So he proposed to his companions, and then his mother, that it might be a good idea for the inhabitants of Langley Hall to host a small supper and card party. The suggestion was heartily and wholly agreed upon. The logistics of execution, however, proved somewhat difficult.

For one thing, when surveying the stock of formal plate in Langley Hall, they found only nine full settings—each in need of a thorough cleaning. When presented with the idea of hosting such an event, their housekeeper, Mrs. Elsie Downs, grumbled prodigiously. She huffed about the inconvenience that a dinner for nine would put on the small staff of Langley Hall. She said over and over that none of the servants were prepared for events of such high protocol as an informal dinner and card party.

Such protestation might have spelled the end of their meager planning, but Hudson would not allow the plan to be abandoned. It had taken him only a moment to fully comprehend the benefits and opportunities of an evening with Diana in such close company. So, it was Hudson who went to Elizabeth's house, hat in his hand like a solicitor of missionary funds, and asked if she might lend one or two footmen to make the event possible.

Elizabeth's vanity was fully gratified by Hudson's acknowledgement of her talent for hosting. She was all too happy to oblige his request for assistance. However, when she suggested they might move the card party to Eastbey Abbey and expand the invitation to scores of further guests, from his hasty reluctance she divined that his desire was for a purposefully small party.

It was Captain Tanders, discussing the requests of the young man that night in Elizabeth's chambers, who suggested that the hosting of a successful party might be the confidence boost the boy needed to work up the courage to propose to Diana. Thus, Elizabeth took a very restrained and supportive approach to her assistance of Mr. Birch. This restraint, Constance remarked, was remarkable.

The party was planned for eight attendees. The four of the Langley Hall tenants, Lady Elizabeth Dormer, Constance, the Reverend Samuel Astley, and Diana.

The omission of Benjamin and Maggie was a situation of long consideration. It was communicated to the Howards by Elizabeth very delicately to avoid giving offense. In addition to the lack of plate and chairs, it was Hudson's design that the two card tables should be divided by age. To his mind, two persons in the middle of young and old would only add confusion. However, no great explanation was needed. Benjamin and Maggie were all too happy to be excluded. They longed for another evening alone, dining tête-à-tête and feeling free to luxuriate in their mutual adoration all over the house, not just in their private quarters.

The date of the party was settled for a Friday night, and invitations were accepted by all intended.

~

By now, the papering and reupholstering projects were well underway in the Wuster Park estate. The whole house smelled of glue. More than once, a room would need to be suddenly vacated to make way for the workmen and craftspeople making alterations to it. In this state of slight disarray, the Howard household found ample reason for being away from home in the pursuit of interests and comfort. Benjamin resumed his regular attendance at the mill offices, sorting through the papers as the sounds of the clacking looms rattled in the background. Diana and Maggie drove out in the carriage or rode on horseback every day to call on Elizabeth and Constance. There, Diana would be set to some task, and the remainder of the party would vaguely supervise.

Her skills in fancy needlework had improved. She was able to add to the decoration of her own wardrobe when instructed. Despite Elizabeth's bonnet-trimming tutelage, she still lacked the sartorial instinct that inspires other young women to continually make and remake their outfits afresh. Her watercolors were still sloppy, but none of her companions felt the need to criticize her soggy creations, for her enjoyment of the process was obvious. Her French language skills were limited to basic greetings, the days of the week, and the colors of Elizabeth's ribbon collection. They might have tried to improve this further, but it was discovered that Hudson's knowledge of French was equally sparse.

Sometimes, when they spent the day at Elizabeth's house, Captain Tanders would play music for them. Dancing lessons would commence, with Maggie playing the lead. But the summer air hung heavy in their little valley, and it was equally likely that they would spend an afternoon lazily fanning themselves as they took turns reading aloud.

The Reverend Samuel Astley, having been told of Diana's scholarly deficiency, lent to her a large atlas that had been a gift from Elizabeth. Some days, Maggie would instruct her young charge to pick a page from the great book and study it. Sometimes she would be quizzed about the page. Other times, she would go to bed without having told anyone what she had or had not learned that day.

When given the choice of what to read, Diana had discovered two books in the Howard library to be of especial interest. One was a large book of botanical engravings, hand colored and fascinating to the horticulturally inclined. The other was "*Théorie et Traité de Jardinage*" which contained numerous diagrams of formal French garden designs, but unfortunately no English names for the plants contained therein.

Such was to be the extent of Diana's education, it seemed, for no other masters had ever been sent for or secured. With such a prospect as Hudson Birch, what need was there?

# Forty-Five

On the morning of the Langley Hall card party, there remained just one thing left to secure. This mission sent Hudson out alone on his horse to New Glenbury. It was the search for suitable wine. The Langley Hall cellars were empty, of course. In the name of economy (long since abandoned and unneeded in every other regard), Mrs. Bellwood did not approve of taking wine with meals when it was just family dining at home. So, off to the small wine merchant's shop in New Glenbury Hudson rode. In this wine merchant's shop, he encountered Benjamin.

Benjamin had come to get a bottle of Spanish wine. Maggie had mentioned her enjoyment of a specific bottle after a late afternoon visit to Eastbey Abbey. Tonight, since Diana would be at the Langley Hall card party, Benjamin wanted to treat Maggie to an especially romantic evening. The paperhanging in Wuster Park had been completed the day before. Now only the upholsterers remained, needing another week or so to complete the redecoration.

Benjamin had instructed Mrs. Rollins that the evening was to have minimal intrusions by staff. As a result, the ever-industrious woman had organized a servant outing to a New Glenbury assembly. Only she, the cook, and a few of the more essential or disinterested staff would stay in to oversee dinner for the Howards. On such a special occasion as a quiet house and a room to themselves, Benjamin felt it was only fitting that they should have a special bottle of wine to enjoy.

Seeing each other at the wine shop, both men looked suddenly rather embarrassed. It was as if they each felt they should not be discovered there. Then, recalling that they were both men of the world and of an age when drinking a glass of wine with dinner is no shameful secret, they both adopted an overconfident posture to disguise their own discomfort.

"For your card party tonight?" Benjamin asked in a tone of studied casualness.

"Yes. We don't typically have wine with meals. I say, not that I don't have wine with meals. I do, when I'm at home. But then, the Langley Hall cellars are, well . . . empty."

"Oh yes, I had heard they didn't have many comforts left there for you."

"I say, it's been very comfortable, certainly. In other ways, no. Yes. You know?"

Hudson remonstrated himself inwardly for his jumbled and rambling answers. Benjamin loomed in his imagination as the ideal of a wealthy, well-traveled country gentleman. Hudson was in awe of the way Mr. Howard seemed to perfectly balance his interests in trade with his position in the community. Hudson aspired to be like him one day.

Benjamin, on the other hand, felt like a stodgy old duffer talking to the fresh-faced boy from London. He was wracking his brain for droll things to say and feeling very anxious about his own out-of-fashion slang. He remembered his own mind at twenty and how the married men of his acquaintance had seemed so dull. He remembered how his friends at his clubs had scorned the attempts of older men at fitting in with the bachelor set.

"Do you expect a good party? Good-sized party, I mean."

"I say, yes we do. Well, no. I mean, there will be eight. We have two card tables. So, it's perfect," Hudson stammered. Then, remembering that Benjamin and Maggie were not invited, he bumbled forward with "But I am, I mean . . . I do wish that we had more card tables. But then, the dining table at Langley has only the ten seats and just nine sets of plate. We could have, I mean, we *might* have borrowed some but I think that Noah and Ellis . . . I think they had an idea for . . . it was not my design."

Before the young man could stammer himself into a deeper pit of insecurities and confusion, Benjamin spared him the trouble by expressing his own happiness at the evening's prospects.

"We've had so many craftspeople in and out with the redecorations, you know. My wife and I are just looking forward to a quiet night at home."

He said this and then felt himself to be as ancient as a grandfather—a quiet night at home, indeed.

To Hudson, this man's cool aloofness to the pleasures of society only expressed an admirable sophistication. Clearly, the company of a card party was beneath such a fine man. Hudson hoped that he, too, would one day be grand enough to eschew such frivolities. That was what it would mean to be a gentleman, he thought.

Turning his attention back to his errand, Benjamin requested one bottle of the wine Maggie had mentioned. Then, thinking that this singular order might make him look dull and miserly, he signaled for the merchant to bring three more bottles. Hudson, not wanting the elder cousin and temporary guardian of his dear Diana to think him some sort of lush, ordered just two bottles of wine. To this small order Benjamin raised an eyebrow, which threw Hudson into uncertainty.

At last, Hudson asked Benjamin if he could recommend a certain number of bottles for a small card party. Four was the recommended number. So, in some confusion, Hudson ordered four more bottles. Benjamin had no desire to appear as a censure to the youth, and he departed quickly before the math of libations could be further muddled. Each man left the other's company feeling certain that he was now regarded as a great fool.

# Forty-Six

DIANA AND MAGGIE were each looking forward to the night's activities. In the hours leading up to Diana's departure for the card party, the two cousins played lady's maid to each other. Dresses were selected with care. Hair was coiled and coiffed, buttons were buttoned, and laces were laced. They each did their best to look especially fresh and pleasant for their evening amusements. Maggie even anointed Diana with a few drops of her French perfume.

Blushing at the splendor of it all, Diana was dressed in one of her new London dresses. It was a fine dark green with yellow trim and clusters of small ribbon flowers adorning her shoulders and breast. Maggie wore her newest evening gown, a light-blue satin shimmering with white ribbon work. When Diana's hair had been secured with a tortoise comb and Maggie's gloves had been buttoned around her wrists, the two cousins surveyed each other with satisfaction.

"I imagine you're excited to go to a party without your cousins tonight."

"No."

"No?"

"Well, I suppose I'm excited for the party. But I'm nervous, too."

"You'll be fine. It's a nice, casual card party and you'll have Constance and Elizabeth to look after you."

As if on cue, Mrs. Rollins now knocked on the door. Waiting a moment, she poked her head in to announce that Lady Dormer had arrived to pick up Miss Huxley in her carriage. The supposedly nervous Diana bounced down the stairs and out the front door without so much as a backwards glance. Once she was gone, Maggie felt a sudden pang at her departure. She had an urgent impulse to chase after the girl and impart a million small warnings followed by a million encouragements. But she knew that the best she could do for Diana was to let her go without fuss so that she might not give in to worry about her first flight from the nest without her cousin by her side.

It was as Maggie stood on the landing, watching the lanterns of Elizabeth's carriage recede over the landscape that Benjamin first saw her. When she looked up at him on the stairway above her, the sudden rush of sentiment he felt nearly caused him to tumble down the stairs. His obvious startled stumble caused them both to laugh. They were laughing, arm in arm, when they entered the candlelit hall to enjoy their romantic dinner alone.

Benjamin was delighted by the cheerful chatter of his wife, and Maggie was touched that Benjamin had gone out of his way to get the wine she had so offhandedly mentioned. The couple was having such an agreeable time relishing the rare quiet of their expansive home that they were quite surprised to find, when their meal concluded, that they had already consumed one of the four bottles of wine. As they rose from their seats at the table, they found they were quite tipsy. Off to the drawing room they went.

Feeling that tea would be just the thing to restore their composure, they waited for Mrs. Rollins to bring the tray.

To break the silence, Maggie began, "I don't know if you feel this way, but I must say I am very pleased that we didn't need to go with Diana tonight. Don't mistake me, I find our time with the Langley Hall party almost invariably agreeable, but you know it's a bit . . ."

"Wearisome?" Benjamin prompted.

"Yes, exactly."

"I know what you mean. I chanced upon Mr. Birch this afternoon at the wine merchant. It was just, oh I don't know, painful. As if I don't know how to talk to his set anymore. He feels almost foreign to me."

"I feel that way about the older ladies, too. Constance and Elizabeth have been so kind to me these long months, and I do value their friendship. But I can't help feeling that they look down on me a little."

"Maybe the way we look at Diana is the way they look at you?"

"I know. I do see that. I just feel I'm not ready to be quite so old, old as in wearing a flannel cap and complaining about rheumatism."

"Or I, falling asleep reading the paper by a fire or feeling too stiff to ride a hunter."

"We're not that old."

"No, not yet."

"But we will be."

"Yes."

As the couple sat and pondered this, Mrs. Rollins arrived with the tea. After filling their cups and taking a few sips, Maggie spoke up again.

"Getting older is not so bad."

"Oh yes. Much better than the alternative, you know."

They sipped their tea and pondered that dark alternative for a few moments. Then Benjamin offhandedly asked if Maggie would like him to fetch another bottle of wine. She affirmed, and so he did. When they had fresh glasses in hand, they raised them in a quiet toast. Then they sat quite close together on the sofa, sipping and smiling at each other in the dancing candlelight.

~

At the card party, things were going better than most had anticipated. Constance was especially surprised, having very little faith in either the residents or the staff at Langley Hall to host any event that could be described as smooth and easy. She had remarked on this point to the reverend on their ride over.

"These tradespeople can gather all the wealth around them as well as any family in the peerage. But they never seem to get the easy, unaffected manners, that casual elegance of a nonchalant deportment, that so defines the truly highbred of the country."

The reverend owned that he did not often notice such things. When presented, as he was for the remainder of their carriage ride, with numerous examples both literal and literary for his consideration, he eventually conceded and pronounced his wife to be quite right indeed.

Constance was to be surprised, though. The combination of Elizabeth's gentle assistance and Mr. Birch's earnest best efforts combined to create an atmosphere of ease and elegance. Guests and residents alike at Langley Hall found themselves on an unavoidable course to having a good time. Dinner was simple, hearty country fare consisting of several birds the boys had shot that week. The transition to the drawing room after dinner felt automatic and unaffected, simply because the boys and their mother made this transition so often that its action felt habitual and unstudied. Indeed, in the comfort of their usual surroundings, all the Langley party seemed more relaxed than they had been in the homes of their neighbors. The shabby old hall felt quaint and genteel, like a lightly neglected hunting lodge in some remote county spot, visited sparingly but enjoyably for a few short weeks every other year.

Diana looked beautiful in her green dress. Greeting her in their familiar jest, Hudson was eager and attentive to her needs from the moment she arrived. But he never neglected his self-appointed role as host to his other guests. Not long after their meal, the card tables were set up in the drawing room and the whole of the party settled down to play.

~

Back in the drawing room of Wuster Park, Maggie and Benjamin were now very drunk. They did not know this, not at first. Keeping the wine bottle handy by the divan, they had no need to rise from their seated positions. If they had, such an action would have sent their heads swimming. Instead, they only noticed how considerably warm it was in the room and how delightfully amusing their own conversation had become. They were just wrapping up an especially droll series of imitations based lightly on the prodigious awkwardness of Hudson and Diana's dialogue. Each of them had adopted the role of one of the main characters. It had gone something like this:

"Well, I say. I do say. Indeed I do. And, I say: say I do, Diana?"

"The birds in the trees there are the purple lark finch which always sings at spring mornings when there's going to be rain."

"Oh, you don't say? I say!"

And the couple dissolved into a fit of laughter. To any uninebriated observer, the humor would have seemed a bit lacking. But with the help of the wine, Benjamin and Maggie discovered themselves to be wonderful wits.

When their laughter subsided and Maggie took the handkerchief from her eyes once more, her gaze met Benjamin's and her smile became a shy look.

"Benjamin, I think I am quite drunk."

"Yes, I'd say you certainly are."

"And you're not?"

Benjamin considered this at some length, then turned to Maggie. "What were we talking about?"

"You *are* drunk."

"Oh yes, I believe I am."

"Did I ever tell you about the first time I had too much to drink at a party?"

Benjamin turned to Maggie in eager rapture, his mouth hanging open in a wide smile of anticipation. She began.

"Well, I was young and just out. It was London, springtime. I had on this ugly orange dress my sister picked out. Mother and Father were playing lottery tickets, which they never usually do, I have no idea why they were—but it doesn't matter. I had a glass of champagne, which was fine because I was allowed one glass of wine with dinner.

Then Joseph Grimbies gave me a glass of punch, and it was so tasty that when I finished it, I asked for another and then I drank that."

"Oh, punch at a party can be deadly! Deadly!"

"It was, of course! I had no idea. I was used to tea punches, but this was . . . well, this was not that."

"No, otherwise there would be no story."

"Exactly."

There was a long pause.

"So then what happened?" Benjamin prompted.

"What?"

"What happened after you had all the punch?"

"I was drunk."

"And what happened?"

"Nothing. I sat down. Oh! No, that's not true. I spilled a plate of food on my dress."

At this, Benjamin broke into a riotous peal of laughter that quickly infected Maggie.

When their giggling subsided, Benjamin sagely observed, "One very good thing about getting older is being better able to control oneself under the influence of alcohol."

"Oh yes, much better," Maggie said with a hiccup.

~

At the card table where Noah, Ellis, Diana, and Hudson were muddling through whist, the real occupation was conversation. The table of chaperones was proving to be unexpectedly lively. Constance Astley and Lady Elizabeth were both players of equal skill and significant competitive spirit who rarely had the opportunity to play whist. So at that table, the games were played fast and with a great deal of energy. This left the younger people to speak quite openly without interruption.

At first, Hudson and Ellis and Noah had spoken at length about life in town and the many amusements it afforded. With stories of grand entertainments and illustrious persons, Hudson hoped that he could impress Diana with his own significance. But she sat silent. Her expression faded from amused curiosity to general incomprehension. Finally, after another failed bid at name recognition from Hudson, her face showed a marked dejection so potent as to make the boys actually uncomfortable.

The realization that he, Hudson Birch, knew more of society than his highborn object of affection gave no small personal gratification to the vanity of that young man. It was with more pride than surprise that Hudson came to see the truth in Noah's assessment of the girl's position in society. Inwardly, his heart thrilled at the idea that Diana might benefit more from his offer of marriage than he by her acceptance.

Reaching the conclusion of this line of thought, Hudson considered himself very gracious to change the conversation to a subject more agreeable to the young lady. There was an upcoming fair to be held in the wide meadow just north of the New Glenbury market lane, and at its mention Diana became reanimated.

There followed much speculation by the group about what kind of activities and displays they might find at the fair. None of them had ever been to a country fair before, and their collective knowledge of its proceedings was based on secondhand descriptions from daily papers and chatty neighbors. During this discussion, it was noted (with no small satisfaction by the male members of the youths' card table) that they had now consumed two whole bottles of wine.

"I tell you," Noah said, "one of the best things about getting older is getting a better handle on what a man can and can't drink, you know?"

"I say, you're right about that," Hudson intoned. "I remember the first time you ever—"

"Oh, don't tell this story!" Noah broke in.

"Why not? I say, it's a—"

"It's embarrassing!"

"All the more reason. I say, Diana, do you want to hear the story about how Noah once had so much to drink he broke Lady Canstell's inkwell and ruined three pairs of gloves trying to clean it up?"

Before Diana could answer, Ellis cut in, "Well you've just told the whole thing, Hudson."

"I say, I guess I did. Damn."

As this oath slipped out of his mouth unbidden, he looked to Diana in mild horror. She looked at him. Surprise and shame were already coloring his complexion. A thousand "pardon me" sentiments were welling up in his eyes. And she laughed—not a long laugh, but just a huff of humor and the shake of her head, as if to say, "Oh, you silly boy." Hudson lost himself for a moment in the dizzying rapture of her approval.

The card party proceeded, but Hudson was adrift in an overwhelming certainty that Diana was just the type of good-humored, easygoing, unfussy girl that he liked best of all in the world. His ecstatic admiration drove him to distraction.

~

In Benjamin and Maggie's bedroom, the candles were burning low in their holders as the couple stumbled through their evening toilette with some distraction. Maggie was telling Benjamin what Hudson had said to Captain Tanders about his feelings for Diana in moments of peril. She shared how the ladies had all resolved that since no crisis could be safely manufactured, they would just have to wait for the organic arrival of one to save the day and secure the marriage.

For his part, Benjamin was laughing along. At first, he had considered the matchmaking to be an idle pastime of his wife and her friends. It had seemed like the type of gentle meddling that could not produce any real results. Now, eager as he was to see his young cousin happily settled outside his house (but not wishing to send her back to her own home which, from the limited descriptions they had been given, was wholly undesirable), he felt that there was real good in setting her up with the perfectly agreeable and eligible Hudson Birch.

It was only after the couple got into bed that Benjamin alighted upon an idea, which he soon shared with Maggie.

"A carriage trip is just the thing you need, I think."

"A carriage trip?"

"Yes, some sort of longish overnight journey to somewhere interesting."

"You think we should take Diana away from the neighborhood for a few days?"

"No, I think you should plan a trip for everyone to go on together because there's sure to be some crisis along the way."

"How can you be certain?"

"Have you ever once in your life heard someone describe a carriage journey that did not include some minor catastrophe?"

Maggie had not. Indeed, the longer she thought about it, the more she realized the profound wisdom in Benjamin's suggestion. It was a perfect solution. She could have kissed him, and so she did.

When Diana arrived home that night, she was surprised that neither of her cousins was awake to greet her. She was not home particularly late, though the moonless sky had plunged the world into the inky darkness of an early night. Mrs. Rollins discreetly disguised the truth about their tipsy tête-à-tête and hinted that the couple had retired early with headaches as she efficiently helped Diana out of her dress and jewelry before locking up the remainder of the house.

If Maggie had been awake to see her cousin, she most certainly would have noticed the glow of gladness in her eyes.

# Forty-Seven

AFTER HIS SUCCESS at the card party, Hudson once again felt that his impending union with Diana was inevitable. Once again, he said as much to his friends in an after-breakfast ride through the woods. Once again, they each concurred with the assessment. Only Noah offered a caveat in saying, "Unless, of course, she's a terrible snob. You know, one of those types who think a family crest is worth more than any money in the bank."

"I don't think she's like that," Hudson said.

"No! She's a gentle, happy girl," Ellis said in her defense. "I just know she and Melissa are going to get along, even if Melissa's father is just a wine merchant. They both know such an awful lot about fruit."

When no one disagreed with this assessment of the compatibility of the ladies, Ellis then pivoted the conversation entirely to his Melissa. Her letters had begun to arrive less frequently, each one shorter than the last. His worry at this development was all-consuming, and there was little talk of anything else for the rest of the day.

Just over the hill at Eastbey Abbey, Elizabeth and Captain Tanders were having their first and last argument. It often went like this for Elizabeth, though it had been many years since such scenes had played out in her sitting room. For a time, after her husband's

death, she had entertained a small series of male traveling companions or house guests. Always, they appeared under the flimsy guise
of some subservient position—estate manager, drawing master, Italian translator—or of being some distant cousin. No matter how the
relationship started, it always came to an end when the man in question pushed for a place of more permanent significance in her life.

In her younger years, she had been *nearly* tempted into accepting
an offer of marriage from a man acting the part of her estate manager. He had been a kind, sensible person of exceptional personal
charm. Elizabeth still sometimes read his letters, which she kept tied
up in a black ribbon in the secret chamber of her writing desk. But
the knowledge that accepting his proposal meant sacrificing her full
financial independence and ceding over her hard-won fortune was,
at length, unthinkable. So was Captain Tanders' offer.

It was easy for Elizabeth to say no to his request that he might be
hired on as stable manager. She was growing tired of his perpetual
company. His lovemaking and saucy compliments were certainly enjoyable, and she thought with a small pang that it was a pity he had
never had occasion to write her a letter. Then, thinking longer about
the subject, she realized she was not actually sure if the man was fully
literate. This was of no importance. She did not want his company
any longer. So, she bickered with him as a prelude to his dismissal.
She did not need to bicker with him, but it felt more dignified to
argue first rather than just send the man packing with cold calculation.

For his part, Captain Tanders didn't seem surprised by the turn in
her spirits. In truth, he had known the night before when he broached
the subject of the stable manager position and saw the little frown dart
across Elizabeth's face. Privately, he had already secreted a few small
items into his trunk and was planning on inquiring with the post driver
in town about any news of his since departed band mates.

When Diana and Maggie came to call that afternoon, the somewhat subdued Captain Tanders informed the younger girl that she
could now consider the borrowed flute to be her own. He told her
to think of it as a gift. He knew she would soon be supplied with a

better one, and probably a better flute master, too. But he felt sure that when the candlesticks were discovered missing, his kindness to the young lady would be a noted point in his favor and a point against calling a bailiff.

Captain Tanders calculated correctly that Elizabeth wouldn't begrudge him some candlesticks and a few of the plated snuffboxes that littered the house. When she let him know that night that it would be his last in her house, she was generous in spirit and in spending. She sent him away with a full purse and secured from him a promise to pay call if he was ever passing through New Glenbury again.

And just like that, the one-legged flute player of such good humor was gone from their lives. He took with him the secrets of his friends, their warmest wishes, and some candlesticks for good measure.

# Forty-Eight

A COUNTRY FAIR is always a lively event. The New Glenbury population was composed of only a handful of fine families, some independent farmers, a smattering of shopkeepers, and one hundred or so factory folk from the Howard Linen Mill. While these people saw some of each other in town and in church each week, the fair was one of those rare occasions that threw them all together at once. But what fun could there be in making polite conversation outdoors with the people you encountered every time you went out of doors anyway? Anyone who has been to a small county fair will tell you: plenty.

The tight-knit nature of a rural community shows its full advantage in the assembly of all citizens united in one place for one purpose. Because everyone knows or knows *of* one another, there is no standoffish shy reserve. As tenants and laborers don their sincerest manners, they feel free to greet their landlords and fine neighbors cheerfully—for at a small county fair, all are made equal in their pursuit of enjoyment.

On the day of the New Glenbury fair, the whole valley seemed to hum in excitement and pleasure. The summer was in glorious bloom, and the fields were freckled with wildflowers among the tall grasses. At dawn, the roads became a parade of the finest stock animals that the local farmers could boast. Whistling and waving, the farmers took their pigs, cows, and freshly washed sheep to compete for prizes and inspire the envy of their neighbors.

Amusements of all kinds had been erected in the field to the northeast of the New Glenbury market street. Swings and climbing poles for children were placed near traveling vendors' stalls. A cricket match was to be the chief amusement for the factory men who had no animals or vegetables of their own to display.

More than anyone else in Wuster Park, Diana had been looking forward to the fair. At dinner the night before, she had pressed Benjamin with questions to expand her limited knowledge of the goings-on of fairs. She explained that while there was a fair each autumn in a town near to Yansworth, her family had never attended. Therefore, her knowledge was gleaned from the discussions of neighbors and acquaintances. Benjamin and Maggie exchanged a few words that night in the privacy of their bedchamber about how odd it was that a family of so many children would never attend such a reasonable social event. But then what little they had heard about Diana's household was equally strange.

"I begin to suspect," Maggie said, "that Diana might not be telling us the whole truth about her life there. Surely at least there must be some exaggeration."

"Perhaps. But if it were all a story to keep us from sending her back, I imagine she'd tell us more, not less. You've said yourself how young girls are prone to dramatics."

"Quite right. Well, she is a bit of an enigma. Perhaps before long, though, she will not need our protection."

When dawn broke on the day of the fair, Maggie felt desperately unwell. Her head was pounding, and her eyes and nose both produced a stream of watery discharge. After getting halfway dressed, she let out an enormous sneeze that splattered her dress with mucus. It would have been funny if she had been alone, but having her husband as witness was supremely mortifying. She begged him to quit the room and send Mrs. Rollins.

Mrs. Rollins was summoned, and the two women held brief

conference. Mrs. Rollins was not such an alarmist as to heed Benjamin's notions that a doctor should be fetched right away. She noted calmly that just yesterday, the hedges that flanked the perimeter of the house had begun to bloom. In fact, Maggie was not alone in her sniffling and sneezing. One of the housemaids, a youngish village girl named Tally, had awoken with the same symptoms.

Thus it was reluctantly agreed that Maggie, Tally, and Mrs. Rollins should stay home from the fair. Benjamin and the rest of the house staff would venture out for the day as planned. Diana was so excited by the allurement of the fair that she could not be delayed in her departure to lavish care on her poor cousin. She took only a few moments to visit, asking Maggie to judge her dress and hair for their comeliness. Then Diana skipped out of the room and down the stairs to wait for the carriage.

Off the Wuster Park party went, with all the servants following on foot after the carriage that conveyed Benjamin and the ecstatic Diana.

# Forty Nine

At the fair, Benjamin had intended to accompany Diana the whole day. Maggie specifically requested this attention to her cousin because she knew that Lady Elizabeth would not be in attendance, and Constance would be busy with parishioners. What Maggie had not anticipated, though, was how much individual attention Benjamin would receive. From the moment he alighted from his carriage, mill workers began to greet him. They wanted to introduce him to their families. They wanted him to take note of their entrances in the agricultural competitions. Benjamin was surprised to learn that several of his loomsmen were amateur horticulturists. Among them was a great passion for gourd growing, since the farming practice was largely passive, and the resulting crops both versatile and long lasting.

Soon Benjamin found himself swept along in a tide of social obligations. Diana could no longer be his chief concern. This was of no concern to Diana. After trotting alongside him for a half-hour, she broke away and happily wandered up and down the aisles of erected coops, cages, and pens, looking at all the fine livestock assembled. The women of New Glenbury were more than a little confused to observe the normally shy Lady Huxley speaking excitedly at some length with a pair of village girls her own age. She was admiring their two long-lopped rabbits, which she pronounced "uncommon fine and very good and fat," much to the satisfaction of their owners.

It was here, by the rabbits, that Hudson, Ellis, and Noah caught up with her. Right away, she made introductions between the village girls and the Langley Hall party, an event that confused all involved except Diana. Then, Hudson offered her his arm, and they set off to enjoy the fair as young people would.

To all four of these fair fairgoers, the scene was a bucolic delight exceeding expectations. Noah remarked how he had never imagined so many people lived adjacent to New Glenbury. Perhaps he considered all the soft rolling pasturelands to be the property of the sheep and cows that grazed upon them. Ellis was delighted by the antics of the local children, all rosy-faced and full of adventure. For some time, the quartet watched the maypole dancing before Hudson maneuvered their meandering to the stalls and carts of the traveling vendors.

The fair vendors were exactly the same sort one always finds at these small county fairs. There was the seller of tin rings, the baker of hot pies, the man promising a formula for youth which was actually a bottle of hair dye, and, of course, the fortune-teller. For what fair could ever be complete without a fortune-teller?

Outside the faded tent of the purveyor of future secrets, the small group debated who would be first to go in and have their fortune told. Diana alone was adamant in her refusal to partake. Noah and Ellis wondered if they might not go in together. They tried to, but Ellis soon emerged from the tent's murky depths, having been sent back out. There he sulked until Noah returned a short time later and twopence poorer. Before Noah could regale the whole group with his lately revealed destiny, Hudson plunged into the darkness of the tent and closed the flap behind him.

~

The fortune-teller's tent was very dark. Hudson stumbled as his eyes failed to quickly adjust. When at last he could make sense of the dark shapes around him, he spied the fortune-teller sitting on a large velvet cushion before a low wooden table. Over the table's surface lay an exotic cloth, held in place by fragments of unusual stones.

The fortune-teller's name was Ava. She was a German widow who enjoyed traveling. She spent her summers on tour of the English countryside, telling the same few fortunes for pennies enough to keep herself and her sister comfortable in their little apartment on Lemon Street in the German district of London. Ava didn't consider herself to be in possession of any remarkable gifts of foresight, but she was a keen observer of people. In addition to quick observation, she harbored a reluctant optimism. This made her pronouncements balanced enough in their tone that no matter the actual result of life, her predictions always held up upon reflection. Now, after nearly ten years of such a practice, she was also adept at dodging the trickiest questions of her patrons.

When expectant mothers asked if they were to receive a son or daughter, she would lay her hands on their swollen bellies and say, "Ah, but you will have many children, boys and girls . . ." and then change the subject to harvests, riches, and the misfortune of neighbors, subjects which people were always eager to hear more about.

Hudson fell outside of her usual clientele. She knew from the cut of his coat that he was from London. The tan of his face said he had been in the country some time already this summer. Inwardly, she resolved to warn him about a horse. This was always a safe bet with a man in his early twenties. Riding or betting, they were wary of horses, and it confirmed their suspicions to be warned against the animals.

"Who rides the bay mare?"

She asked as soon as he sat down on the pile of pillows across the table. His eyes grew wide, and his mouth hung open; he seemed so startled, she wondered if he wasn't a little slow.

"Diana," he whispered.

The fortune-teller needed no special gifts to see that whoever Diana was, this young man was in love with her. She drew a breath, preparing her speech about faith and full moons.

"You love her," she began.

Before she could say another word, Hudson interrupted with his astonishment at her so rightly knowing the situation. Indeed, the young man was quite convinced that he sat in the presence of a being of supernatural divination, and so he seized the opportunity to ask the question that was burning in his heart.

"How should I ask her to marry me? I say! Will she have me? Will she say yes?"

This was not the first time the fortune-teller had been asked this question. It was a common one, but not an easy one to answer. Many a long winter evening, Ava sat with her sister by their small hearth and talked through possible answers. What could be said which might be heard as encouragement but not a promise? From her time traveling the county fair circuits, Ava had heard stories from other fortune-tellers. Jilted lovers were always the angriest of clients. Some, it was said, might even be angry enough to follow a fortune-teller from one fair to the next, plaguing them with threats of violence or religious aggression.

To buy herself a little time to consider her answer at length, Ava lowered her head, closed her eyes, and spread out both of her palms on the table as if she were drawing answers from it like a tree draws water from its roots.

Should she recite the poem about spring flowers well-tended? Should she predict a dark obstacle (usually hinted at being a disapproving family member) that would need to be overcome before victory could be assured? She had used the poem already today, so that seemed ill-advised. Ava took a deep breath, and Hudson mimicked her in his anticipation.

"You have searched for a long time, but only recently have you found what you are looking for. The looking has not been wasted. You have learned many things along the way, and they will serve you as you begin the next chapter very soon."

She paused and looked at the young man from under her eyelashes. He was nodding, but not smiling.

"You have long felt that you are not enough, but I see that you possess all that is needed for a lifetime of happiness."

This was obvious, Ava thought, because the cost of this young man's boots would keep her and her sister in meat and coal for a year. The young man was now starting to relax. His nods rocked his body forward like a child anticipating a bowl of sweet milk porridge.

"It will not be long now before you have all you desire."

"Well, I say!" Hudson exclaimed as he clapped his two hands together.

Knowing when to stop talking was as important as knowing what to say. So even though she had not yet come to the heart of her prediction, Ava stopped her recitation and said, "Twopence, good sir."

Hudson happily paid and left the tent in a flurry of self-assured delight.

# Fifty

BACK AT WUSTER Park, Maggie hauled her tired body out of her bedchamber and shuffled down to the kitchen. Expecting to find Mrs. Rollins, she instead found Tally the equally sniffling maid helping herself to thick slices of bread with butter while clutching a damp handkerchief to her red nose. The two shared an uncomfortable laugh before Tally offered to bring up tea and luncheon for the lady if she pleased. Maggie approved this plan, for she did not wish to embarrass herself bungling about in the kitchen in front of a parlor maid.

So back upstairs she shuffled. It was just as she settled down into a comfortable chair in the sunshine of a wide window in the south drawing room that she heard a knock at the front door. No one ever knocked at the front door. If one came to the front door, it was because they were expected. And if one was expected, then one had no reason to knock. Peddlers, knife sharpeners, and other such transient tradesmen who were known to knock always had the good sense to knock at the lower door around the back of the house.

This knock at the front door was singular. Maggie, as she slowly moved to ring the bell for Tally or Mrs. Rollins, could only imagine that it must be one of Elizabeth's foreign servants who had come with a message, not knowing the protocol for delivering it.

She rang the bell in the drawing room. Then she listened closely to the sounds of the empty house, trying in vain to ascertain if Tally was coming up from the kitchen. She heard the knocking at the front door again. Gripped with a sudden, indistinct feeling of foreboding, she would not wait any longer for someone else to get the door. She blew her nose on her handkerchief, smoothed her dress skirts, checked her reflection in the hall glass, and opened it.

There on the threshold stood a young man. Two horses were hitched at the post behind him. The young man's face was tawny and freckled from the sun, his hair a sandy mop. His clothes proclaimed him to be a farmer. He did not look familiar to Maggie, but she assumed he must have come from the fair to deliver a message.

"Good morning, what is your business?" Maggie asked, hurriedly. She hoped it would not be bad news.

"Begging your pardon, ma'am, I am come to see about the Lady Diana Huxley."

"She is not here. Who are you?"

The young man's face fell. "Pardon me, ma'am, is this Wuster Park place, then?"

"It is."

"Then where has she gone? Have they sent her somewhere else?"

"What is your name, sir?"

"I am Charlie McFaden. I come from Yansworth to see about Miss Lady Diana Huxley. Do you know her?"

Maggie looked at the young man before her with new consideration. This must be the son of the farmer who taught Diana how to ride. This *handsome* young man . . . Maggie reeled with the rush of conjecture that clouded her thoughts. Could *this* be the reason Diana's family was so eager to send her far from home?

He was tall and well built. He could not be more than twenty years old. He was handsome. He possessed large blue eyes that looked, even in that moment, like they would rather be smiling. His bearing was warm, his speech soft but not meek. Maggie could see at once that he was exactly the sort of kind country farmer who might delight in teaching a pretty girl about trees and flowers and nursing sick birds and lame dogs.

With a greater softness this time, Maggie answered Charlie.

"Lady Diana is my cousin. She is not here now. She is at the fair in New Glenbury. But she will be back. Will you come inside?"

"Oh no, miss, ma'am, madam, m'lady. No, thank you. I shall go on to the fair and see about her there."

He was just turning away when Maggie caught his elbow and insisted politely but firmly that he should come inside first. Charlie looked uncomfortable with the prospect, but acquiesced.

Inside the front door, Charlie took in the spectacle that was the entrance hall. In this moment, Tally emerged from the kitchen staircase with a tea tray. She leapt back in startled astonishment at the strange man, nearly spilling the tray's contents before Maggie could assure her it was all right. Maggie led Charlie to the smallest of their receiving rooms. She saw that the sight of the hall was distracting to him. She hoped that the relative closeness of the blue drawing room would be less unnerving.

Charlie took a long time to get comfortable. After sitting, he stood again and looked all around him. Then he took in the views from the windows before finally returning to his seat and asking, "Do you know when Miss Diana will be back, ma'am?"

"I am expecting her and the rest of the party to be back before dinner."

At this, Charlie once again stood and tried to take his leave. "It is not yet noon," he said, "and I wish to see Diana presently."

"On what matter do you wish to see her? Is her family well?"

"Her family? Yes, they are well. I want to see that *she* is well. I heard she was given a position here. A maid. And it is a fine house here, I can see. But I want to see that she is well."

"I can assure you she is."

Charlie stared hard at Maggie now. His gentle blue eyes took an air of appraisal. Under his intense silence and this close scrutiny, Maggie continued speaking.

"You have been misinformed, however. Diana is not a maid. She is my cousin. She is here as my guest."

"Your guest?"

"Yes. She has been a guest here for nearly . . ."

"It has been four months since she left Caldflett Castle."

"Ever since she left there, then."

"And she is your guest?"

"She is not my prisoner, if that is what you are suggesting," Maggie said, bristling at this young man's guarded tone and pointed questions.

"Then I should just like to see her right away, and I shall not wait here longer. I thank you."

"Wait, before you go, sit and tell me—Diana has told me about you."

This last sentence arrested Charlie in his hurried exit, and he now met Maggie's eyes with a small smile.

"She has told you about me?"

"Not very much."

"Well, I imagine there is not much to tell. I am only her neighbor."

"Yes, but I know you taught her how to ride. Or, your father did, I think. And so you probably . . . spent much time together," Maggie said delicately.

"Aye, we did. She's a fine rider, too. She's been ever so good helping out with me and my ma and pa," he said without delicacy or deception.

"So, you have come to . . . ?" The unfinished question hung in the air between them. Maggie thought uncomfortably about the second horse hitched outside.

After a moment of quiet consideration, Charlie clarified.

"I have come to see that she is happy. If she is not . . . then I've come to take her back to Yansworth."

"Well, I assure you, Mr. McFaden, she is very happy here."

"She has told you this?"

"Yes, of course."

"I'm sorry, ma'am. But I should like to hear it from her." And for a third time, Charlie tried to quit the room, but Maggie called after him in some haste.

"Charlie! I think you should . . . I would like you to know . . . Diana has made many friends here in New Glenbury."

The genuine warmth of Charlie's smile at that sentence touched Maggie.

"She has? A good many friends? I hope some her own age. She was awful lonesome being always the oldest with her sisters."

"Yes, many friends. And . . . there is a man in the neighborhood, a man I think she is very fond of. And he is very fond of her. Do you see?"

Charlie looked down at his hands where he was turning his old, brown farmer's cap around by the brim.

"I see. You've got her earmarked for him, like a lamb to the butcher. Oh, I see very well."

His tone had the edge of a freshly sharpened plow.

"No! It is nothing so sinister as that. I believe she has real affection for him. She really likes him, I mean."

"I know what the word 'affection' means. I don't need speaking down to."

"Then I will say it plainly. I think she loves this man, and I am certain he loves her. If you care about Diana's happiness as you say you do, then I think the best thing you might do for her is leave. Do not linger to complicate her feelings."

"Complicate her feelings? She's just a girl! Not yet eighteen! Who is this man she supposedly loves after just four months away from home for the first time in her whole life? Some old lord looking for a spring chicken to sire his heirs? Some rich fellow willing to take her for nothing and talk down to her every day of her life? That can't be right, miss . . . ma'am. It can't be right. She is just a girl."

Maggie was startled by this sudden impassioned outpouring of words, and it took her a few seconds to arrange her thoughts into a reply.

"No," she explained finally, "he is not an old man. He is a young man. A good man. Not titled, but from a family of . . . good standing."

"Rich, you mean?"

"Yes."

"Rich as all this?" Charlie asked, gesturing around the room.

"Yes," Maggie said quietly.

Charlie lapsed into a spell of thoughtful silence before speaking again, this time in a low and slow voice of great consideration.

"I only want to know that she is happy. If you think this man will be good and kind to her, well then I suppose I've nothing to do but offer congratulations. But if she isn't happy . . . because I know that even a fine house like this, with all your land and servants, I know that is not all it takes to be happy, I do. Well, if she isn't happy . . ."

He trailed off, but just as Maggie was about to answer him, he started again, more to himself, seemingly, than to her.

"She always was a baron's daughter. It's right then that . . . I just want to know that she is happy. I only want to speak with her."

During his breaks of deliberation, Maggie had considered how best to navigate this difficult situation. Now she put her thoughts into action.

"You cannot see her today, but I will speak to her tonight. If she wants to see you, I will send for you. Now you must go. And you must not go to New Glenbury, for the inn will be full and I do not know that—"

"I understand. If you will give me your word, your word as a lady and as a woman, that you will tell her I am come in friendship to see about her—"

"Indeed, you have my word."

"Then I will go to the town west of here."

"Shrewsbern."

"Shrewsbern. And I will stay in an inn and wait for you to send for me tomorrow."

"*If* she wants to see you."

"*When* she wants to see me."

Charlie rose one last time from his chair, went to the door onto the main hall, and opened it. Tally toppled backwards at the action. It appeared that she had been "cleaning the keyhole" just a moment before. Charlie helped the girl to her feet and then he took his leave. Without exchanging a word, Maggie and Tally climbed to the top floor of the house as quickly as their phlegmatic breathing would permit. There they looked out the dormer-windows at the young man with his two horses. When he reached the road, he steered west to Shrewsbern and spurred the horses to a trot.

"I want you to stay here and watch the road. If you see him heading back towards New Glenbury, come tell me right away."

Tally was thrilled with this conspiratorial (and conveniently easy) occupation for her afternoon. While she worried for a while that she would be chastised for her eavesdropping, all of that seemed forgotten by the time Mrs. Rollins brought up luncheon to her sentinel spot. There, over a plate of cold tongue and potatoes, Mrs. Rollins asked that the girl repeat all she had heard and observed until she was certain that the information gleaned by the maid could not be enough to cause any real problems if it was repeated, as it surely would be, to the other staff of Wuster Park.

This task accomplished, Mrs. Rollins rejoined her mistress and did her best to make the lady as calm and comfortable as she could be while her anxious mind turned over the sudden and strange visit of the young farmer from the north.

# Fifty-One

Buoyed by his interpretation of the fortune-teller's foretelling, Hudson rejoined his friends and the dear Diana in spirits so high that even Ellis's eternal optimism was rendered dull in comparison. He listened rapturously and asked many urgent and ridiculous questions as Diana pointed out the fine features of the goats and pigs currently paraded in the ring for judgment. He bought sweet pies for a few young children and even danced the maypole, towering over his fellow dancers, not one of them more than ten years old.

He felt alive and free. The anxiety of uncertainty was lifted from him, and with it went all his reservation about the type of man he was meant to become. He was, he felt at last quite certain, to be a spry old country gentleman with a clever, industrious wife to run his estate. He saw an endless summer stretching before him with more maypoles and bleating goats and game birds roasting for dinner. And Diana, lovely Diana, the modest, beautiful daughter of a baron. She had come to rescue him from being just another man with a brand-new name and brand-new fortune. Never again would he find himself considering the waspish, ambitious girls of his own set.

The girls of his set, Hudson felt, would never understand gentility. They would spend their whole lives degrading the simple pleasures afforded by true refinement. They would practice instead that mock gentility, speaking harshly to the servants and adding up everyone's dinner bills at the end of a party the way his mother did. As he saw it now, every girl he had ever met before Diana had reminded him of his mother. But Diana was nothing like his mother. For this reason alone, he might have married her. That he should also be guaranteed happiness and success in his proposal, why, it was too much ecstasy to hold inside.

Already, he was thinking of their honeymoon. They would not go to the Continent. What would Diana want with the Continent? He knew she, too, would think the whole thing dreadful and daunting. Instead, they would travel the whole of the country to find the most dear, secluded spot: somewhere with plenty of shooting, and good soft downs for riding, and not too far from the seaside. . . . They would find the most perfect wild, free, and beautiful place, and there they would build their own estate, bigger than the ungenerous comforts of Langley Hall, but smaller than the overwhelming scope of Wuster Park.

It would have all the simple country charms of a cottage, but it must also have a billiards room. And there must be plenty of card tables. And there should be a big hall for dancing because they must have dances, at least two a year. The decorations would be modern and elegant, made of the best of everything so that no one visiting would ever mistake their station in the world. And just as Hudson was debating whether to locate the formal gardens to the north or south of this great, contradictory fictional estate, Diana's foot slipped on a slick patch of muddy earth, and she flew forward towards the ground.

Hudson caught her. Technically, he was already holding her by the arm as they were walking. As she slipped, her body twisted towards him, and he was obliged to put out his other arm. Thus, he caught her. He caught her around the waist, and he clutched her to him. She did not fall. She was safe. But Hudson's arm stayed longer and held her tighter than was strictly necessary, and then he was holding her longer than was even really appropriate. Some of the villagers cast sidelong glances at the pair, who had long since been abandoned by Noah and Ellis.

The moment was too much for Hudson. Feeling her soft, supple body against his, her breast pressed firmly and warmly upon him, it was all he could do to manage the words, "I say, Diana."

She thanked him, very demurely, and wriggled free from his close embrace before lowering her eyelids in the modest feminine fashion which smote his heart.

Hudson dropped to his knee. In fact, his knee landed in the exact spot of slippery mud that he had just rescued Diana from. But this was of no matter. Now there was just one thing left to do.

"Lady Diana Huxley, will you do me the greatest honor of becoming my wife?"

# Fifty-Two

THE WORLD FROZE. The air around them rung in silent vibrations. All the eyes of the New Glenbury villagers were drawn to them instantly. The young lovers had been the subject of so much gossip all summer that this obvious and public action could not have gone unnoticed. All the people of New Glenbury had seen Hudson and Diana frequently riding out together, strolling, and speaking at length after church or in town. Rampant speculation was fueled by the oft-shared observations of the staff at the great houses of the neighborhood, who overheard many conversations concerning the pair. So now, nearly all the village was following the story of the poor baron's daughter and the rich fishmonger's son. And here, in the warm summer sunshine of the county fair, they paused to witness what would become of this great romantic conspiracy.

The bleating of a sheep broke the spell of sudden silence. A ripple of laughter at the little lamb's timing only confirmed what Hudson and Diana felt in that moment, that everyone was watching and waiting for what might happen next.

And what did happen next?

Diana withdrew her gloved hand from his grasp on stunned instinct. Hudson's smile vanished.

"Diana?"

"I'm sorry," Diana said, quietly. "I don't think I understand you."

"What is there to understand? I'm asking you—"

"I think you are confused. Or it is a jest, isn't it?"

"A jest? Is that what I am to you?"

"I mean, you cannot be serious. Marriage with you—it is impossible."

"Impossible?"

"Hudson, don't be ridiculous."

Diana looked around her for an escape. Still on his knees, Hudson felt his great joy come crashing down around him, lighting a fire in his temples.

"Get up before people see—"

"You bitch."

His words came out like the snapping of a dry branch. A collective gasp and then a flurry of activity ensued as the citizenry tried in vain to pretend that they had not just witnessed this dramatic refusal. Having hastily made his way over to the site of the sudden spectacle, Benjamin was at last by Diana's side. Taking both her shoulders, he steered her away from this most mortifying situation and towards the carriage. Their hasty retreat was expedited as the entire crowd, in conspicuous inattention, parted before them like the Red Sea before Moses.

Hudson, stumbling further in the mud before being able to follow after them, began to shout.

"Diana! Wait! Diana, come back!"

When she did not turn back (no, not even before the carriage door closed behind her), his temper fully ignited.

Benjamin turned back on her behalf.

"Mr. Birch, you have nothing more to say to my cousin. I suggest you return at once to Langley—"

"Langley Hall be damned! Your cousin has . . . your cousin has . . . your cousin is a lying, stupid—"

Benjamin slapped him. The action startled both men and the whole of the village watching them. Then, before getting up onto the carriage box and driving the harnessed horses back to Wuster

Park, Benjamin turned and hissed to Hudson in a low voice.

"How dare you make such a display? I thought you were better than this. I thought you were a gentleman."

Benjamin wished that he could not hear what Hudson said next. But his shouts over the noise of the hastily departing carriage reached him easily.

"Not her! She never forgot what I am! She never forgot what my father is! She is saving herself for a duke, at least!"

And because Benjamin heard it, he knew Diana heard it, too.

# Fifty-Three

MAGGIE HEARD THE clatter of the approaching carriage and rushed outside onto the gravel entrance so she might speak with Diana directly. But when the carriage halted, the young girl burst from the box and flew past her cousin, into the house in an indomitable rustle of ribbons and skirt. Seeing immediately that something was wrong, Maggie thought first that, despite her instructions, Charlie McFaden had slunk unobserved to the fair. When Benjamin had tossed the reins of the carriage to a footman, who'd had the foresight to hop on the back of the carriage knowing he would be needed, Benjamin too clattered off the box with an unusual swiftness that startled Maggie.

"Benjamin, what has happened?"

"Oh, it was awful, Maggie. Really awful. We need to see to Diana right away."

The pair rushed into the house and up to the door of Diana's bedchamber. Finding the door locked was no small surprise. Maggie knocked at it determinedly.

"Diana, open the door. What has happened?"

From behind the great oak barrier, Diana's voice weakly permeated, obvious in its sorrow and tears. She begged that they would go away, and not ask her anymore about it.

For a moment, the couple stood on the threshold and debated

silently in an exchange of eyes. Should they call for a key and open the door against her will? Should they coax her into conversation through the barrier? At last, it was settled between them that giving the girl time and space would not be so bad. It would give the two of them time to regroup and decide their next moves.

Alone with her husband in the drawing room, Maggie plunged into conversation.

"What happened? What did Charlie do?"

"Hudson, you mean?"

"Oh yes, did Hudson and Charlie fight?"

"Who is Charlie?"

"The man Hudson fought with?"

"Hudson didn't fight any man!"

"Oh."

"Who is Charlie?"

"What happened at the fair?"

It took a long time for Maggie and Benjamin to untangle their knotted narratives. They recounted the events of the day individually and independently until all was known by each. It was thirsty work, and the arrival of the tea tin and urn (now cold) was evidence that no one belowstairs could draw themselves away from the gossip and suppositions brought on by their own uncovering of all the goings-on that day.

"So she must love this Charlie fellow then," Benjamin concluded. "For why else would she turn down a match with Hudson?"

"It looks that way. But a marriage with Mr. McFaden would do so little for her . . . so little for her family. And Hudson is as good a match as she might ever hope to achieve. I cannot believe he proposed. I suppose I expected him to do it soon. I was hoping for it. I just thought Diana was hoping for it, too."

"Maybe she will change her mind."

"She could never have him now, after what has passed. Such a display. Such a temper! How awful."

"He was very upset, it's true."

"More than very. I never heard of such behavior except in novels."

"Maybe that's the problem. These young people have only seen the world through those books. Maybe he thinks himself well and justified in his declarations."

Benjamin considered inwardly some of his own literarily inspired notions and actions, not without some embarrassment.

"Well, I hope not. I hope he comes to repent his actions very much and has the good sense to quit New Glenbury before morning."

# Fifty-Four

HUDSON WAS, AT that moment, in the process of quitting New Glenbury as quickly as possible. After his raucous remonstrance of Diana, Noah and Ellis had (with some difficulty) maneuvered their impassioned friend into his carriage. There they left him under the guard of the enlivened Mr. Downs. The old butler had not seen this much chaos since the Langford squire had gambled an entire dining set, lately inherited, on a horse race he had just decried as being not worth watching. Now Mr. Downs stood watchman and made knowing looks at all his friends as they passed by trying to get a look at the red-faced youth so contained.

By merciful providence and utter predictability, Mrs. Bellwood had managed to miss the startling events. Really, the whole scene had been over in a few short minutes, so it was not terribly surprising that she would miss it, her powers of observation being so limited. With the flimsiest of pretenses, she too was hustled into the carriage and whisked back to Langley Hall in near silence. Still, she must have sensed some odd energy in the coach, for, despite the silence of her traveling companions, she did not doze.

As Noah and Ellis ushered their mother into Langley Hall, Hudson took off towards the stable. There he mounted the only ready horse, an old Langley farm plodder with two white hooves and a soft mouth.

Without heeding for a moment the concerned calls of his friends, he galloped off and away from New Glenbury. The wind of his flight stung his eyes and gave further cause for the tears that there flowed.

He might have ridden all day and the rest of the night. He might have ridden all the way back to London. He might have done all these things had he felt more confident in his navigation and less ashamed of what he would have to tell his parents when he arrived unexpectedly home, covered in mud and dressed for a country fair. So he stopped instead at the next town over, Shrewsbern. He told himself it was just for a steadying pint and to inquire about directions. But the tavern at the Grey Swan Inn was such a fine and inviting place to drink in sorrow that he indulged that impulse at length instead.

Shrewsbern was a town of fickle fortune. It enjoyed none of the steady prosperity of its neighbor, New Glenbury. Instead, it had booms and busts of plenty and poverty largely tied to the price of wool. As a result, the town had a hard-worn feel about it, as if even in good times it was prepared for bad. The tavern at the Grey Swan was especially gloomy that day, as many of the regular patrons had gone to enjoy their drinks out of doors at the New Glenbury fair. This left only the cranky proprietor and a few grumbling old men who nursed their penny pitchers. Dark enough on the inside to need (but not have) candles burning during the day, the tavern was the perfect place for Hudson to hide from the world in his anger, shame, and regret.

It was nearly an hour and several pints of ale later that Hudson bothered to look about him. By then, his eyes had adjusted to the darkness, and his anger had fully given way to shame and regret. He wished desperately that Noah were there with him. He would have even settled for Ellis, provided he promised not to talk. However, he had instructed his horse be hitched around back, so unless his friends were actively inquiring about him, it was unlikely that he would be found. He did not feel well enough to go back to Langley Hall, and he quietly hoped that, after nightfall, he would be offered a room at the inn which would require no effort on his own part to secure.

Indeed, the youth was despondent. So depressed by his own actions, so certain in his unforgivable status, and so utterly lost to good society was Hudson, he felt sure that life as he knew it would be forever divided into before and after this very day, as long as he lived.

# Fifty-Five

IT IS NOT every day that one sees a rich young man splattered with mud crying in a dark tavern in a forgotten town.

Charlie McFaden, tired of anxiously pacing his small room at the Grey Swan, descended the uneven stairs to the dark tavern below in search of a meal and a drink. He noted the crying youth right away, but thought very little of him. However, over the course of eating his hearty stew and contemplating his glass of porter, he began to wonder about this unusual feature of the otherwise unremarkable tavern.

In a quiet exchange with the monosyllabic barkeep, he attempted to determine the regularity of this apparition. The barkeep's quick shake of the head told him that the young man was as mysterious and unusual to him as he appeared to Charlie. Charlie sat with this information for a while. On his second pint of dark oaty porter, he began to let his imagination assemble a narrative.

Perhaps, he supposed, this rich young man was the same rich young man who was going to make Diana his bride. Perhaps he was here in this bar weeping because Charlie's arrival and plans to return Diana to her home had foiled his ambition. The longer he observed the distraught patron and the more porter he consumed, the more likely this story seemed.

Charlie had been staring and thinking for quite some time when he noticed that the young man was now also looking at him. He felt a sudden wave of fear. What if he were to be shot? What if the young man blamed Charlie for his disappointment? Charlie knew that London gentlemen were always demanding satisfaction and shooting pistols at each other. Then he recalled that even if he, Charlie, had correctly determined the young man's identity, there was no possible way for the rich boy to have divined Charlie's—unless, of course, he knew where Charlie was staying. It occurred to him then that the rich young man might be here waiting to fight him. The only reasonable thing to do, it seemed, was retreat to his room and hope the door would hold fast if he were discovered.

But something in the forlorn young man's eyes made Charlie's compassion bold. So, in this boldness of spirit, he approached the young man at his solitary table and took a seat.

The sad young man was quite drunk. Charlie saw it as he sat down and the gentleman's eyes had trouble registering the movement with sufficient speed or clarity. His face also showed no malice, which was reassuring. However, Charlie himself was not free from the effects of drink. He realized, after settling into his seat, that he had not made any further plan of action. So, the two young men looked at each other in silence for some time while Charlie calculated what to do next. At last, he spoke.

"You seem to be having a rough go of it, eh?"

Hudson, overcome with a sudden wave of shame, realized that even in this dark, dreary place, he could not fully hide his sorrow. He dropped his head so suddenly and violently upon the table that Charlie thought the lad had fallen dead before him. When he saw that Hudson was drawing shuddering, sad breaths, he regained his own composure and began to speak in the low, soothing tones he employed when his horses were ailing.

"Whoa, hey now, you're all right. You're all right. Take it slow, there. You're all right."

Hudson lifted his head slowly, not even trying to conceal his tear-streaked face.

"What's the trouble, then?"

"I . . . I have lost all that is most dear to me."

Not very specific, Charlie regretted. He was forced to go out on a limb in his hopes of gaining the truth.

"Some girl, then?"

Hudson's face contorted into a mask of sorrow, and all he could do by way of answer was nod.

This must be the man, Charlie concluded. There could be no other.

"Ah, well that's too bad. You are young, yes? You'll find another. You'll feel better soon."

"No. No, I will never be happy again," Hudson said with no small touch of pathos, and Charlie, despite his well-developed empathy, was made to suppress the inkling of a smile.

"I know it feels that way, I do. But you're young and life is long. Why don't you tell me what's happened and see if I can't—"

Charlie had not time to finish his offer of assistance before Hudson burst into rapid explanation. His telling of the romance did little to inspire sympathy. It was not for lack of sentiment, though, but perhaps because of an excess of those emotions which make our own logic so fuzzy and render many a short story long and a long story short.

What Charlie really took away from the jumbled and distorted narrative was that Hudson had proposed to Diana and was now heartbroken with no understanding of her reasons for refusal. He had long since abandoned his initial idea that Diana was too much a snob to have him as a husband. He had been sitting in the tavern replaying all her most unfussy and egalitarian moments. Despite what he had shouted at the fair, he knew in his heart that there must be some other reason for her rejection. He was tormented, because his own rash behavior meant he would never be allowed to know it.

Charlie was not prepared with an answer when the young man, upon concluding his tale, asked, "What should I do? What do you think?"

Naturally, Charlie was tempted to tell this sad, spoiled man to flee the county and never return. But his own nature was too honest and too feeling to allow him to give advice in bad faith. He pondered the question at some length before giving his honest reply.

"I think you should stop drinking tonight. Get some sleep here in a room, and go back to your friends tomorrow before you give them much worry."

"And after that?"

"Well, I don't know. In my experience, there's little use in rushing things. In time, your feelings might change. Her feelings might change. A great number of things might change. Tonight, I think you had better eat something and go to sleep."

As if by magic, but more certainly by the benefit of eavesdropping, the innkeeper came by with two bowls of stew. Charlie nodded his appreciation. The young man looked at his serving skeptically, swirled his spoon around it a few times, and then reluctantly took a bite. Upon first taste, his appetite was aroused; he soon devoured his own bowl and then the rest of Charlie's bowl, which he was offered after eyeing it keenly. Color and vigor returned to Hudson's face, and Charlie could feel the calmness of exhaustion overtaking the young man.

"How about you head upstairs and get a jump on the night?" Charlie gently suggested.

"I say, you know the girl I'm talking about, don't you? Lady Diana Huxley?"

Charlie's eyes grew wide with shock at the young man's sudden perception. Then, as Hudson continued, Charlie realized he was not as discovered as he'd originally thought.

"You will have seen her in the village. She rides a bay mare very often."

Charlie realized that Hudson thought him a local and assumed he knew Diana at a distance.

"Ah, yes. She's a very pretty girl."

"The most beautiful. She's more than that, too."

Charlie could not resist the temptation to hear this lordly man's impression of his wildflower friend.

"Oh aye? What's she like, then?"

"She's kind. She's sweet. She's gentle. But also strong. And I say, she's the smartest girl I ever met. She knows every bird and plant. She can tell you when it's going to rain, and where the birds will fly in the winter. She saved my life—twice, actually. Maybe that's why she said no . . . doesn't want to marry such a fool that can't even swim."

Charlie stifled a smile at this embarrassing admission. But he was gratified to hear that the young man saw Diana's true virtues. It was a comfort to know that he loved her honestly—not just for her pretty face. Knowing this, Charlie felt the last prickles of animosity towards the gentleman dissipate, leaving behind a tender sympathy informed by his own sadness at missing the same girl when she left his life so unexpectedly.

# Fifty-Six

Having stayed home from the fair, Elizabeth was the last to learn of Hudson's failed proposal and insulting outburst. The language barrier between her staff and the others of their station in New Glenbury made it difficult for the particulars of gossip to be easily conveyed. So it was nearly two and a half hours before Heloise relayed some version of events close enough to the truth to alarm Elizabeth into immediate action. She called for her carriage at once and set out in a hurry for Wuster Park. However, as she saw the gate of Wuster Park swing into view, her courage and certainty failed her. She slid open the carriage window and shouted that the driver should not turn there, but proceed instead to the rectory.

She did not need to go all the way to the rectory, though, before her mission was accomplished. Constance was walking at as brisk a pace as the fine summer day would allow on the road to Wuster Park when Elizabeth's carriage came to a stop and admitted her as a passenger. The lane was too narrow and too rutted to permit an immediate reversal, so they proceeded away from their ultimate destination for another half mile before a wider place would allow for a turnaround.

In that time, the two friends compared the accounts they had each heard of the events at the fair. They speculated on Diana's reasoning. They resolved that Hudson should be stricken from the list of eligible partners. And they concluded that the original three-year plan for Diana's edification should be resumed immediately.

They had just begun the composition of an advertisement for a flute master when the carriage stopped before Wuster Park, and they exited to await admittance to the great house.

Wait they did. Though it was now some several hours after the bulk of the Wuster Park staff had returned from the fair, the house was still in disorder. Diana remained locked in her room, while Maggie and Benjamin waited in anxiety and inactivity for the next step to present itself. At last, a footman opened the door and directed the ladies to the blue sitting room, where they met with Maggie and Benjamin.

Once again, the full narrative of the day's events was explained, including the baffling coincidence of Charlie McFaden's visit. It was not until the conclusion of such retellings that dinner was finally announced.

What a dour, confused dinner it was. The plan of cold cuts and fruit had been abandoned by Mrs. Hellens, the cook, who felt that in times of crisis, hot, savory dishes were the only thing to serve. However, Mrs. Rollins was adamant that there should be no further outings of any of the staff that day or the next. So, ingredients were limited to the current contents of the larder and cellar. The result was an odd combination of winter root vegetables in heavy gravy, a chicken lately killed, and an abundance of meat pies which had been meant for the staff that evening.

No one remarked on any of this, though, as no one remarked on much of anything. The group was painfully aware that the attending footmen would be quick to report all their conversation belowstairs. Nor did any of the party feel so strongly in any course of action as to be bold enough to recommend it. So, they ate mostly in silent contemplation. At the conclusion of the meal, Maggie requested a plate to take with her up to Diana's room.

There she knocked gently on the door and said softly, "You

don't have to let me in, but I've brought you some dinner."

Maggie could hear the sound of light footsteps approaching the door. There was some hesitation, but then, to Maggie's relief, she heard the smooth click of a lock. Diana opened the door.

The girl had been crying; that much was very plain. Maggie had no wish to press her for conversation. It had been resolved by all that the subject of Charlie's visit should not yet be made known to Diana. So, when Diana stood aside and wordlessly invited her cousin into her bedchamber, Maggie was apprehensive. Maggie possessed enough self-awareness to know that silence had never been one of her strongest virtues. She placed the dinner tray on the small table by the window and handed Diana a small dish of sliced apple. Diana took the little dish and sat down on the bed.

Maggie could see that the girl was exhausted. Her face had that drawn, pale expression which reminded her of Diana's first days at Wuster Park. As Diana ate the sliced apple, Maggie silently buttered a piece of bread and brought it to Diana with a glass of water. Both were consumed with little hesitation or grace. Maggie felt that she should leave, having nothing to say that she could not be sure would not give more pain. When she attempted her exit, she saw how Diana's face fell. So Maggie continued to stand awkwardly by the bed.

Eventually she asked, "Diana, would you like to go to the chair?"

Diana remembered herself and rose to take her seat by the window at the little chair and table. Once settled, she picked at the dinner plate with only vague comprehension. Maggie sat on the footstool by the end of the bed. After a short silence that felt long, Diana spoke.

"Are you going to send me home?"

"Send you home? Goodness, no. Unless you want to go home. Do you want to go—"

"No."

"Then we will not send you home."

Diana seemed relieved by this for a time. Then another thought clouded her face.

"But you are upset with me?"

"No! Of course not. You've done nothing wrong. But . . . well, I must own that I am a bit confused. I thought you were very fond of Mr. Birch. And of course, now I would not have you see him. Of course, of course. I am just . . . surprised is all."

Maggie managed to stop talking, in a paroxysm of self-control prompted by the certainty that the more she spoke, the greater her chance of causing pain.

"I was surprised, too, when he asked me."

"No, I wasn't so much surprised to hear about him asking you. We'd all been expecting that. I was surprised you said no. I thought you liked him."

"I did like him. I do! It's just not that simple."

"Is there . . . someone else?"

Diana looked up at her cousin with obvious confusion.

"Someone else?"

"I know about Charlie McFaden."

Maggie heard herself say this, and lamented it instantly.

"What? How do you know of Charlie McFaden?"

"You mentioned him to me. I know you were fond of him when you lived back home in Yansworth."

Diana spluttered an incoherent rebuttal.

"You think because I . . . as if I'm . . . You cannot . . . I don't. I don't know what you're talking about."

"I confess, Diana, I don't know what it is that you want. I thought you were very fond of Hudson."

"I am. I was . . . I mean . . . I have been, yes."

"Then why did you refuse him? It is an eligible match."

"I . . . it's complicated. It's not because I didn't like him. Only, I barely know him. He knows nothing about me. Nothing about the truth of my situation. When we meet, we jest and chat. We never speak on anything serious. He hardly knows me at all. Not the real me. And what do I know of him? Marriage is forever, Maggie. When you choose a husband, you place your whole life in his hands.

You hope for a protector, but you might find a jailer. Such a decision cannot be made in haste. Only a fool would . . . I'm sorry. I know you and Benjamin married very quickly but . . . I simply could not trust . . ."

At this point, Diana's eyes filled with tears again, and she rose from her seat. Turning away from her cousin, she looked out the window, wringing her handkerchief in both hands and trembling. Maggie stood up and came towards her. When she placed a comforting hand on her cousin's shoulder, Diana flinched so suddenly that Maggie instinctively drew back a few steps.

"You know, it wasn't as if I had so very many options, Diana. I only ever received one other proposal."

Diana turned to her cousin with silent inquiry. Maggie was deeply relieved to discover this new topic of conversation held some distraction for her depressed guest.

"I never told you? No, I suppose not. It was when I was eighteen. Freshly out. My very first season, actually. It was no great romance, I assure you. Just Anna Heath's odious brother, Winston. He was drunk at a picnic. Because Anna was trying to secure an offer from Gerald Jeffries, I thought I would help smooth things over, leading Winston away and sketching his silhouette. It was the first time we'd ever been anything close to alone, and . . . Oh goodness, it pains me now to think of it. But yes, he proposed. At first, I thought he was joking. When I laughed, though, he seemed to take it as an affirmative. I then had to tell him, as politely as I could, that I was not interested in marrying him. He didn't like that. He made such a fuss, called me all kinds of names I won't repeat."

Diana was listening to her cousin with keen attention, and Maggie wished that her story might have been a longer one. She continued.

"And well, what did I say? 'Winston Heath, you shut your trout mouth!' Which, you know, was not the boldest or the brightest thing to say. Indeed, I am embarrassed to remember it. Only, well, it was quite true. He looked like a trout. Big downturned lips and a long jaw. When girls used to talk about him, I heard him called 'dignified' and 'stately.' That's what they say about the Hapsburgs, too, and we have all seen those portraits. . . .

"I don't know how the story of it got round. I certainly didn't tell anyone. He must have confided in a friend. But the effect was . . . Well, it made quite a splash. There was even an engraving of it in a print shop window for a few weeks. Suddenly, everyone was under the impression that I was this wonderful wit. I got invited to all the best parties, and wherever I went people wanted to ask my opinion, thinking I would have something droll to say. I suppose I didn't measure up. For, the next season, I wasn't invited as many places. The only lingering effect of my *supposed* social triumph was that boys were forever afraid I was going to make some joke about them. So, you know, when Benjamin came along . . . Well, I was very happy to meet someone who wasn't shy of my talking. I was twenty-eight, you know. I'll be twenty-nine soon. I think my parents just thought I'd live with them forever. I was starting to think that too. So, when I met Benjamin, and he was so insistent, so kind . . ."

Diana had been listening with interest, and she now took her cousin's hand.

"You are happy. You chose well. You two are a good match. Everyone sees it."

Now it was Maggie's turn to grow misty-eyed.

"Thank you, Diana. I'll give you some more time. Please try to eat something more before bed."

Leaving the room, Maggie felt a rising respect of Diana's rationale for refusing Mr. Birch's marriage proposal. It was true that her own courtship and engagement had been a hasty one. It was true that it had worked out very well. But what if it had not? What option would she have had then? In these considerations, at last, Diana's reluctance made perfect sense to Maggie.

Night fell in New Glenbury. All over the hills and valleys of the sleepy town, the melodrama of the rejected proposal was told and retold. Each retelling placed less emphasis on truth and more emphasis on the comedic folly of it all.

In the candlelit glow of the Wuster Park estate, Maggie and Benjamin were now wondering what their responsibility was in this situation. Were they duty bound to Diana's parents in reporting this unfortunate occurrence? Constance and Elizabeth had unanimously advised them against mentioning the event to anyone under any circumstances. The older women had solemnly promised to flatly deny that such an event had ever taken place. They trusted that the river of time would soon sweep away the muddied waters of gossip and truth.

Indeed, Elizabeth had already explained to Heloise (who she trusted would relay the message to the rest of her coworkers) that the whole situation had been a misunderstanding. When returning home from Wuster Park, she clarified to her lady's maid that the occurrence had been a combination of accident and imagination. Constance was retelling the details in grave soberness to the reverend. Together, they were trying to decide if a sermon on the ills of gossip could be preached the next day, or if such a lecture would only draw more attention to the situation.

As the night drew on, sooner or later, nearly all involved and uninvolved persons retired to their beds and slept. Only Diana, sitting at her small desk, lit by a sad single candle, stayed awake. Slowly, carefully, and with many false starts and stops, she was composing a letter.

# Fifty-Seven

THE NEXT MORNING, Hudson awoke with a snort. Immediately upon opening his eyes, he regretted that morning and its blinding sunlight should ever see him in such a condition. He had passed the night in the unmoving sleep of the drunk. Half his body ached from its continued pressure on the hard inn bed. The other half of his body ached with the effects of having consumed entirely too much drink. His slowly waking intellect recalled the vague outline of his evening: the hurried ride from Langley Hall, the copious amount of beer consumed, the hearty stew, and the kind stranger. Not even his prodigious hangover could blunt the razor-sharp recollection of his conduct at the fair. This was how Hudson learned that drinking to forget is only a temporary solution to a persisting problem.

As he paid the innkeeper with his remaining pocket money from the fair, he looked around the Grey Swan for his kind and mysterious stranger. It occurred to him that he must look quite frightful in his rumpled, unshaved, and unwashed state, for he received many odd looks in return from the grouchy morning drinkers. He was almost tempted to join their ranks and give drinking to forget another try. Since his limited capital was already exhausted, he thought it more gentlemanly to return on his own to

Langley Hall than to be found hiding out in some dark alehouse.

He rode his horse as quietly as possible back to Langley Hall. He walked him in the grass beside the road to avoid the crunch of gravel that gave him such pains in his delicate condition. Mercifully, Hudson passed only a few farmers and no familiars on his route. He returned home to Langley Hall before anyone of more consequence could spy him in this wretched condition.

Upon his entering the hall, the most unusual thing happened. Mrs. Bellwood began to shriek. Hudson was not sure what to do or where even to look as she commenced in a violent admonition of his sudden quitting of Langley the night before. From her assertions that his abandonment was wholly unprovoked and irrational, he was sure she still operated in ignorance of his earlier actions with Diana. He prayed that her ignorance would persist always. Still, her fury at his seemingly random desertion of his abode was enormous. She swatted him, she shouted at him, she stomped her feet and declared that he had given them all such a fright.

She'd been sure, just sure after all, that he had gone mad, been taken ill with brain fever, been robbed by highwaymen and held ransom by bandits, eloped to Scotland with Diana, decamped with itinerants, been drugged, bound, gagged, and all number of dramatic fates which Mrs. Bellwood knew plenty about, because she always read the trial reports in the London papers.

Like a vicious sheepdog, she barked at him as she advanced, herding him against his conscious thought down the hall and into his own chamber. Once he entered his room, the pitch of her panic subsided almost entirely. Her goal had been accomplished. Hudson was home, in his bed, safe at last. Without a moment's hesitation, therefore, she transformed back into the quiet, caring Mrs. Bellwood whom Hudson thought (until recently) he knew so well. She gently advised him to take off his boots, change out of his clothes, and freshen himself up while she fetched his breakfast.

Just before quitting the room, she added without a shade of

irony, "And do try to be quiet, Hudson dear. I don't want you to wake the boys."

She departed, and Hudson sat motionless on his bed, his ears still ringing with the reverberations of her remonstrance.

# Fifty-Eight

CHARLIE AWOKE EARLY that day, not a little surprised that he had actually managed to sleep. All night he had been thinking about Diana, Hudson, and the great house at Wuster Park. All of his plans now lay in confusion around him.

He had come from Yansworth with such a clear purpose. On the long journey by horseback, he had practiced his speeches of indignation and benevolence. He had imagined finding Diana scrubbing floors in a cold and imposing fortress. Her doleful eyes and wan face had been his North Star. He imagined her running to him, throwing her arms about his neck, hailing him as her rescuer, and delighting in his promise to return her home.

Now, he had reason to pause. If her cousin was to be believed, then Diana was happy here. She was not working as a servant, but staying as a guest. She had even made friends. This was the most surprising revelation of all: Diana with friends. Always, he had known her as a shy, lonely girl with only the company of her younger siblings. He liked the idea that she had friends here. And she was a baron's daughter. She had always been a baron's daughter. Wuster Park, or a place like Wuster Park, was where a baron's daughter belonged. Would she want to go back to her home in Caldflett Castle? Could she really be better off there, where no one noticed or cared about her?

He would just have to ask her. Then, he considered all the drama which must surely be unfolding at Wuster Park as a result of Hudson's rejected proposal. Charlie wondered if he would be permitted to see her or if his visit of the previous day would even be remembered.

His visit was remembered. All morning, his request to see Diana weighed heavily on Maggie's mind. She struggled to chart a good course of action. Constance and Elizabeth had been so firm in their resolution that the best way to handle the situation was to simply pretend it never happened, but Maggie could not align herself with this attitude. After their conversation the night before, she felt that Diana was more than entitled to her feelings and that she was owed a great deal of compassion. However, she did not wish to confuse the girl with the sudden and ill-timed appearance of Mr. McFaden. She was not convinced that the shock of the situation would not prompt Diana to make a hasty and (in Maggie's opinion) poor decision to leave Wuster Park and return to her home, which would offer no comfort except familiarity.

Still, she knew that Charlie was waiting and he would not wait forever. The fact that Diana had not yet left her room was of little comfort. Diana's windows faced the road, and Maggie was certain that the caprices of fate would not allow a second visit from Charlie to escape Diana's notice. Maggie wrestled with the idea of simply sending Charlie word at the inn in Shrewsbern that Diana had no desire to see him. But the promise he had elicited from her made such deception an impossibility. She thought of writing him a long letter explaining the situation in detail, begging him to depart unseen. Then, she was not sure if such news would encourage or deter the impetuous youth. She thought of leaving Wuster and going to see Charlie herself. Only she did not want Diana to be left without trusty female counsel for even a moment.

Maggie felt trapped. Her morality and motivation were at odds, the tension inside her most pressing.

At long last, she knocked softly and let herself into Diana's room. Expecting to find the girl in bed, Maggie was surprised to see her looking up from the small desk in the corner. Diana did not seem displeased to see her. Maggie took this as an invitation to sit in the stuffed chair near the window.

"Diana, my dear, we have something we must discuss."

"I know. First, please, do you think someone can take this letter to Langley Hall?"

Diana handed her cousin a folded letter consisting of at least three pages of thick paper. It was addressed to Hudson Birch, in Diana's neat, restrained hand. Maggie studied the packet, unsure of how to navigate this request. Diana, taking her hesitation as disapproval, went on to explain.

"I know you and Mrs. Constance say that it is improper for a girl to correspond with a boy. Only I must offer some explanation, some apology—"

"You owe him no apology! Why, it is he who should apologize to you."

"I'm sure he would. But really and truly, I don't want to see him again. I can't. And I must tell him the truth. He was so good and kind to me."

"Diana, I cannot have this letter delivered to him."

"It has nothing bad in it; I swear it does not. I swear, and you know I do not swear. You may read it if you like. Read it first. Check it for spelling, too. I will rewrite anything you think is wrong, only I must tell him. Please, Cousin Maggie. Please, at least read it."

Maggie, stalling for time and burning with curiosity, opened the unsealed missive. There she read the following:

*Dear H,*

*I know it is not proper for me to write to you, but I must.*

*I knew you were fond of me. You were always so kind and sweet. But I never let myself imagine you were fond enough to want to marry me. If you knew me better, you would see that I am not worthy of such an offer. That is why I must write, so I can help you understand why I had to refuse you.*

*Please, Hudson, do not think that I do not like you. I do like you. It is only that we are so different. I am sure if you were to marry me, you would be disappointed to know me better.*

*You said in anger that I was too proud of my father's title to marry you. I am not. I have no pride in my father. He is a gentleman in title only. He is far from a gentle man.*

*Caldflett Castle is not the grand palace I have let you imagine it to be. It is a crumbling, lonely place with fewer comforts than even a mill hand's cottage. Would you believe when I came to stay at Wuster Park, it was the first time I ever had a room to myself? It was the first time I was ever waited on at table or driven in a private carriage. Imagine my feelings here in a world so new and strange. I have been happy—confused, surprised, all of those feelings, too. But above all, I could not help but be happy here. Then I met you.*

*You are the newest and strangest thing of all here. You come from London, a city so big I saw one hundred carriages pass my window the first day I arrived. You live there as if it is nothing. You know all the best places to go. You know the names of all the theaters. You have the nicest boots and clothes, always so clean and pressed. And you were kind to me, so truly kind to me, when you did not need to be. You had no reason to be.*

*I think now, as I look back, I did not want to believe there was any reason other than your good nature that you were so kind to me. But I suppose I have to admit that I knew your kindness was more than just simple courtesy. Then again, the rules of this place, this life among such comforts, are all so strange. I told myself I was making something from nothing.*

*Perhaps I should have stopped you from your attentions after Lady Dormer's ball. Yes, I know I should have. Only, I liked you so much, you and your good manners and your sweet questions. I felt that you enjoyed listening to me. I felt happy when we were together. I never thought that you would consider me as a wife after such a short time—you, who have so much and know so many things. And I who only know about birds and trees. I didn't allow myself to dream that you would want a wife who could give you so little and was not even worth your parents receiving.*

*So, you see, it is not you that is the reason for my refusal. It is I. I know too little to be a credit to you. I know too little of your world to be any good in it. I would embarrass you; I know it. In time, you would come to dislike me. I will not say too much, for it is a sin to speak against a father. But I have seen what an unhappy marriage makes for a home. I do not want that for you, and I will not be the cause of it.*

*I will admit that your reaction to my refusal was as much of a surprise as your offer. I have heard cruel words, both worse and more. Hearing such words from you, though, I know you must have been very hurt. That is why I had to write you this letter, so you might know that it was nothing against you, your character, your family, or your most generous offer. It was only myself, and knowing that if you knew more about my true circumstances, you would have made no offer at all.*

*I hope in time you can forgive me for the wrongness of not discouraging your attentions. I have already forgiven you your unhappy words. I know they do not reflect your character. I will instead think only of your kindness, though I know we shall never meet again. I wish you nothing but happiness, for you are a good man and deserve greater happiness than I can give you.*

The letter was unsigned, a demure and thoughtful gesture for a girl so lacking in the finer points of delicate etiquette. For a moment, as Maggie concluded her reading, all thoughts of Charlie McFaden were eclipsed. She felt only a sad tenderness for not having supported Diana enough that she should see her own worth. How ridiculous, Maggie thought, that a girl of seventeen should be apologizing to a man who had shouted at her in public. Then, the few sad details of Diana's letter made it clear that such ill-tempered outbursts were not new to her. She probably was in the habit of apologizing for others' faults.

Maggie wanted to tell Diana this. She wanted to help her cousin understand that she was not the ignorant burden her letter portrayed. Maggie reproached herself for not having built the girl's confidence through encouragement rather than emphasizing to her all she did not know of polite society.

Maggie did not know how to say all of this. So she said instead,

"Diana, I cannot have this delivered. I . . . I am sure that Hudson has left Langley Hall by now."

Maggie had not known it was possible for the girl's face to fall further, but it did. Apparently, she was capable of great depths of unhappiness.

"If we have the address, I have enough set aside to include the postage."

"No, Diana, it is not the logistics of the letter which makes it undeliverable. It is the . . . well, it is not right that you should apologize to him. Don't you see? It is he who should apologize to you."

"Yes, I know he was wrong to shout. But I was wrong, too, in encouraging him. I really just never thought he was thinking of me that way. Don't you see?"

"Well, what did you think?"

Maggie could not help but air some of her frustration at this rather dense perception.

"I thought he was, you know . . . flirting. Idle flirting, like Captain Tanders and Lady Dormer. I thought because he was bored and didn't have his London pursuits . . . Mother always said that the men from London can't be trusted. I didn't think he was being underhanded, only just having a little fun. It didn't seem wrong because you and the reverend's wife were always around. I know now that it was. I hope you will not be too mad at me. I never meant to be a discredit to you."

"Oh Diana . . ."

Maggie searched her mind for something else to say. Then, because it was the only subject which occurred to her, she ventured on to the original reason for her entry.

"We had a visitor yesterday. Mr. Charlie McFaden."

Diana looked very confused.

"Charlie was here? Why?"

"He wanted to see you."

There was a long pause. Diana's face clouded in consideration. Her feelings remained inscrutable to her cousin.

". . . I suppose he was on his way to his sister's in Kent?"

"No, he came to see you. He wants to see *you*." Maggie looked at Diana significantly, but Diana's expression yielded no clue to her inner contemplations. "Do you want to see him?"

"He's still in New Glenbury?"

"He is in Shrewsbern."

"To see me?"

"Yes. He wants to know that you are happy here."

"It's a shame he didn't visit two days ago, then." And Diana gave a shy laugh at her own sad little joke. Maggie was forever caught off guard by the sporadic manifestation of her cousin's wit.

"Diana, do you want to see him?"

"Yes. . . . But do we have to leave Wuster Park?"

"No, no. I'll send word for him to come here."

A clear look of worry passed over Diana's countenance.

"Do you think something bad has happened at Caldflett? Did he say?"

"No, Diana. He said your family is well. He just wanted to come see that you are well."

"I don't know what to say. Is that why you asked me if I was in love with him yesterday? Because he came to visit? You don't know him like I do, Maggie. He's just very kind. It doesn't signify. He doesn't mean anything by it, I'm sure."

"Diana, I think it is time for you to consider that maybe the men in your life *do* mean something by their actions."

Maggie said this last statement and suddenly felt very tired. She sounded like a sensible old woman. She left the room hoping that the finality of her words might give them the weight needed to sink through and make an impression on Diana's consciousness.

She was halfway down the hallway when she realized she was still holding Diana's letter.

# Fifty Nine

CHARLIE DID NOT hesitate for a moment when the messenger arrived for him. All morning, he had been waiting at the Grey Swan in his cleanest shirt and trousers, hoping for the summons to see Diana despite his doubts about the likelihood of that occurrence. The boy, a young groomsman from the stables of Wuster Park, was wholly unconcerned with the reason for his mission and not in the least bit curious about why he would be instructed to summon the guest on foot and insist on a return to Wuster Park by the same means. It was of no concern to Charlie, either. His quick strides kept the boy at a trot on the return journey.

Diana and her cousin were in a different room than the one he had been admitted to the day before. But the grandeur of the space was no distraction from the sight of Diana as she shot up from her chair and crossed the room to greet him. She stopped short before him, close enough to touch. Neither knew what to say. Her blue eyes held his in an unblinking attention. After a breathless pause, she spoke.

"It is very nice to see you, Mr. McFaden."

Though her sentiment was warm, her formality was cold.

"Charlie is as good as ever for me, *Lady* Huxley."

"Then you must call me Diana, of course."

"Why, I'm not sure I can. I hardly recognized you in such a

place. You are surely too fine to be plain old Diana."

Charlie had meant this as a joke, a gentle teasing, but his tone betrayed a sincere insecurity. She was changed. She was not the girl he knew from home. Somehow, she had become a woman. He saw it, and she knew it. Diana offered him a seat.

Maggie was keenly observing this interaction, though not quite comprehending its true meaning. She motioned to the footman to call for tea so Charlie and Diana might discuss the news of their familiars. The conversation was slow to start. Charlie reported with more detail than even he expected about the health and happenings of Yansworth, as Diana nodded along with rapt attention. Maggie was amused by the girl's obvious and unfeigned interest in some of Charlie's more agrarian reporting, such as how many ewes the Collins clan could boast of or what the south field of the Grangers was to be planted with in the fall. It was some time after the tea had been served before conversation caught up to the present moment. When Charlie had been exhausted in his own reporting, he finally ventured to ask Diana about her time at Wuster Park.

With considerable interest, Maggie listened to her cousin describe the merits and surprises of life away from her home. Diana's tone was measured but pleasant. There was a great deal of time spent in reporting the number and variety of shops in New Glenbury. Her trip to London was recalled with much exactitude. Diana had enough tact not to boast of her material circumstances or the significant finery which now surrounded her. But she confided to Charlie how much she enjoyed having a room of her own. Her clothing spoke on her behalf of the generosity that was obviously being lavished upon her.

For a time, as Charlie listened, he wanted to believe that this was actually some deception. He considered that perhaps Diana was being dressed in her cousin's things and made to falsify reports of her own happiness. He could see that she was burdened with some deep concern, true. But she was also at ease in the grand space, with her delicate dress and with the thin china of her cup. It was clear this was no departure from a life Diana now considered regular. Her circumstances were truly changed, and for the better.

But was her heart the same? Charlie wished he could know. Was she still the kind, observant, interested girl who had ridden alongside himself and his father, asking about the birds and the trees? She treated him as if his patched corduroy trousers and dusty hobnailed boots were perfectly at home on the thick carpet and brocade chair. In this, at least, he took comfort. In this, at least, he could see that she did not resent him for his arrival.

Beyond that, it was also clear that she was healthier. Her complexion was warmer, her cheeks fuller, and her eyes brighter. He did not need to ask to know that she was well cared for here at Wuster Park. The knowledge washed over him in tremendous relief and then, with a pang of sorrow.

For so many months now, he had imagined himself her rescuer. He dreamed of whisking her away by night and bringing her back to his home, his family. When she left so suddenly and mysteriously, they had all felt her absence. He recalled his mother, looking out the lone glass window of their little cottage and fretting over the fate of the neighbor girl she had loved nearly as a daughter. He had imagined what Diana's gratitude to him would be, saving her from a life of servitude and then giving her the freedom she always wanted.

Now, he saw that to take her from her new world would be both an impossibility and an unkindness. As she talked about her flute lessons and the fine walks she took in the park, Charlie's heart sank slowly within him. He wrestled with accepting the sad truth: Diana needed no rescuer. She would be happier here than she could be back home in Yansworth. Once again, Charlie reminded himself that Diana had always been a baron's daughter.

"Charlie, why are you looking at me like that? Is something wrong?"

Her words recalled him to the present moment. Charlie noticed that Maggie was also watching him closely.

Taking a deep breath and collecting himself, he managed to say with an almost convincing confidence, "I am just so happy to see you so well. We've all been very worried about you. But you seem very much at home here."

He glanced towards Maggie before continuing so that she might understand his conclusion.

"I am pleased to see you so well settled. This is the right place for you."

Diana shifted nervously, for she was unsure how to respond to such a weighty statement. Maggie came to her rescue.

"Mr. McFaden, would you like to come out with us for a walk and tour the park? I am sure Diana would love to show you—"

"Yes ma'am, I'd be delighted to go on a ramble about the grounds if it's not too much trouble."

"Trouble, nonsense. You are our guest. Diana and I will just fetch our bonnets, and we shall be down directly to start off."

Maggie stood, but Diana did not. She looked at her cousin plaintively.

"Would you get my bonnet for me, Cousin Maggie?"

Maggie considered, then nodded and departed. What harm could there be? She would be gone only a moment.

Charlie watched the door close behind her. Then, Diana turned to him. Her face was more familiar to him now. It wore no mask of restraint or gentility.

"How did you find me, Charlie?"

"Did you not want to be found?"

"No. I only—"

"I saw your sister. I thought she was you. She was wearing one of your dresses. She told me you'd gone."

"It all happened so fast. I didn't have time to explain."

"You could have sent a letter."

"I know."

"Why didn't you?"

There was a short pause that felt like an eternity.

"I didn't want to say goodbye," Diana said flatly. Her eyes met

Charlie's; both of them shone with unspilled tears.

"Why did you go, Diana?"

"Because I could not stay."

Before she could say more, Maggie bustled into the room with both bonnets, ready for a long walk. Oblivious to the air of unspoken sentiment lingering between the two, Maggie was now sure that Charlie saw the truth of Diana's life at Wuster Park. Whatever dark fate the young man had imagined for his friend, Maggie was confident he did truly want what was best for the girl. And though she remained in subdued spirits, Diana was being distracted from her recent unhappiness. It was obviously doing her a world of good. Maggie had resolved, therefore, to make the day as nice a one as ever they had shared. So, on her errand for the bonnets, she also sent word that a full and hearty luncheon should be laid out for them upon their return.

They set out.

In the absence of questions he could not ask, Charlie asked a great many questions about the expansive Wuster grounds. In the beginning of their journey, Charlie was polite enough to direct his questions to Maggie. However, as Diana was the only one of the women to possess any knowledge of the park and its maintenance, it was soon settled that all questions should be directed to her.

In the absence of answers she could not give him, Diana answered Charlie's questions about the park grounds with astounding detail. Maggie learned more about her own grounds and gardens on that walk than she had in her entire time living at Wuster Park. It was after admiring the trout pond, the ha-ha, and the great oaks in the wood that Charlie mentioned with a tone of gentle regret that he had recently planted some beds of campanula and irises along the south side of his cottage.

"Just as I said you ought?" Diana asked with a note of tenderness.

"Yes, just as you said."

"How is the effect?"

"They'll need another season to fill in, but I am sure you'll be pleased with it . . . when you come to visit."

Some ache in his voice caught Diana's attention. She smiled through her own sadness.

"I should like that very much." And then she continued with more restraint, "I should like to see my family."

"Oh, and they should like to see you here, I'm sure."

"Yes," Diana replied. "Yes, I'm sure they would. Can you imagine Nat and Nan in the drawing room here?"

"Oh no, you couldn't let them inside!"

Maggie was about to reproach this insinuation about the limits to her hospitality, but when she saw that both Charlie and Diana had laughter in their eyes, she knew it was only meant in jest. She let them share their moment of levity before suggesting they might turn back for luncheon.

To Maggie's great delight, Benjamin was intent on joining them. That morning, he had trusted the navigation of what he anticipated to be an uncomfortable meeting to his wife's capable care. Having heard from Mrs. Rollins that Maggie had seemed in cheerful spirits when ordering a large luncheon, he resolved to join the party and support her.

They ate out of doors on a plainly set table heaped with the bounty of summer. Charlie was a quick observer of his hosts and mimicked their manners well enough to give the impression that he had eaten in fine company before. The arrival of Benjamin prompted Charlie to ask questions of a more detailed, businesslike manner which only the owner of the estate could answer. Charlie wanted to know where he pastured his flocks in the winter, how he kept the spacing of his wood thin enough for riding and thick enough for birds to roost. He asked so many questions so intelligently that Benjamin, forgetting himself and the circumstances of his guest's arrival, asked plainly if Charlie would consider coming on as a groundskeeper.

Charlie replied with a gracious calm.

"Oh sir, I do thank you. But no. Any land I farm is to be my own, and I like it that way. I am honored by your offer, I am. My father has worked hard that I might have my independence. But if I might make a suggestion . . ."

"Oh do, please."

"You might consider planting a few trees on that hill above your trout pond. I can see it would do well with more shade. The willow, while very nice, gives only a little to just one corner."

It was heartily agreed that this suggestion was a good one, and the merits of different trees were then discussed by the visitor and Diana at some length.

At the end of the luncheon, Maggie was tempted to extend an invitation to supper. Before she could, Charlie saved her the consideration, mentioning that he needed to resume his journey. He took his leave quickly, smiling but not meeting Diana's eyes as he said the pleasantries expected and promised to pass on her well wishes to her family.

Diana watched him go in contemplative silence. She alone knew how much she had missed him. She alone knew how relieved she was to see him go. He was halfway down the long approach before she mastered her emotions and turned to her cousin.

"As you can see, Cousin Maggie, Charlie and I have had nothing but friendship between us."

# *Sixty*

WHERE WERE CONSTANCE and Elizabeth? Did they come to regret the effects of their meddling? Did they devote themselves to the more traditional charities of the English countryside? No, dear reader, they did not.

As Maggie was watching Diana's face fall and her heart return to its sad present predicament, Constance and Elizabeth sat in Constance's drawing room, sipping lemonade and discussing in great detail how the failures of others had caused their well-laid plans to go astray. Between the two of them, they agreed that if Benjamin had been more attentive at the fair, if Captain Tanders had been more prescriptive in his advice, and if Maggie had been more unflinching in her instructions, then really this whole situation could have been avoided. They felt sure that, in the absence of these errors, they would be planning a wedding breakfast instead of instructing Mrs. Astley's cook to bake conciliatory shortbreads to send over to Wuster Park.

Their official position, which they repeated often and always in the days that followed, was that nothing had happened. The whole event had been a misunderstanding, a collective fantasy spun out of a few loose threads of observation on a busy afternoon. Shockingly, this approach of denial and distraction was actually working. Doubt was now as prevalent as certainty as to the exact events between Mr. Birch and Lady Huxley at the fair.

Elizabeth had come to the ingenious conclusion that further muddying the waters with conflicting reports would serve to discredit the originals. With that purpose in mind, she had placed a large order for beef with the all too obvious accidental inclusion of the dinner guest list showing both Hudson and Diana to be invited. That this beef would be served to her own staff was irrelevant. Reports quickly circulated that the two young lovers were not on such bad terms as various reports would make necessary.

Then, Constance made a point of discussing with some shopkeepers at length how fond Miss Diana was of Mr. Ellis Bellwood, and how she thought the pair of young people a very handsome couple. This obvious scheming became more believable as it filtered through the mouths of the townsfolk of New Glenbury. At last, no one—not even the eyewitnesses of the event—could be really certain what they had seen that day at the fair. Besides, there were other scandals which soon overtook the botched engagement. Old farmer Radcliff was said to have come into some money. And one of the Linden boys was being expelled from his apprenticeship.

All around New Glenbury, time was passing as it always did. It marched on and on, with each summer day stretching into a golden sunset. The wild roses on the lanes bloomed and then burst. Their petals tumbled down the dusty roads in the evening breeze. Time passed everywhere for everyone, except for Hudson and Diana. In their borrowed estates, they each contemplated the other, insensible to the days slipping past them. Diana grew pale from sitting indoors all day, and she could not even be tempted by the offer of a fine trot over the park. Hudson stayed mostly out of doors, walking up and down the overgrown gardens of Langley Hall. Occasionally, he picked up a fallen stick or branch and thwacked at the undergrowth with it as if to startle pheasants.

For their parts, Ellis and Noah tried to console, engage, distract, and advise their friend. He seemed to only half hear them. He was too eager to agree with all they said and then soon forget whatever action he had promised to try on their recommendation. Maggie likewise tried to coax Diana back into good spirits. She sent away for horticultural catalogues and even stealthily invited their flock manager to let a few sheep loose into their small formal garden. She hoped that any damage they might do would be of interest to Diana. However, the sheep, so fat and happy in their normal daily diet, took very little interest in munching on the flowers and box hedge of the garden. They simply wandered around like nervous visitors. The sight of their wooly bodies outside the drawing room window could not even extort a smile from Diana. She was miles away in her own thoughts and cared little for the trouble a stray sheep could make.

Finally, Maggie could think of nothing else to do, and she appealed to Benjamin that they might all go back to London. There was new work to be inspected at his townhome, after all. They both agreed that the change of scenery might do something for Diana's spirits now that all other attempts had been exhausted.

Only after the plan had been decided was Diana informed. She took the news with the most animation she had shown in the last two weeks. She was adamantly against it. She begged to be excused. She wished to see nothing of London now, or ever again. She could not, she would not, she must not; on and on, she protested.

Maggie feigned ignorance of her possible reasons for the refusal, until Diana firmly and plainly said, "I cannot and will not go to London. I just know, I just know that if I go I will see him, and I cannot."

Maggie then made many promises that they would not appear in public. She assured Diana that they were only going to check on the house. She promised that any company they would have would be by invitation only. Yet Diana would not agree. Finally, Maggie had had enough.

"Diana, you are coming with us and that is final. London has more than one million people living there. If you are going to stay inside the whole day long, you run no greater risk of seeing him in one drawing room than any other. Besides, we do not even know that he is in London. Langley Hall has not been given up, and he might have gone anywhere else as likely as London."

Diana heaved a heavy sign of frustration and resignation. Inwardly, her mind was turning. Langley Hall had not been quitted. That meant that New Glenbury was as unsafe as London. Her only real option of total safety was to go home to Yansworth. However, she thought, things were not so bad yet as to want that. Things would probably never be that bad, Diana reflected, unless she were wanted to serve as bridesmaid for Hudson's wedding. That alone might be enough to tempt her into retreating back to that comfortless, crowded cold castle.

Then, she reproached herself. If Hudson were to be married, she should only be happy for him. That was what she knew she must truly feel, for any other feeling would be most ungracious. Diana knew that one cannot refuse an offer of marriage and then condemn the refused to a life of loneliness. One day, she knew, she would have to be happy for him. Because the date of this impending eventuality remained unfixed, it loomed even more ominously in her conscious mind. She tortured herself with impossible calculations.

Hudson had taken four months to fall in love and offer to marry her. So then, if he met a better, prettier, smarter girl, it would probably only take him a few weeks to fall in love with her. Perhaps, even now, his parents were arranging for his happiness. Yes, each day Diana dreaded that she would hear of his new attachment. Then it could be only so long before she would inevitably see him in public and have to offer her congratulations. The thought of it was torturous enough to occupy her entire day and leave her exhausted, falling into a fitful sleep each night.

Hudson could not think of the future the same way Diana did. He simply could not imagine it. He would not imagine it. Though he knew he should quit Langley Hall and return to his family in town, he did not want to close the book on this chapter in his life. As long as he was here in New Glenbury, the story did not feel over. He could look back on it, replaying over and over every small moment of their interactions. He could think of her walking in Wuster Park with certainty as to the degree of sunshine she was enjoying. In his most poetical moments, he could even imagine that the eastern breeze caressing his face had first blown Diana's ribbons and skirts before traveling over the hills to meet him.

He tried to talk to his friends about this, but Noah was vague in his sympathies and cold in his advice. Ellis, on the other hand, continually turned their conversations to his own anxieties for Melissa. His beloved had not written more than a few spare lines to say she was quite busy but that they should be in touch when Ellis was returned to town. It was for this reason that Ellis pressed Hudson so hard to return to London. But Hudson could not. He was not ready for this summer to be over, even though the grasses were already growing brown and stiff in their last dry weeks of heat and sunshine before fall.

# Sixty-One

THE DAY BEFORE the Wuster Park party was to depart for London, Diana came to Maggie in her bedchamber.

"Cousin Maggie, I beg your pardon, but I should like to speak with you, please."

The formality of tone arrested Maggie's attentions to her trunk, and she turned to face Diana.

"I have come to the conclusion that I will travel with you and Cousin Benjamin to London. Please don't interrupt me. I have come to the conclusion that I will travel with you and Cousin Benjamin, but only for the purpose of having my letter delivered to Mr. Birch. I should like to have it back. Please return to me my letter at once for this purpose, thank you."

Then the girl stood trembling at the force of her own direct speech. Maggie paused, unsure of what to say. Finally, she began to speak, but Diana cut her off.

"If you do not have my letter, I will write another. But I would prefer to save you the paper, which I know is very dear."

Maggie opened her mouth to protest, but Diana broke in once again.

"If you do not have specific criticism for the content of the letter then I can see no reason that I should not have it delivered."

Once again, Maggie tried to speak, but when Diana broke in once more, Maggie stood up and said, "Enough of this, Diana. You may have your letter back if you wish. Going to London will do nothing to help its delivery. I have heard just this morning that Mr. Birch has not quitted the neighborhood and still resides at Langley Hall. If you wish him to know your feelings so much, you might as well walk the letter over yourself."

Diana was startled by this outburst, and Maggie instantly regretted her harsh tone. She saw how it had unsettled the young lady. But, trembling as she was, Diana stood rooted to the spot. After a few moments, she extended her hand in an unmistakable gesture of request. Maggie went to her writing desk and took the letter from its inner drawer, then placed it in Diana's outstretched hand. The moment it touched her palm, she took it and fled the room.

Maggie lamented that her own youth had been spent in such a bland fashion. She did not know how to reason with the unreasonable feelings of young love. She hoped the news of Hudson's presence in New Glenbury would make Diana more excited for her trip to London, or at least more amenable to the idea of venturing out of the house once they had arrived. She was not foolish enough to count on any such blessing.

~

Diana wasted no time. She would not even pause long enough to reread her own letter. She felt sure that in another moment Maggie would change her mind and come retrieve it. So, without further hesitation, she raced downstairs to the kitchen. There she stood, observing the bustle of activity which always made her feel so small and unworthy. It was Tally the housemaid who first caught her eye and came quietly over to Diana to ask what she needed. Owing to her involvement in the activities of the big house on the day of the fair, Tally considered herself more directly concerned in the drama of the upstairs and had less shyness in offering her services outside of bed making and carpet beating.

"Do you know Langley Hall?" Diana asked, her hand extended with the envelope.

"Yes, miss. Would you like me to take it to Mr. Birch?"

"Yes, please." Rather than be offended by the presumption, Diana was relieved that she did not need to explain herself further.

"Should I wait for a reply?"

This was not a question Diana had anticipated. In fact, her plan was now fully exhausted. In a moment she said, "No. No, just come right back."

"Very good, miss."

And Tally hurried off to tell Mrs. Rollins that she was being sent on urgent business to Langley Hall and not to expect her back for some time because she had been instructed to wait for a reply. Tally of course had no intention of waiting, but she did very much fancy a trip into New Glenbury to talk to the butcher's handsome new apprentice.

# Sixty-Two

THE LETTER WAS left unceremoniously with Mr. Downs at Langley Hall. The aged butler tossed it on the hallway tray without a word to anyone about its arrival. Hudson was out of doors when it arrived. It wasn't until dusk that he made his way reluctantly back to the house to eat and spend another brooding night dropping tricks at whist. Loath as he would be to admit it to himself later, he saw the letter on the tray when he came in. Not knowing the handwriting, he assumed it was an invitation to some shabby country ball where gentlemen were wanted. He resolved to leave it until after supper. Supper came and went, and his thoughts on the letter were never recalled. It was therefore not until the next morning at breakfast that Diana's letter was finally put into his hands.

Upon reading the first line, he stood bolt upright, sending his chair clattering backwards and throwing all his friends into confusion. But Hudson could not hear them. Wholly absorbed by the letter, he would not even put it down to properly fasten his own boots over the legs of the exotic silk pants he wore at breakfast before dressing for the day. He was already out the door and rushing to the road in the direction of Wuster Park when he stopped short and became suddenly aware that the letter contained no instructions for his action.

But action he must take. He knew this. It was at this moment that Noah and Ellis caught up to him, panting and inquiring what the devil he thought he was doing running out of the house half-dressed so early in the morning. Hudson attempted a coherent reply, and the effect was admirable. He was able to communicate that the letter he'd received was from Diana and that he must now see her. He said a great many other things in the process, but they meant very little to anyone, and very little to himself, upon reflection.

The boy was frazzled; that was plain to see. He was also determined. Knowing how stubborn he could be, his friends did what they could between themselves to complete his attire and send him on his mission more completely dressed. Noah gave him his coat, which was too long in the sleeves and too tight in the waist. Ellis attempted to untuck his trousers, which had been consumed by his boot in his haste. His neckerchief was in the process of being retied but then, unable to wait any longer, Hudson ran off, still unsure of his actual mission.

The activity of running spared the young man from having any further consideration to his purpose. Speed was his objective. He must see Diana, and soon. However, Hudson was not expecting speed to greet him in the opposite direction. So, when the coach carrying Diana, Maggie, and Benjamin to London swung around the soft curve in a wooded section of their drive, the horses were as startled as Hudson at their mutual apparitions. Each leapt backwards in a spectacular display of chaos.

There was much shrieking, horse and human alike.

Hudson did not recognize the carriage right away, for Wuster Park kept several, and this particular coach was used only on journeys of significant distance or luggage. When Benjamin burst from the door to see what had caused their sudden dramatic halt, Hudson, never particularly gifted in math, managed to put two and two together. He began right away to shout.

"Diana! Diana! Is she in there? Diana!"

Maggie poked her head out of the window and, at first, mistook Hudson for a highway robber or a madman. Indeed, he looked half-mad. His outfit suggested he had dressed in the dark, and his eyes had a feverish glitter she did not like the look of. Diana heard the shouting and moved to the window. Maggie prevented her attempt to survey the scene. She took this rebuff with an indignant huff of frustration and waited for the revelation of the next startling development in her life. In just four short months, her existence had been transformed from one of scarcity to one of abundance. What had felt impossible was proved possible, and so what might happen next was utterly unknowable.

Benjamin was by Hudson's side as soon as he had calmed the horses. The boy had taken quite a tumble, and Benjamin wanted to be sure he was not seriously injured.

"Stop shouting, Mr. Birch! What are you doing?"

"I have to see Diana."

"So you attack my carriage?"

Hudson ignored the question. "Is she with you? Is she inside? I say, is she hurt?! Diana!"

"Stop, stop, stop. You look as though you've gone completely mad. Do your friends know where you are?"

"I . . . I suppose I do appear—" Hudson looked down at himself and began to lament. "Oh Lord, I do look like something awful. I say. What was I thinking? What am I wearing?! I hope you and . . . I wasn't . . . I wasn't trying to stop your carriage. I didn't even know you would be out. I was coming to Wuster Park. I got a letter and I wanted to see Diana. Lord, look at me. I say, I'm glad I didn't see her. I would not have her see me like this."

The ladies had heard none of Hudson's reply over the sound of the panting horses and the conciliatory coachman. To them, it sounded as if the conversation had ceased. This silence was far more terrifying than any shouting could be. Diana, unwilling to contain her curiosity any longer, escaped out of the opposite door from Maggie and ran around the coach just in time to see Hudson admonishing himself and showing Mr. Howard his comically long sleeves.

"Hudson?"

Her voice startled both men, but it was Hudson whose mortification caused him nearly to faint. As neither could answer her in this moment, she walked ever closer.

"What are you doing?"

Finally, Hudson found a handful of words.

"Your letter. I got your letter."

"Oh, I understand."

"You do?"

"No. Not really."

"I'm sorry, Diana. For stopping your coach and scaring the horses. I say, you aren't hurt, are you? I'm sorry for . . . I'm sorry for everything. I got your letter. And I'm sorry."

"That will be very sufficient, Mr. Birch," Benjamin broke in, and he attempted to lead Diana back to the carriage.

"No sir, please. May I just have a moment, just a moment to collect myself and . . . and then speak to Miss Huxley?"

Before Benjamin could answer, Diana answered for him with a firm and resounding yes. Hudson took a deep, relieved breath.

Walking some ten paces away, he attempted to collect himself. He ran his hands through his hair. He tucked in his shirt. He rolled up his sleeves. He took a few more deep breaths and collected himself into his most proper posture.

Then he approached Diana and said, in an air of studied casualness with only a note of tender anxiety, "I say, is that you, Lady Diana Huxley? What a coincidence. I never imagined I'd meet you here."

Benjamin might have expected many things, but he had not expected this. Right away, he was ready to be offended. Then Diana began to laugh. Then Hudson began to laugh. The two young people laughed so hard that tears wetted the corners of their eyes. Diana was the first to catch her breath.

"Look at you," was all she managed to say before laughing again. This set Hudson to laughing as well. And then Benjamin, unable to prevent himself, also began laughing. An unfamiliar cackle chimed in to the chorus, and the three outside the carriage looked back to see the coachman was now laughing.

At this, Maggie stuck her head out of the carriage window and yelled, "What on earth is going on?" which sent them all (coachman included) into a fresh fit of hysterics, and none could answer her.

Benjamin held up one hand as if in pause, and then retreated to the coach. Finally, the laughing spell was broken.

"I say, Diana, I am so sorry. I am so sorry for this, and for what I said at the fair. I should never have put you in that position. It was all so foolish and I didn't mean it. I say . . . I just got carried away. I've never met anyone like you. I've never felt this way before. I think, I say, I guess I wasn't thinking. I just had you in my arms and, well, I wanted to always have you in my arms. I never meant to hurt you. I say. And your letter . . . Oh, I just couldn't let you think that you weren't good enough for me. Because you are. You more than are. Your letter proves that. I'm a fool, and I know it. I want you to know it."

"I know it."

There was a pause, and then Hudson said in his usual self-assured manner, "Well, now that we both know what a great fool I am, I suppose I had better let you go on to . . . I'm sorry, where are you going?"

"London."

"London, of course. I say, well, don't let me detain you any further. Only . . . Diana, do you think, I mean, do you think we could still be . . . I say, if I were in New Glenbury, next summer . . . could I call on you? In friendship. Could I call on you?"

"I would like that."

"You would?"

"Very much."

"Well, I would like that too. Very much."

The young people stood with locked eyes and shy smiles. Eventually, Hudson stuck out his hand. Diana took it, pressing it warmly, wordlessly telling Hudson he was forgiven, and would not be forgotten. Then she turned and reentered the carriage. As the wheels began to turn, crunching the gravel underneath, Maggie ventured to ask what it was that Hudson had said to her.

"He said he was stupid and that he was sorry," Diana succinctly summarized.

"Did you forgive him?"

"Of course, Cousin Maggie. He really is very sorry."

"I think he's quite mad."

"I rather think I'm starting to like him," Benjamin said, surprising his listeners as they rattled down the road to London.

Hudson stood under the green canopy of oak leaves, the light falling in shafts through the dissipating dust of the departing carriage. He felt whole and calm for the first time in a long time. He could see her again. Their story was not over.

If you enjoyed reading *Accomplishments and Accomplices*,
please leave a review on Amazon or Goodreads. Share your
copy with a friend, or request it at your local library. Each
one of these small actions helps enormously. I want this book
to reach every reader who will appreciate it.

# Acknowledgements

My sincerest gratitude to my enthusiastic early readers, Kathleen Richards, Scott Lydon, Alison Sprague, Kate Brunette Kreuzer, Stephanie James, Julia Weed, and Bland Simpson. Your gentle feedback and encouraging words gave me the motivation to make this novel what it is today.

Thank you to Millie Shephard and Mary Lee Malcolm who each provided invaluable insights into the publishing and self-publishing process.

Heartfelt appreciation to my dear and talented friend Hannah VanWoert who designed my cover and website, making each far lovelier than imagined.

Erin Wilcox is the greatest editor on the face of the planet. Thank you, Erin, for agreeing to work on my book even when you had better things to do.

I am eternally grateful to my Instagram community who have continually showed me that softness and silliness are still wanted in a world of harsh realities.

Thank you to my wildly supportive parents who have (for some strange reason) always believed in my dreams.

And thank you to my husband, Kevin, who has given me the greatest gift of all: time to realize my true purpose.

**Grace Ellen Queen** is originally from a small town in the Appalachian Mountains of North Carolina. Her early experiences there informed her fascination with the beauty of nature, the joys and struggles of rural life, and the complex dynamics of intergenerational drama.

After receiving a degree in Creative Writing from the University of North Carolina in Asheville, she headed out west. Now she resides in Seattle, Washington with her husband, Kevin, and her oversized Cavalier King Charles Spaniel, Beans.

When not writing, she can be found wandering aimlessly from one room to another, wondering where she left her favorite pen.

Follow her cottagecore adventures on Instagram:
@the_paperbackprincess